Prai

Legs and the Two-Ton Dick

A deliciously dirty romp through the streets – and the bars, strip clubs, and strange living spaces – of San Francisco. In *Legs and the Two-Ton Dick*, Melinda Bailey weaves oddball characters, unlikely settings, and a first-rate plot into a satisfying murder mystery. I hope this book is the start of a series, because *Legs* needs to live on!

~ Paula Harrington, author of *Mark Twain & France*

A more motley crew of mystery jockeys you won't easily find, at least not one this fun, that's for sure. It's not everyday that characters this dysfunctional are such a crack up. Think Scooby Doo meets Charles Bukowski. The death of a classic rocker and the details surrounding his murder set the stage as the sillier side of the rock star mythos gets trashed like a 5-star hotel room. A binge-worthy, delusional limo ride that sucks you in from page one.

~ Jim Fourniadis, author of *The King Lives*

A local rock star on the verge of a comeback overdoses in a San Francisco recording studio. Sad, but unremarkable – except that someone murdered him. Video evidence implicates his wife, but she insists she didn't kill him. Is she lying, or did his bandmate, his mistress, or an obsessed fan give that fatal dose? Finding the truth rests in the hands of a struggling actress, a failed former cop, a flamboyant radio host, a conspiracy-loving hacker, and the swearingest caretaker in the China Basin neighborhood.

In this underground tour of the City by the Bay, Melinda Bailey captures the feel of its edges – where free love turned into polyamory, where everyone is always working and rarely employed, where strippers behave better than doctors, where junkies are family men and actresses are avenging angels. The stated mystery is who killed the local rock star working on his comeback, and that is solved. What remains ineffable is the chosen family that brings the killer to justice and exonerates the innocent, a motley crew of hustlers and weirdos who allow each other to live as they choose, embracing one another around all their quirks. A satisfying, believable, hard-boiled mystery, and as precise and loving a portrait of post-dotcom San Francisco as exists in fiction.

~ Karen Spiegelman, editor and journalist

LEGS *and the* TWO-TON DICK

MELINDA BAILEY

TRUTH SERUM PRESS

First published as a book June 2018 by Truth Serum Press

Any historical inaccuracies are made in error.

ISBN: 978-1-925536-37-9

Truth Serum Press
32 Meredith Street
Sefton Park SA 5083
Australia

Email: truthserumpress@live.com.au
Website: http://truthserumpress.net
Truth Serum Press catalogue: http://truthserumpress.net/catalogue/

Also available as an eBook
ISBN: 978-1-925536-38-6

Truth Serum Press is a member of the
Bequem Publishing collective

http://www.bequempublishing.com/

For Zelda

For my fun friend Michelle the songstress!
Happy reading and thank you for all your support. I appreciate it and you!
Luv xoxo

Contents

Prologue

Porter Nepal wondered if this was the day he wouldn't make it out of bed. He had not subjected himself to the humiliation of the industrial scale in quite some time, but he guessed he was now a little over nine hundred pounds—nearly at the one-thousand-pound mark. The phrase one-thousand-pound man seemed to go better with headlines like "Had to be Buried in Shipping Container" or "Found Dead in Pile of Macaroni" than "Loses Eight Hundred Pounds by Sweating to the Oldies." A weight that required a comma seemed impossible to escape alive. It was like some kind of metabolic gate where anyone weighing nine hundred ninety-nine pounds or less could still turn it around, but that one extra pound meant infected bed sores, certain death, and a team of firemen coming to cut your corpse out of your house.

Beep. Beep. Beep.

The diet barbeque-chicken pizza his housekeeper put in the microwave every morning was ready, which meant he'd been stuck in bed for four hours. Moment of truth. He tried to push his leg toward the edge of the bed, but couldn't move it. He tried again. Nothing. He was still stuck. This was the beginning of the end. He'd started to mentally make out his will when he realized that he wasn't paralyzed by fatness. His leg was just caught in the sheets. Slowly, he slid his leg along the sweat-soaked sheet, inch by inch, like a glacier made of fat.

“Woof.” Butter, his less-than-svelte yellow lab, stared at him with a ridiculous amount of expectation considering his predicament. Port stared at the ceiling. The dog walker was late, but maybe she could hold on a little longer until Von arrived. “Woof.” Butter could not hold on.

“Yes. You have to pee, and I am trying not to die a humiliating death. We both have problems.”

At that, Butter laid her chin on the bed and issued forth a noise that was one third yawn, one third whine, and one third bark. “Growlch!”

“Growlch is right. I’ll just bite the bullet and do it then, shall I?” Butter backed away from the bed, wagging her chubby tail. Port kicked at the sheet until it released his calf, swung his legs over the side of the bed, pushed up with both arms, and with less effort than he’d expected, got himself to a seated position. “Like Lazarus from the grave,” he announced with reserved triumph.

Butter whined from the doorway. Port pushed on the bed with his hands and sunk his feet into the floor. He wobbled—one slip away from falling back into bed and into oblivion. He hoped death would come before the television cameras arrived. Then, in a move that truly felt like resurrection, he somehow wobbled upright. He waved his arm in a flabby flourish. “You shall live another day, you magnificent beast, for your master has made it to his feet.” Butter turned and ran toward the kitchen.

There was a scream. He tensed—ready to spring into action, his old police instincts kicking in. He chuckled. Apparently, his instincts were unaware that he was no longer a fit, hundred-seventy-five-pound police detective but a Jabba-esque pile of goo who could not spring into anything, even if he were to be fired from the world’s largest catapult.

He listened for another scream but heard only laughter and accordion music. He’d forgotten that his neighbor and best friend, Farmer Ted, was hosting one of his silly all-day parties. For some strange reason, Ted had invited him to his Pirates Versus Nuns Carnival even though Port hadn't left the house in three years.

Butter backed her ample rump up to the front door, smacking her tail against it with a *Thumpity, thumpity!* As if to say, "Let me out now, or the tail gets it." The SFPD had trained Port to evaluate hostage situations, and this crazy dog meant it. He walked toward the door as quickly as his fat feet would carry him, which was not quite as fast as an old man recovering from hip surgery. When he finally reached the door, he pushed it open as Butter nosed her way out. "Let the wild rumpus start," he said, as he always did. Butter took two steps and peed directly next to the front step, as she always did.

Port looked out over his little corner of China Basin. It was nothing more than a gravel parking lot bordered by a rusted chain link fence, two rows of warehouses and a dusty little beach. A small weather-worn sign down by the water read "Welcome to Deadman's Gulch," which was odd because if you made it to the water, you'd already been through the entirety of Deadman's Gulch.

There was another scream. He looked up as a girl dressed in a pink wig and a leather bustier ran by him. She was holding a garden-hose contraption in the air that spouted bubbles instead of water. A bubble landed on Port's face and popped directly into his eyeball. He rubbed his eye and grumbled.

"Sorry about my bubbles." The girl smiled at Port.

He looked down at the tiny red belt that she had cinched around the bustier, giving her figure an unnatural wasp-waist effect. He mumbled something that probably sounded like "bubbly eye" and looked away—embarrassed that a wasp-waisted girl had caught him being grumpy and fat. He blinked a few times with his eye pointed at the ground, letting the tears and soap flow to the ground. When the deluge stopped, he looked up. The girl was gone, and a familiar figure was riding toward him on a unicycle.

"Porterhouse Steak! To what do I owe the pleasure, sir?"

Port blinked and rubbed his eye until he could see Ted clearly. With his red-and-white striped stocking hat and a well-worn eye patch over one side of his glasses, he looked very much the part of pirate—a pirate who slept in grease-stained black jeans.

"I'm not joining in on your silly little reindeer games, Farmer Ted."

"Pirate games. Silly pirate games." Ted maneuvered the unicycle in front of the door and carefully but easily kept upright in that one spot. He was quite good at it, but that was the problem with Ted. He put an inordinate amount of effort into useless pursuits like balancing on a wheel and throwing weird parties. Even the nickname thing. Ted's real name was Mason Gruber, but Port called him Farmer Ted—based on a character in the movie *16 Candles* who claimed to be King of the Dipshits because if there was anything that Ted was king of, it was The Dipshits. Done. End of effort. Ted couldn't be satisfied with giving Port just one nickname in return. He had to roll out a string of different riffs on the name Port (Porterhouse Steak, Portola Park, After Dinner Port, etc.) to prove his endless font of useless creativity.

The problem was that Ted possessed a font of useful creativity for computer programming, but instead of revolutionizing the product of some local tech company, he'd perfected the art of dipshittery. He was against anything that threatened to allow him to make a living wage—anything legitimate, that is. Ted once sold baby aspirin at thirty dollars a pop to guests at his own party, claiming that he'd taught them all a valuable lesson about the drug trade that was worth much more than thirty bucks, but when Port hired him to code Dickopedia, he refused payment. Port argued that Dickopedia was essential to his PI business and thus a valuable service, but Ted just ranted about not wanting to become another circuit breaker in the tech machine. It wasn't surprising, then, when Darla showed up at Port's door, eight months pregnant, tearful and tired of Ted and his Pirate Mace charade.

"Pirate Mace! Need some fuel for your journey?" A young man dressed like a pirate who shopped exclusively at discount stores offered Ted a giant lollypop. Ted waved him off. The motion disrupted his balance, and he fell off the unicycle, landing hard on his feet with an ungraceful hop. The unicycle flew up in an arc that threatened to knock him on his head, but Ted ducked and caught it by the seat with one hand. The wheel spun as he held the cycle up in the air.

A few party-goers cheered. One man yelled, "Do it again, Mace!"

"Here, you try it, smart-ass." Ted handed the unicycle to the man and walked over to Port. "What are you doing out in the daylight? Aren't you afraid you'll turn to dust?"

"Yes, but I'm waiting for Princess Flabby to complete her morning proclamation."

"Get on with it, Butterball!" Ted grabbed the dog by the jowls and kissed her nose. Butter licked both sides of his face, mussing up his well-waxed mustache. He twirled the ends before giving her another quick peck.

Suddenly, Port felt every one of his thirty-eight years and at least eight hundred seventy-five of his nine hundred plus pounds. His hand gripped the doorjamb in an effort to keep his weight from sinking into his overworked knees. He often thought about his knees. The human knee joint was about the size of a grapefruit, and it wasn't fair to place the weight of an entire shipment of grapefruits on top of them.

He leaned against the doorjamb and called out for Butter. She ignored him and squatted in front of a Mercedes. Port looked around. If one of the dipshits complained about one little, steaming pile of dog crap and asked him to pick it up, he'd be sunk. He hadn't bent over in years.

A man with salt-and-pepper dreads turned the corner on an old bike that was decorated liberally with what appeared to be butt plugs. Von. As his bike hit the pebbly surface of the parking lot, the front tire wiggled back and forth and his dreads bounced up and down. Von took one arm off the handlebar, leaned back on his seat and nodded casually at Port. Port nodded less than casually. Von glanced at the pile behind the car and pointed to a compact package of purple bags attached to his belt. Von was the Batman of dog poop. Despite the searing pain that was traveling from his knees into his shins, Port smiled.

Port was about to start the laborious process of peeling his carcass off the doorjamb when he saw his upstairs neighbor, Irina, holding a red cup and looking at once bored and bewildered. She was a ceramic artist who worked exclusively in baroque saucers and plates depicting details of Napoleon's invasion of Russia. (The one possible exception was a Mount Everest-shaped sugar bowl she'd made for him as tribute to his ancestral homeland, but she'd still included a tiny group of 19th century soldiers huddled under the mound of sugar that formed the mountain's snowy peak.)

Her face brightened when she saw Port. She waved. Port waved back and considered calling her over, so he could, yet again, remind her to never accept an invitation of any kind from Ted, but his knees reminded him that he was about to collapse. He turned slowly away, planning to plunge his enormous rump into his custom-made chair and leave it there until late afternoon, but before he'd even taken a few shuffling steps, he heard a scream—not the high-pitched, playful scream of bubbles and kink but the low guttural scream of terror.

His instinct kicked in and told him to run out the door. Stupid instinct. How was he supposed to squeeze through something as dainty as a door? He would have to go through the garage. His stomach flip-flopped at the thought of it.

A few months ago, Port had a nightmare where Darla and Johnny Depp set fire to the warehouse. The famous actor lit match after match, tossing them toward the blazing entryway while Darla stared though the blackened skeleton of the warehouse at what was left of the back bedroom. He couldn't see it through the smoke and flames, but Port knew his dead body was there, burning slowly to a large pile of fatty ash. The next morning, Port called a contractor to cut out the living room wall and put in a door to the garage large enough to maneuver a forklift through. He also bought a forklift.

As he lumbered across the living room and pressed the button, it felt strange—as though he were lumbering across his own grave. He hadn't expected to use the door while he was alive. The door rattled open, slowly. Port took a deep breath and shuffled through the garage and out the docking-bay door. Despite an increasingly distressing and persistent tightening in his chest, Port felt a small thrill as he blinked in the bright sun before stepping out into Deadman's Gulch. From behind him, the microwave beeped three times.

A scream came from the water's edge. He spotted a girl in a nun's costume standing on a makeshift raft about two feet from shore. The water was shallow enough that she wouldn't need to know how to swim to get safely back to dry land, but even from about seventy-five feet away, Port could see she was in trouble.

He pushed on, his extensive flab collection wobbling unpleasantly as his knees sent distress signals in the form of searing, grinding pain. He was about to give up when he heard splashing at his feet. He'd made it to the water. A crowd had gathered around the raft—including the dollar-store pirate. Ted kept telling her it was okay, as if she were having a bad trip. This wasn't drugs. She was having a panic attack. Port had had them before, only without quite so much screaming, he hoped. Ted continued talking her down. "It's okay. It's oh...oh, holy shitballs!"

Port tried to say, "Get her off the raft," but he was using what precious air he could suck into his body to push his gigantic calves through the water, so it came out as more of a tiny squeak that sounded like "farf!"

"Did he just say farf?" Captain Dollar Store said.

Ted gaped at Port, his lower jaw hung so low, he had to close it to say, "I think so."

"Farf," Port said and realized that he was not going to convey any thought more complicated than "farf" with the small amount of air currently wisping about in his lungs. Worse, he realized that he, Porter Nepal, a nine-hundred-pound ball of goo who could barely pick up a slice of diet pizza, would have to pick up an actual girl—a girl with long blonde hair, sea-green eyes and an incongruously tight nun's costume. He considered having a panic attack himself, but then his arms lifted as if attached to helium balloons, and he picked her up. He was so surprised, he almost dropped her but instead, he boosted her awkwardly over his shoulder and lurched to the shore.

Back on dry land, his knees ordered him to collapse, but at his size, collapsing might be catastrophic. He wobbled before taking a deep breath and throwing himself backwards onto his bottom. The landing hurt more than he'd expected, considering all the padding he had back there. He looked up at the thin clouds whipping across the blue sky and imagined tomorrow's headline: "Nine Hundred Pound Man Beaches

Self. Breaks Forklift." The worst thing was that she would witness it all. Maybe she wasn't watching. Maybe she'd run off to sob in her car. He looked up to see that she was still there and, to his horror, looking at him.

"Thank you," she said. Maybe he was delirious from lack of oxygen, but he didn't detect any disgust in her voice.

There was a hand on his shoulder. "That was pretty kick ass stuff there, Portlandia."

Port hung his head. His elbows sunk into the shelf of fat he'd installed on his torso. "I think I'm going to need help getting back in." He expected Ted to panic and call the fire department. Instead, he felt one arm under his shoulder, then a second arm under his other shoulder.

"Oh Porter! That was just the most astounding thing," Irina said, attempting to lift his massive girth.

"Stop, you can't take the weight."

"It's okay," Ted said. "We're stronger than we look."

He was right because they somehow managed to drag Port into the warehouse and to his chair.

"Do you need anything?" Irina asked.

Beep. Beep. Beep.

He'd made it out of bed, saved a girl from ankle-deep water, and thanks to his surprisingly strong friends, had avoided the forklift. Port figured that after three miracles in one morning, breakfast would be nice and asked her if she would retrieve his pizza from the microwave.

Chapter One

Talia was naked, standing on the bridge again, and this time, he was going to kill her. A motor boat sped by, chopping up a thick, frothy wake. Horns blared. Angry voices yelled out of the darkness, demanding that *something* happen. She was suddenly acutely aware of her body's imperfections (patches of cellulite where her legs met her butt, eight extra pounds of pudge on her hips, she'd only shaved one leg that day). The giant lunged at her. The tire iron cut through the air with an audible *whoosh*. She closed her eyes and leapt into the uncertainty of the black water. She opened her eyes just in time to see the whirring blades of the outboard motor—too late to get out of the way.

Talia opened her eyes again. Kirk blinked at her. She stared at him for a while and then said, "I have to quit my job."

"Meow," Kirk said, without taking any time to consider what she'd just said.

"Coffee. Coffee first. Then you get fed."

While pouring Kirk's kibble, she realized two things. One, Toby had already fed the cat and two, she couldn't quit her job. It was an acting job—a real acting job. It was what she'd gone to college for, what she'd moved to California for and what she'd wanted to be when she grew up ever since her mom took her Boston to see The Nutcracker. Everyone else in the audience was watching the performers' feet, but nine-year-old Talia barely noticed their feet. She was watching their faces. And now, twenty-nine-year-old Talia wrote *actress* on forms that asked for her occupation, and when people asked, she would say, "I work at the Crime Museum. I do the re-en*act*ments." She always emphasized the third syllable. She acted. She was an actor. Quitting was out of the question.

*

Talia left ten minutes late and had to run to catch the 30-Stockton. The bus was crammed with commuters carrying sharp-cornered bags. The only place for her to squeeze in was near the door, so she had to step out every time someone got on or off. At her stop, she leapt off the middle step and onto the sidewalk. She ran down Jones, side-stepping the tourists who'd congregated around the t-shirt shops. She ran across the parking lot and around to the side door of the Crime Museum—only two minutes late for her shift.

She ran down the stairs and into the caverns and slowed to a quick walk when she emerged into the open common area from the narrow, low ceilinged hallway. Grimey said that the caverns were a holdout from when the crime museum had been a speakeasy. They stretched all the way out to Jefferson Street and sometimes, when it was quiet, the faint rattle of the F-train could be heard. The rooms were dank-smelling but well-lit and scattered with costumes, snack bags and quarter-filled bottles of Jack Daniels. (Grimey always said, "Work tipsy, not drunk." It was a rule they almost always followed.)

Talia banged open her dressing room door and tossed her bag on her table. Lucy was in what Talia called her mermaid position: stretched out, legs on one chair, her hips on another, while she leaned on one elbow as close to the mirror as possible as she carefully applied bright red lipstick. She turned from the mirror and smiled. "How do I look?"

"You look like the perfect...um...murdered hooker?"

"Wrong." She looked back in the mirror, threw her reflection a pouty kiss and then dragged a perfectly manicured hand across the lipstick, creating a large, cherry-red smudge that went half-way up her cheek. "Murderous hooker."

"Ooh! Nice role." Talia swiped on some nude lipstick that was true to the fifties-era secretary she was playing but washed out her complexion.

"Yeah, well..." Lucy looked at her own reflection. "I don't like to complain about a paying gig, but I'm starting to feel like my roles are limited because I'm the black girl."

Talia took her flip wig out of her bag, pulled off the hairnet and patted down the fly-aways. The only roles she could remember Lucy playing were hooker roles: crack, prison and now, murderous. "You should complain. Maybe Grime would let us switch."

"Really? You'd let me play Kitty Genovese?" Lucy looked at Talia and raised an eyebrow. "Could you really give up that fabulous wig?"

Talia looked in the mirror, pulled the brunette wig over her head and tugged at the curls that flipped up from the middle of her neck up to her earlobe. It was poofy and outdated, like something Annette Funicello would wear to go surfing, but the color made her eyes pop even with the pale lipstick. "It's not the hair, Loose. It's the rest of it."

"Oh yeah." Lucy recoiled. "It's a pretty gruesome story line. Still..." Lucy waved her eyeliner at Talia's reflection in the mirror. "She was a badass."

Talia tucked a few errant blond hairs under the wig and stood up. "Yeah. A dead badass."

She walked up the stairs, out of the caverns and into the theater. Lucy was right. Kitty Genovese, a tough, deep-in-the-closet lesbian from Queens, was a badass. Living with the constant fear of being found out must have desensitized Kitty to the point that walking home late at night was no big deal. So, that was how Talia played her—tough, tortured and desensitized—even as sound of the footsteps grew louder and closer.

When Winston Mosely caught her, she fought fiercely, but he was too strong. He threw her to the ground. That was the cue for the lights to go out. The crime museum couldn't show a rape. There were kids...and Midwesterners. They had changed the timeline of the attack and put the rape in a more tasteful place—before the murder—because necrophilia was never tasteful, no matter how old you were or what part of the country you were from.

A scrim painted to look like an apartment building was reeled down with a *squeak*. Talia lay on the floor and stared up at the dusty back of the scrim. Cobwebs dripped off it like ivy. The windows lit up: her cue. Talia screamed as the callous shadowy inhabitants turned away from poor Kitty Genovese and her plight. One of the silhouettes was making a pot of tea. Talia had the urge to yell, "Hey lady, put down the kettle! I'm getting raped down here." But that wouldn't go over well with the kids or the Midwesterners.

As the scrim went back up, Talia stumbled to her feet and ran out onto the brightly-lit stage. The lighting went from soft yellow to harsh red. The music switched from mostly violins to mostly violas—a sure sign of doom. George Springer sprang from the shadows. He looked crazed—extremely crazed (George was a bit of an over-actor). One of the tourists, an older lady in khaki shorts and a sweatshirt appliquéd with the letters *SF*, gasped audibly.

Talia looked up at George. Only he wasn't George anymore or even Winston Mosely. He was the man from her dream, and instead of the prop knife, he held a rusty tire iron. She looked behind her. The water was there, dark, swirling, and...red? Had she already fallen in and been chopped up by the blades? The giant raised the tire iron. Talia screamed. George brought the knife down on her chest, plunging the blade harmlessly into its sheath. The strobe lights came on. The music hit a crescendo. Talia continued to scream. George stared at her, frozen. The lights went down. Talia continued to scream.

"Our Kitty seems to be more resilient than the real one," Phil, the guide, said with a chuckle after Talia finally stopped screaming.

A man in an Alcatraz windbreaker whispered to the older lady, "method actor," and she nodded, staring at Talia.

George knelt on the floor next to her, shoving the blade of the prop knife into his palm over and over. Talia wiped away the tears that wouldn't stop flowing.

*

"Are you fucking crazy?!!!" It was a text from Lucy. She was right, but what could she do? She couldn't afford therapy without a job, and she couldn't work at the crime museum without therapy. She turned on the radio, opened her laptop and clicked onto Craig's List.

"Oh em gee, dudes!" Toby's voice devolved into the half-squeal, half-growl that was the hallmark of his on-air KGAY persona, Toby the Flaming Rock God. "You all know my fag hag, Teabag...." Talia held her breath. Toby often talked about her on the air, always using the nickname he'd given her in college, but he usually let her know before he did it. There was no warning this time. "She quit her job at the crime museum. How do you quit the crime museum? All she had to do was stand there and *pretend* to be stabbed. It wasn't like she was *actually* getting stabbed."

"I don't know, Toby. Maybe her boss was a jerk? Or maybe he was sexually harassing her. I've met Teabag, if she worked here, I'd totally harass *that*." Vick the Straight Metal Freak was KGAY's sole straight on-air personality, a fact he often made unnecessarily clear.

"Oh, come on! They don't call him Grimey for nothing. That filthy hippy couldn't sexually harass a bar of soap, never mind a woman." There was a pause. "Just kidding, Grimey. You know I love you."

Talia smiled. Grimey would be getting a bottle of single-malt Scotch from Toby. He sent one every time he made fun of him on the air. Grimey, a dedicated Deadhead, never listened to KGAY and was always surprised and appreciative of the intermittent deliveries of free booze.

She turned the radio down and went back to the job hunt. She dismissed the first five job postings because they offered "no compensation." The next two postings required that applicants be "comfortable with nudity." Talia wondered if it meant her own nudity or someone else's as she clicked on a listing with the subject line "2 Ton Dick Needs Legs."

"Let me begin this job posting by saying that the Legs I require are not for a sex thing. In fact, I absolutely forbid anyone who answers this ad to ever consider having anything that even resembles sex with me, but I am sure that won't be a problem for all but the most fervent chubby chasers amongst you. No. Chubby is not the right word for what I am. I am a magnificent specimen of man's ability to pile obscene amounts of flab onto a human skeleton. The only difference between me and an elephant is fifty pounds and a PI license, which is why I need to hire a person of normal weight to do the leg work required by my occupation. No experience necessary, but if you do have training or experience of

any kind—anything from working as a security guard at Bug's Market to acting as a docent at the Crime Museum, please include it in your reply."

Talia wasn't overly superstitious, but she read her horoscope every day, and she believed in signs, especially obvious ones. This was an obvious sign. She couldn't apply, though. Toby had helped her put her résumé online when they'd first arrived in San Francisco, but she didn't have the link anymore. She could ask him when he got off work, but she didn't want someone else to take the job that was clearly, and cosmically, hers. She sent a quick response, lying about why she wasn't sending her résumé, and promising to send the link as soon as her server went back up.

*

Talia arrived at Julio's just as Toby walked in. He held the door open for her. "You're late."

"I'm always late. As my best friend, you should know that," she said. It took thirty minutes to get anywhere in San Francisco. It was an odd fact, but a fact that most of the city's citizens agreed on. Talia refused to believe it, and she almost never gave herself more than fifteen minutes to get anywhere.

"I'm still hoping you'll change." Toby waved over Julio, the hip, mustachioed owner, and ordered a round of Long Island iced teas.

Talia took a sip and winced. It tasted exactly what gasoline with a splash of Coke should taste like. "What's in this?"

"I have no idea." Toby smiled as he took a long sip.

Julio tapped their change on the bar. "Me either. No one ever orders them but this guy." He pointed at Toby.

Her phone rattled against the bar. She picked it up to silence it but accidentally answered it. "Hello, my name is Porter Nepal. You responded to my listing today. Is this an acceptable time to call?"

"Oh...yes. We're at a...at a store. I mean I'm at a grocery store. Uh...grocery shopping." Talia expected to be laughed at, hung up on, or both.

"Grocery shopping at the grocery store? That's important stuff. I won't keep you, then."

"Two more drinks, lady and gent?" Julio said loudly. Talia motioned at him to be quiet, and he backed away, holding a finger to his lips.

"They're giving out free samples. Hold on a second." Talia walked out the door but found the sidewalk crowded with chatty smokers, so she ducked into the alley and stood next to a dumpster. "Sorry about that."

"Not at all. I was just looking at your résumé, and I think you might be perfect for the position."

"My résumé? But I...I didn't send it."

"Well, yes...right...that is true. But you mentioned that you had one online, and since I had your full name...I hope you don't mind, but I did a quick search for it."

"Oh! I guess I could have done that myself when I sent the email, but I've just been so busy with my...errands." Just then, a girl walked by with a man who must have said something outrageously funny because she didn't just laugh, she scream-laughed.

"Grocery shopping, right?"

"Right." Why did that girl have to scream-laugh? Why couldn't she have just giggled? "I'm not really grocery shopping."

"Really?" He sounded unsurprised.

"I'm out with my roommate at a bar." She must have been wrong about that cosmic sign because she was surely about to lose a job she'd never even had.

"Detective work does call for a certain amount of deception."

"I can do that...that is if the people around me would just *keep quiet*." She said the last bit loud enough for the scream laugher to hear and, hopefully, feel the appropriate amount of shame.

"Would you be able to come in for an interview tomorrow morning?"

Talia stepped out of the alley. This was not a conversation to have while standing next to a fossilized pigeon carcass. "Yes. Great. Um...." Nine would be impossibly early—especially since she was sure to have a few more drinks to celebrate her new job opportunity. Eleven was too late. Only people who stayed up all night drinking considered eleven to be *morning*. Ten was respectable, sober even. "How about ten?"

"Perfect! Do you know how to find a neighborhood called Deadman's Gulch?"

"I know exactly where that is."

Talia walked back into the bar. Deadman's Gulch. Maybe it was another sign—a bad one. "Hey, remember that guy I told you a.... What's wrong?"

His eyes were brimming with tears. In over ten years of friendship, Talia had only seen Toby cry twice: once when his first broadcasting job (an oldies station called WSHK, The Shark) fired him for coming out and then again when Linda Ronstadt lost her voice. Something bad must have happened. A red-hot ball of dread bloomed in her chest. Toby pointed at the television. The news was on, and the anchorman was talking about Buster Bones. Everyone in the bar stood and tilted their heads up at the screen. Buster Bones was dead. Worse than that, he was murdered.

When the news finally cut to commercial, Julio tearfully unplugged the jukebox. He plugged it back in, and the crowd lined up to play Buster and Crunch Pup songs. The first song was a Crunch Pup song, "Dark Star." Toby nodded at Talia: his choice. Everyone remembered that song from classic radio playlists but not well enough to know all the words. They mumbled along with the verses and raised their voices to a drunken shout during the chorus.

A few rounds in, people started to talk about their brushes with Buster. Julio served him a drink once and said he tipped like a rock star but didn't act like one. Toby ran into him in the elevator at KGAY, and the two of them discussed New Wave bands from New York and the fact that the term New Wave didn't mean anything anymore. The girl at the corner of the bar had run into him at Amoeba in the discount vinyl section, and he helped her choose an album: *Rock and Roll Survivors* by Fanny.

The best Buster story, though, came from the bar's sound man, Dusty Trails. "I was working at The Fillmore and Crunch Pup was in one of those new bands showcases. A very long time ago." He paused and laughed softly. "Then, last summer, I'm at The Great American Music Hall when Buster walks in for sound check. I was going to introduce myself and then tell him that I'd run sound for him back in the old days. But before I could say a word, Buster walks over to my booth and says, 'Cool, man. I'm glad they got you for this, Dusty.' Couldn't believe it. Ol' Buster must have worked with hundreds of sound guys over the years, and he remembered my name and took the time to...." He raised his glass and choked back a sob. "To Buster." The crowd raised their glasses in silence.

Chapter Two

When Talia got to Deadman's Gulch, it was five past ten. The last time she'd been here it had been sunny. Today was gray. The buildings were dark gray, the gravel road was a whitish gray, the industrial cranes were green gray, the bay was a bluish gray, and the sky had a steely gray cloud cover. In the middle of the grayness stood an older blonde woman in a white jumpsuit splashed with brightly-colored paint. She was using a garden hose to fill a large plastic tub that was also white and speckled with paint.

"I'm sorry to bother you, but I'm late for an interview. Do you know where number ten is?"

The woman lifted her arm and held the hose up by her shoulder. The water splashed at her feet. "Are you looking for Port?" She had a thick accent—Russian, probably.

"Yes."

"He's right over there, but...."

Talia started walking toward the large gray warehouse. "Thank you."

"I don't think you're prepared for what you are about to see."

"It's okay. Port warned me." Talia said over her shoulder.

As Talia knocked on the door, she heard the woman say, "Then I know you are not prepared."

The door was opened by a woman wearing a stained t-shirt and threadbare sweater. Her dark hair was pulled into two messy braids that peeked out from underneath a faded black kerchief decorated with skulls and crossbones.

"Hi. I'm looking for Porter Nepal."

"We've been expecting you." The woman smiled—an odd, knowing smile that made Talia wonder if she were the butt of a joke. Was it because she was late?

"Darla, just open the door before she thinks we're all crazy people!" a man's voice yelled from inside. Darla kept smiling as though she hadn't heard him.

"I'm sorry I'm late. I got lost," Talia lied.

"Late? I thought you were five minutes early?" Darla, who was making a point of not opening the door, turned toward an area that Talia could not see. "You said she would be fifteen minutes late, but it's not even ten past."

"I don't think you're crazy at all," Talia said. Another lie.

"Darla! Let her in before she runs away from this loony bin."

Darla flung the door open. Talia had expected the space to be decorated in traditional San Francisco warehouse style: all stainless steel, movie posters, and ironic shag. It was pleasantly jarring to see it decked out in polished wood, antiques and well-faded oriental rugs. The only nod to warehouse design was the open layout.

In front of the entry area there was an office area with three television screens on the back wall and a mahogany desk, large enough for several workstations. To the left was a kitchen where Tibetan prayer flags were strung across a small window. To the right was an enormous living area, dotted liberally with sofas and overstuffed chairs and featuring a play area for a baby or toddler.

"Hello, Miss Green." He must have been sitting at the desk the whole time. Why hadn't she noticed him? Maybe it was because he was small—about the size of a ten-year-old child.

She blinked, opened her mouth to say something and then closed it again. The man wasn't small, but his over-sized chair and clothing gave the illusion that he was. He was an average-sized man—an attractive one who, with his dark complexion, thick hair and brown eyes, reminded her of the brief yet intense crush she'd had on Frank Langella after watching *Dracula* in junior high.

"I'm Porter Nepal, but please call me Port. Excuse me for not getting up, but I'm glad to meet you. Formally anyways," he said, and that was when she realized they'd already met.

*

Ten hours later, Talia was at The Blue Cat, an upscale bar on a downscale corner of North Beach, drinking a Manhattan with extra cherries and watching the door for the mark so she could tail him. She'd never waited for a mark or tailed anyone before. She'd shaken a tail once by running across Market Street to lose a crackhead who'd been following her, but that didn't really count because crackheads are notoriously easy to shake.

Initially, she'd turned the job down and walked out the door, but then Darla chased her out and explained all of it. Body Dysmorphic Disorder. Port thought he was fat, and nothing anyone did or said could change his mind. Darla must have caught on to Talia's initial attraction, though, because she also said, "Listen, I love Port like the crazy brother I've never had, but this is a guy who has put seven hundred imaginary pounds of fat between himself and anyone who would get close to him. You'd be smart to keep things as professional as possible, and if you think you can't do that then you really should run away...as fast as you can."

A man walked in. Not him. Talia picked up Dicko and typed in the word *mark*. A dossier for Richard "Drick"

Wayland, and all his personal information (some of it disturbingly personal) came up on the screen. His current internet activity was displayed on a crawl at the bottom—that was how she knew he was coming to this bar. He had tweeted about "heading to The Blue Pussy for a beaver hunt." According to Drick's GPS data, the beaver hunter would be arriving any second.

"Can I buy you a drink, Blondie?"

A lot of men called her Blondie: men in bars, men on the bus, her drama teacher. She didn't mind it really, but she didn't turn her head for it. She looked toward the door and then at the man who'd made the offer. Shit. It was the mark. She shoved Dicko back in her purse, and as she did, her elbow hit her Manhattan spilling it, extra cherries and all, on her dress—her *white* dress. "Damn! Why did I have to get extra cherries?"

"Another of those for the lady. Easy on the cherries," Drick told the bartender and then handed her a wad of cocktail napkins.

"Excuse me, ah.... Can you wait right here?"

"How about I come help you?" He put an arm around her waist and squeezed—it was like being caught in the coils of a horny boa constrictor.

The bartender came back with her drink. "No men in the ladies' room, please," he said robotically, as though he'd had to say that particular phrase a lot.

She ran into the bathroom, turned on the sink and slapped at the stain with the wet cocktail napkins, trying to dilute the bourbon and cherry juice before it set. Out of curiosity and desperation, she plugged "spilled Manhattan on white dress" into Dicko. It came up with the names of two cleaners in the neighborhood who could handle catastrophic stains and then vibrated a quiet alert. Drick had just sent a tweet, a reference to the "beaver hunt" he'd mentioned earlier: "Snared one!!!"

She generated a fake smile as she opened the bathroom door. Drick wasn't at the bar. She looked around. The bartender pointed at the door. Talia ran outside. He was about a half-a-block away, talking on his cell phone. She walked toward him and typed "following mark on foot" into Dicko.

It came up with: *Stay one block behind mark.*

A whole block? How would she keep up? What if he ducked down an alley? She looked up to check how far behind him she was and nearly walked into him as he stood with his arms crossed around his chest. "Are you following me?"

She stumbled back a step. The only instruction Port had given her was to check Dicko before she did anything, and she'd already screwed that up. "Um, no...I just...I'm sorry, I...."

"No, no. I'm the one who's sorry. Sorry I walked out on such a supremely sexy woman." He spoke directly at her chest. "The name is Drick."

"Alex Owens." Talia held out her hand, hoping he would just go in for a plain old vertical grab and handshake, but he grabbed her hand horizontally, which meant he was going to kiss it. And he did. His lips were either very wet or he had slipped the top of her hand the tongue. She slid her hand away and wiped it on her sweater.

"Excuse me. I just have to finish this text."

She typed, "The mark is hitting on me."

A red, square button appeared on the screen. *Press the record button and flirt with mark.*

"Sorry about that." She tried to look into Drick's eyes but they were on a stakeout of her cleavage. "That was my date. I told him not to bother showing up."

On the short walk back to the Blue Cat, Drick suggested getting a hotel room and listed three sexual positions he wanted to try with her, as well as several household items he would incorporate into their lovemaking—a bottle of spray cheese, a make-up mirror and a portable flashlight.

Once at the bar, she was glad to see her drink waiting for her and took a large sip. "You move fast and weird but all that stuff you just said sounds—"

"Exhilarating?" Drick swirled his index finger into her drink and then sucked it.

"Complicated." She pushed the contaminated drink across the bar. "Do you mind if I meet you at the hotel? I need to...um...get a Brazilian wax." The bartender retrieved her glass just as she said the word *wax*. He shook his head.

"Hells yeah!" Drick tried but failed to get a high-five from the bartender.

She stared at him, mesmerized by his repulsiveness, and then smiled. "Let me just see if I can get a last-minute appointment." She took out Dicko and typed, "Caught mark on tape offering to have sex with me...and household appliances."

Congratulations! Job Complete.

Once in the cab, she called Toby. "Oh my god. Ew! I cannot believe that weirdo wanted to bring a bottle of squeeze cheese into it."

"Spray cheese," Talia said.

"Even worse."

"How is that worse?"

"I don't know. Higher salt content? CFCs? It's all gross. I hope, though, that all you have to do is get hit on by gross dudes. What if you get a murder case or something like that? That would be scary, Tea."

"Port said that ninety-nine percent of my cases are going to be following suspected adulterers, like Captain Beaver Hunter."

"What about the other one percent?"

"What do you mean?"

"Well, maybe they're going to be murder cases."

"I'm just an assistant. I'm sure it'll be a long time before I get a murder case, Tobe."

Chapter Three

"We've got our first murder case," Port said.

"It won't be dangerous, will it?" Talia asked, pouring herself a cup of coffee.

"Well, it is a violent case—an armored car heist that turned deadly."

"Holy crap." She put her coffee on the desk and sat in her chair, careful not to kick the dog, who'd spread out like a furry oil slick under the desk.

"Yes, but I misspoke. It isn't really our case. It's Detective Nguyen's."

"Detective? Like another PI or like a cop?" she asked, gently nudging the dog so she could put her foot on the floor. Butter accommodated, moving to the side, stretching out, and laying her head on Talia's foot.

"Exactly like a cop," Port said. "Brad and I were on the force together. He usually only asks my help on cases that I can solve without leaving the warehouse." He opened his laptop and typed as he talked. The light from the screen made the hollows of his face appear dark and gaunt. It reminded her of a book of optical illusions she had when she was in the third grade. Most of the images were lines and patterns that seemed to move, but her favorite was a drawing of a Victorian woman looking in the mirror. If you looked at the drawing a different way, it looked like a skull, with the woman's head forming one eye and the reflection of her head forming the other eye.

Port was talking to her and saying, "...investigating any successful armored car robbery. They are always put together by the man at the top who lives out of town and keeps his hands clean, there is always a middle man, and there is always one inside man."

"Why just one?" Talia blew on her coffee and sipped. It was cold. What time did Port get up in the morning that his coffee was cold by nine a.m.? "Couldn't there be two inside men? Rules were made to be broken, right?"

"Wrong. Rules were made to be followed." He smiled at her. "Two inside men might argue, which might lead one to snitch on the other, which would expose the middleman, which could lead to the man at the top. That is why the police always start with finding the inside man. The problem is that the bad guys know this, so the middlemen almost always go out of their way to leave him dead."

"So, is the inside man dead?"

"That's what we need to find out. Two men were shot. One died." He tapped at his keyboard and pointed at one of the TV screens on the wall. It displayed two photographs—one of an older man with close-cropped salt-and-pepper hair and a uniform shirt that was buttoned to the top and another of a young, blond man with a scraggly beard. "Here's the driver, Jason Brandt. Single, twenty-three years old, from a well-to-do family in Marin. Worked for the armored car company since dropping out of Stanford two years ago. Brandt was shot twice in the chest and died. The passenger is Victor Diaz. Forty-five. Been with the company for twenty years. He has a wife and three kids: ages six, four and two. He was shot in the head and is currently in a coma at San Francisco General. So, what do you think, Miss Green? Gut reaction."

"I think it was the young guy."

"Ah, but what if I told you that the older guy has a rap sheet?" Port said. "Nothing recent. Shoplifting, weapons charges, aggravated assault. Which makes sense if you knew that, from the ages of fourteen to twenty-two, Diaz was involved in a Mission District gang called The Norteños."

Talia nodded, but she had never heard of The Norteños and thought the only gang activity in The Mission were the gangs of bloody-Mary aficionados she and Toby competed with for tables at popular brunch spots on Sunday mornings.

"So, why do you think it was the young guy? Is it because he's dead?" Port shifted in his chair in a way that seemed to take an inordinate amount of effort.

She looked up at Victor Diaz and his primly buttoned shirt and shrugged. "Diaz just doesn't look like the type."

"True enough. But maybe he needed the cash for his family. Desperation can turn just about anyone into The Type." He peered at his laptop screen. "He has some significant debt. Credit cards, hospital bills, his wife has student loans...about a hundred grand in all."

"I probably have almost two thirds of that in student loans and credit card bills, and I'm not even close to going into a life of crime. Was he about to lose his house or something?"

Port looked at his laptop and shook his head. "He lives in a rent controlled apartment in the outer Richmond. They've been there for fifteen years, so maybe your gut is on to something. His financial situation only shows us part of the picture, though." He turned his computer screen so she could see it.

"You hacked into his Netflix account?"

"Hack? I resent the implication. A friend of mine did. A good detective should always be able to hack a little and know someone else who can hack a lot. So, what does this say about Victor Diaz?"

"Well...." She pulled the laptop toward her and scrolled through the list of movie titles. "Disney princess movies. Probably for his kids. Dancing movies—*Lambada*, *Strictly Ballroom*, *Billy Elliot*, *Dirty Dancing*. Probably for his wife. Oh! I hit a vein of romantic comedies. Probably for date night. Date-night movies are always chick flicks."

"Always?"

"Of course." She looked up from the laptop. "Men have no problem snuggling up with a movie they hate because they know it will lead to sex and don't mind the trade-off. Women already see sex as a trade-off, so why would they compromise with the movie choice?"

"Women see sex as a trade-off?" He raised an eyebrow.

"Yes, but only on movie night." She smiled at him until he broke eye contact.

"And, well...um, which movies belong to our suspect?"

Talia shook her head as she scrolled. It was all dancing, princesses, romantic comedies, or all three. "He doesn't have any. Maybe he doesn't like movies."

"The account is in his name. He wouldn't get an account if he didn't like movies, so that means the dancing movies are his, which makes total sense."

"It does?"

"It does if you know that Victor Diaz likes to dance."

She laughed. "How do you know he likes to dance?"

"Why else would he rent so many dancing movies if he didn't?" He winked at her and then turned back to the laptop and clicked a few keys. "I admit my thesis seems a bit thin at the moment, but.... Aha!" He pointed up at the big screen on the wall.

It was a website for Caliente, a *Salsa* club on Valencia. Underneath the club's logo was a picture of an elaborately costumed couple executing an impressive lift.

"Wait...is that?"

Port widened his eyes. "Victor Diaz and his wife. To be honest, I checked the website of the *Salsa* club closest to Diaz's house, hoping to just find a number we could call, but there he is—in all his glory."

"There he is." She stared up at the screen, and then turned to Port. "But how do you know he's not just doing this for his wife? He watches chick flicks for her."

"Miss Green, a man will go dancing for his wife, he will even learn to dance for his wife, but he will never wear sequins for his wife."

She laughed. "So, you're saying that the costume had to be Victor's idea?"

"Absolutely. Now, let's compare the image of a family man who loves the art of the *Samba* with Brandt's viewing history." He turned back to his laptop and whistled. He put the list on the big screen.

"*Reservoir Dogs*, *Bottle Rocket*, *The Usual Suspects*, *Heat*, *Ocean's 11*...these are all crime movies," she said.

"Not just crime movies. Heist movies."

"Which means my gut feeling was right."

"Well, it means that we should be focusing on Brandt." He pointed at another laptop. "Take that and check Brandt's Facebook account while I sort through his tweets."

The other laptop was closer to Port than it was to Talia, but she leaned across the desk and slid it toward her. She scrolled through pages of rest-in-peace posts from Brandt's friends. "What am I looking for?"

"Pay attention to any odd status updates or check-ins from about a week ago. That's when a middleman would've recruited him. They don't like to recruit inside men too early because time to think means time to get cold feet...or snitch."

"A week ago, he was at Krav Maga. I guess he takes a class every Wednesday night at a place called the Dragon's Den."

"Sounds promising. Keep digging."

Talia found an album Brandt had labeled "Kickin' Butt in the Dragon's Den." Some of the pictures had been tagged. There was a plumber in Daly City, a stay at home dad in San Francisco, and an IT specialist in Menlo Park. None of them seemed like the type to plan an armed robbery.

"Is there anyone at the Dragon's Den named Spider?" Port said without taking his eyes off his screen.

"Not that I've seen. Why?"

"Because about a week ago, Brandt was apparently 'Meeting Spider at Bill's after Krav Maga tonight.'"

"What do you think the meeting was about?"

"Weird self-defense moves? Or perhaps they went to the same finishing school?" He shrugged. "Or just maybe, while all the secretive machinations between the man at the top and the man in the middle churned away, the man at the bottom went and broadcast it all over the Internet."

"Would that make the middleman Bill or Spider?"

"Do a map search for Dragon's Den. See if there are any bars nearby that might...."

"Here it is," she interrupted. "Bill's Billiards. A sports bar across from City College, three blocks from the Dragon's Den."

"Which would make Spider our potential middleman. Speaking of, have you seen this guy in your investigation?" He pointed at a large man in a photo of a Krav Maga class on the Dragon's Den homepage. His face was mostly hidden by his shoulder-length black hair, but the tattoo on his lower bicep was visible—a spider.

"I saw him, but he wasn't tagged, so I don't know who he is."

"Sure, you do." He tapped the screen.

Talia looked at the picture and then back at Port. "No, I don't."

"Have you ever taken a class like this?"

"Not exactly like that, but I've taken kick-boxing and hip-hop kickboxing and kick-boxing yoga and a self...Oh!" She saw it. All the people in the picture were doing the same move except for Spider. "He's the instructor."

"Which means he works there, and that means I can do this." He picked up his phone.

"Hello, Dragon Den? My name is Cryson, and I'm interested in signing up for your Crab Rangoon class. ...Crab Maga, yeah, that's it. ...Uh huh, Crab. That's what I said." Port had inexplicably adopted a weird Southern accent. "Let me ask y'all something. I was told by my friend...." Port looked at Talia expectantly. She stared back at him, wondering what he was expecting. "My friend is the one who told me about this class and his name is...." He pointed at her laptop. She finally got the hint and turned her laptop around. It was on the plumber's page. She pointed at the name.

"...Dave. His name is Dave Hernandez. Dave said that I should take the class from the guy with the spider tattoo. Do you know who...? Uh huh. Gil...Trenton? Listen, I live not too far from y'all, and I happened to walk by there last night. I looked in the window, and the feller I saw giving the class didn't seem to know what the heck he was doing. That wasn't Gil, was it?...Oh, I see. A substitute?" Port raised his eyebrows at Talia. "Gil called in sick, huh? Well, I can't wait to take this class...Huh? My credit card? No! I'm too excited. I'm coming down there with cash right now." He hung up.

Talia laughed. "I never knew you were such an actor, Port."

He laughed. "I thought you were laughing because you were imagining the looks on their faces when all of this...." He waved a hand awkwardly over his torso. "Tried to squeeze into their little dojo."

"Yeah. That's funny." Talia wasn't laughing anymore.

He nodded. "You're right. We should get back to work."

Talia drummed on the desk in celebration. "So, what now? I'm ready for my next case."

"That's too bad because it's just past ten, and we've got nothing to do until our meeting with the Feather Sisters at four, but not to worry. I'm an expert on killing time."

*

They spent the remainder of the morning drinking coffee and playing alternate rounds of cribbage and Trivial Pursuit. After the third round of cribbage and the fourth round of coffees, they invented a game they called Cribby Pursuit, which consisted of playing cribbage and answering trivia questions for extra peg points.

Port threw a triple run on the desk with a slap, rousing Butter. She emerged from under the desk, yawning and stretching, and sat next to his chair as he methodically pegged out his sixteen points. "Don't worry, girl. Your friend will be here soon."

"I get a question because you scored more than ten points." Talia handed Port a Trivial Pursuit card. "You know, this would make a great drinking game."

"Drinking? So, detective work isn't as exciting as you...." The door clicked shut. "Was that Darla?" Port dropped the card on the desk, shifted in his chair, and looked at the closed door.

Despite his capable appearance, one of the unspoken aspects of Talia's job included even the smallest tasks, like standing, walking and looking, so she stood up, walked across the room and looked out the small window next to the door. "Yep. She's taking the baby for a walk."

The door banged opened. Darla struggled to pull Belisa's stroller inside. Talia held the door for them, but before the stroller was all the way through, Darla grabbed the door with such force that Talia's thumb bent back uncomfortably. Darla slammed the door shut and peered through the window before turning on Talia, who was still rubbing her injured thumb. "Are you crazy?! There's a creepy van pulling down the road."

"This is a warehouse district," Port said. "I'm sure plenty of vans drive around here, bringing goods from one place to another."

Darla shook her head. "Not this van. It's disguised to look like a Bug's Market delivery van."

"Those will be the groceries then," Port said.

Talia looked out the window. A young man was unloading boxes from the back of a delivery truck. "Yep. That's the grocery guy."

"Maybe. You can't be too careful," Darla said.

Port raised his index finger in the air. "Au contraire, you can be too careful. You are living proof of that." He paused. "Hey, hold on. This is cause for celebration. You went outside...with the baby."

Darla threw up her arms. "Of course I did. A new study says that exclusively breastfed babies are in danger of getting rickets from lack of vitamin D, and I can't give her formula."

"Why can't you give her formula?" Talia asked, wondering if it was an allergy or something specific to babies born with cleft lips.

Darla looked at her as though she'd asked what was wrong with feeding her baby vodka. "They put ground-up glass in baby formula."

"Who puts ground glass in formula?" Port said.

"*Them*, Port. Don't be so naïve." Darla lifted the infant out of the stroller and smiled at her. "Isn't that right, *mija*? He's naïve." Belisa, a dark-eyed baby with a small vertical scar on her upper lip and a mass of dark curls framing her rosy face, flapped her arms and giggled. Darla thrust the baby at Port as though she were a chubby little weapon. "Here. Hold her while I call the cops."

"Which *Them*? The old monster movie about giant radioactive ants *Them*...." Port bobbled Belisa in one hand, the other gripping the arm of his chair tightly as he worked at shifting his weight to accommodate the baby. "Or the '60s-garage band, fronted by Van Morrison, *Them*?" He held the baby on his lap as awkwardly as he held anything. He even held coffee cups backwards, as if his fingers were too fat to grasp something as delicate as a cup handle. Belisa grabbed Port's hand and casually chewed on his finger. "Yow! Someone is teething. Where is Ninja Mouse?" Darla picked up a toy from the stroller and threw it at him. Port caught it.

Knock. Knock.

Darla peered out the window, clutching her phone. "Who the hell is it?"

"It's Brett. I've got your grocery order."

Darla opened the door, keeping her body in a ready-for-a-fight stance. Brett slunk in, craned his neck around Darla, and waved at Port. "Hey Port. Hi Belisa."

Darla advanced on him. "How do you know my baby's name?"

"Uh...you told me." Brett backed away until he bumped into the counter. "I'm here every week."

Darla softened her stance. "Oh yeah. Brett, right?"

There was a voice outside the door. "Hey! Who stole the key?!" Butter responded with a low woof.

"Darla. Did you take the hide-a-key?" Port said.

She held up a plastic rock that was disguised as an actual rock. "Oh, I'm sorry. Was I supposed to just wait around while we all got axe-murdered by a homicidal grocery delivery guy?"

Brett leaned out of the refrigerator he was stocking with skim milk and mineral water. "What was that?"

"Not you," Darla said.

Port sighed. "The dog walker needs the hide-a-key to get in so he can walk the dog."

Butter looked at Darla and then at the door. She barked softly. Darla opened the door. "You're on a short leash, Von!"

Von slunk in, scratching his head. "Was it something I said?"

Darla glared at Von as she grabbed Belisa from Port and sang, "Time for breakfast."

For a full fifteen seconds, the three men searched for a spot on the wall that would represent the furthest point in the room between themselves and the female breast that was about to come out of Darla's sweater. She rolled her eyes at Talia as she settled onto the couch. "Christ, it's like none of these guys have seen a boob before."

"I've not seen one in a very long time," Port said, holding a hand in front of his eyes.

Von nodded and as he did, his Adam's apple jutted outward. Everything on Von jutted: his knees, shoulders, wrist bones. Standing in the middle of the kitchen with his joints jutting and his limbs dangling in random directions, he looked like an erector set that had been arranged in the shape of a man and draped in a Mr. Bungle t-shirt. "They haven't changed much. They're still fleshy orbs with nipples in the middle of them."

Brett dropped a large bag of apples onto the counter with a *thunk*. "Oh jeez! It's too early to talk about nipples. Can we talk about something else like...oh! What about Buster Bones? Super tragic, right?"

"Crazy tragic. That cat was the soundtrack of a lost nation." Von sniffed. "I lost my virginity to 'Black Star.'" He wiped his eyes on his sleeve.

"Yeah, well, I preferred Crunch Pup's deep cuts. 'Waylaid' was all over my push mix," Darla said, her voice cracking.

"What's a push mix?" Von said. "Is that like a booty playlist?"

"Shut up, Von," Darla snapped, cradling the baby with one hand. She used the other to wipe tears from her eyes with short, quick movements, as though she were trying to slap her emotion into submission. Then she leaned her head back, exhaled and let the tears flow down her temples. "I'll tell you one thing for sure. Whoever did this can go to hell and burn forever."

Chapter Four

It was nearly four-thirty when the Feather Sisters—busty, hippy, heavily made-up, dripping in costume jewelry and draped in the feather boas that had earned them their nickname—glided in on their platform shoes. The pair apologized for their lateness and pounced on Port, giving him two long, simultaneous kisses on each cheek.

"Have a seat, please...um...ladies." Talia waved at the two chairs she'd placed on the other side of the desk for them.

The Feather Sisters stared at her, not moving from where they'd perched on either arm of Port's chair.

Talia stared back and said, "Can I offer you something to drink?"

Thorny Feather, a tall brunette dressed entirely in emerald green, lit up. "Ooh! You know what would be divine? Oat straw tea."

"I think we have chamomile."

Thorny nodded without hiding her disappointment.

Rosy Feather patted her intricately coiffed, cherry-red hair. "That sounds lovely. May I have whiskey in mine?"

"Mine, too. If you please," Thorny said.

When she came back with the tea, the Feather Sisters were seated in chairs on either side of Port. "Our operative, Talia, was meant to follow your boyfriend, but he ended up propositioning her instead."

The Feather Sisters glared at Talia.

"I'm sorry." Talia clunked the tea cups on the table. "I couldn't find any whiskey."

Port reached down into the bottom drawer of his desk, grunting from unseen effort. "I have just the thing to take the edge off this afternoon's unpleasantness." He held up a bottle of Dewar's and poured generous shots into their cups.

"Maybe he was just flirting with you. Drick is a very sexual person," Thorny said.

"I was meaning to ask you about that," Talia said, more edge to her voice than she'd hoped. "Why is he Drick? Shouldn't he be either Dick or Rick?"

Thorny shrugged and looked at Rosy. Rosy looked at Talia and said, "He has trouble making up his mind."

"That's evident," Port said and then cleared his throat. "What I mean to say is that the evidence against him is quite damning."

"Oh, Drick." Thorny ran two jade-polished nails under her eyes, wiping away tears and smearing her mascara into two thick, black lines. She gulped her tea and then held her cup out to Port.

He poured another shot. "If you don't mind me saying, in my experience, once a person, or *persons*, arrive at my door, they are already, at least on some level, aware of the indiscretion."

The Feather Sisters looked at each other. Thorny nodded. Rosy sighed. "Last week, we were at a party. We all dropped E, and while Drick was giving another girl a backrub, I overheard him say something to her. Oh! It's too awful to even speak of." Rosy took a pink handkerchief out of her sequined purse and dabbed at the black tears that continued to spill onto her cheeks.

Thorny put a hand on Rosy's shoulder. "He told that little trollop that he was in an open relationship."

Talia and Port gaped at the sisters. Even Darla, who had been reading on the couch, looked up from her book.

Thorny nodded. "E-related back rubs are one thing, but we are most certainly *not* in an open relationship."

"We should be enough woman for him," Rosy said, still weeping.

"Women," Thorny corrected.

Port poured a little more in their cups and smiled. "My dears, I can say, with somewhat suspect authority, that the two of you should be more than enough for any man."

Talia pushed her glass toward Port for a shot as well.

He started to pour and then stopped. "Isn't that diet grape soda? Wouldn't you prefer a proper mixer?"

Talia glanced at the Feather Sisters. "Hit me." Port poured her more of a shot than she had expected, and she downed her strange cocktail with barely a wince.

Port opened his laptop. "I'm sorry, but some of this recording might be hard for you to hear."

He clicked a few keys and Drick's voice oozed from the laptop's speakers. "*Listen, Blondie, we're both adults. Why don't we go to a cheap motel and do something despicable?*"

Talia put her head on the desk and closed her eyes as Drick listed his litany of despicable acts. When it was over, she lifted her head and was met with raccoon-eyed glares from the sisters. Port's cheeks were flushed. Darla was quietly but openly pointing and snickering at Talia from her spot on the couch.

"I can't believe he was going to do that thing with the flashlight," Thorny whimpered. "That's our thing." The sisters collapsed into each other's arms.

"It's okay," Talia said. "I'm sure you will find someone else. Maybe even two someone elses."

Rosy looked up at Talia. "Oh, I know we'll get another boyfriend."

Thorny sniffled. "We have a waiting list."

"Just like a good preschool," Darla said matter-of-factly.

The door had barely shut on the streaked-yet-sparkly pair when the warehouse filled with laughter. They were still laughing when a door slammed and a man said, "Damn it! Did I miss the Feather Sisters?"

They all turned toward the kitchen to see a man standing by the open side door. When Talia first met him, he'd been dressed like an urban pirate. Now, he was dressed like an '80s-era roadie, with a Slayer t-shirt and a coil of cable clipped to his belt. She recognized him immediately, though, as Pirate Mace because of his habit of twirling the ends of his mustache like a cartoon villain, which seemed both an affectation and a parody of an affectation at the same time.

Darla stopped laughing. "What do you want, Ted?"

"Maybe I'm here to see my baby. Did you ever think of that?"

Darla put her hands on her hips and cocked her head to the side. "Are you?"

"No. I know my baby's naptime." He shook a finger at her. "That's a trick question, and you know it, devil woman."

Darla turned to Talia. "Talia, this is the other half of Belisa's DNA. Farmer Ted."

"We've met," Talia said. "He said he was someone else, though."

"We did? I did?" Ted looked at her, squinted, then smiled and said, "Ah. Sister Mary Aquaphobia. How's it going?"

Talia's cheeks warmed at the unfair nickname. The only reason she'd dressed as a nun was that he'd hired her to play a character for his party. She was supposed to ride out on a dinky raft and engage in a squirt gun battle with a raft of pirates, but the raft started sinking almost immediately. He had built the raft, so her freak-out was his fault. He was the one who deserved a snarky nickname: Captain Sinky, or no! Pirate Dinky.

"Oh shit!" Ted yelled. "I forgot why I came over. There's someone watching the place...in a van out in the...." He pointed toward the front door.

Click-clank.

Darla leapt to the door and locked it before Ted could finish his sentence. "Why didn't you say that in the first place?" She slapped him on the chest.

"Sorry, Darl." He rubbed his sternum. "Yeah. She's doing some covert stuff out there. She's got her cell camera out, but she's all hunched in the seat like this." Ted slumped his shoulders and held his hands in front of his face. "It's a small Asian woman in a surveillance van disguised as a mom van. You know the ones with the bumper stickers of the stupid happy families on the back? No legit person would do that."

Talia peered out the window. "It looks like a perfectly innocent woman talking on her cell phone."

Ted nodded at Port. "Probably CIA. Spooks love suburban disguises."

"I'm sure it's fine. I'll just go check...." Talia moved toward the door, but Darla blocked the way.

"I'll find out what she's up to." Ted ran to the desk, leaned over Port and opened his laptop. Port twisted awkwardly out of his way as Ted banged intently on the keyboard.

Talia sighed. "I'll go ask her what she wants. She doesn't look dangerous." Talia put her hand on the lock, but Darla swatted it away.

"You know who else didn't look dangerous?" Darla said. "Hitler."

"Don't worry. It won't take Ted long," Port said. "He's a computer whiz. He created Dickopedia."

"Co-created. I just wrote all the code. You created the content." Ted clasped Port on the shoulder as he typed. "Don't sell yourself shortly, Portly."

"You mean Dicko? That thing is pretty impressive," Talia said.

Without looking up from the screen, Ted said, "True that, sister. If the government ever caught wind of the full power of Dicko they'd be all over us like a hazmat team on a UFO landing. Oh shit!" Ted threw his hands in the air. "You're not going to believe this. I hacked into that cell phone signal—"

"Hack is such an...em...illegal word," Port said.

"Excuse me, ex-pig. I meant to say that I innocently stumbled upon a cellphone signal, just lying there—out in the open," Ted said, walking toward the door. "Guess who the mom is?"

Tap. Tap. Bang! Bang! Bang!

Darla jumped. "It's okay, Darla," Ted unlocked the door and opened it.

There, on the stoop, stood a small woman wearing high heels and dripping in jewelry, but not the costume kind the Feather Sisters wore. It was Minnie Johnson: Buster Bones' wife, or as of a couple days ago, his widow.

Minnie glared at them. "You should get a fucking doorbell. Why do you make people knock? Knocking is for fucking dogs and vaudeville comedians."

Chapter Five

Talia got up in the morning before her alarm, even though she'd been at the warehouse discussing the case until after midnight with Port, Darla and Ted. She hadn't been this excited since she'd landed the role of Choosy Toilet-Paper Consume. (The commercial stopped running over a year ago, but Toby still taunted her with her one big line, "Three ply toilet tissue? How luxurious!") Minnie hadn't been much help. She'd dropped a pile of cash on the desk and said, "I didn't fucking kill my husband. Talk to Crunch Pup. Those fucking has-beens hated Buster."

Talia licked her finger and touched the curling iron quickly, but couldn't tell if it was hot, so she touched it again, leaving her finger on longer. "Ouch!" She waved her hand in a vain attempt to cool the burn. She grabbed an ice pack and tried again—this time without touching the iron. She'd never used a curling iron, but then she'd never needed to convince a semi-big rock band to talk to her. She needed to get into character, and that meant big hair.

The character she decided on was Maggie Foley, Ellen Barkin's rock-and-roll journalist character from the movie *Eddie and the Cruisers*. Maggie chain-smoked Winstons, wore pencil skirts and pumps, and had big '80s hair. Talia would skip the smoking, though. She'd only had one cigarette before—one of her father's Marlboros when she was ten, and it made her so dizzy she'd thrown up on her Strawberry

Shortcake comforter. Her mother was never able to get the stain out, so it stayed there, for the rest of her childhood, like a splat-shaped reminder to just say no.

By the time she got her hair to the appropriate fluffiness, even she knew she was going to be late. (How did women in the '80s manage to get anything done?) She put on one red pump and, while putting on the other, hopped around chanting, "keys, keys, keys." They weren't on the hook Toby had put by the door so that she would stop losing her keys. She looked all over the apartment before finally finding them on the kitchen counter.

She was victorious for about ten seconds...until she saw the sign taped to the elevator. *Out of service—the mgmt.* She half-ran, half-stumbled down the five flights of stairs to the street. She was late, her feet were already starting to hurt and perhaps worst of all, she suspected that her hairspray was failing. The more she thought about her predicament, the more she felt like crying. Maggie Foley would never burst into tears on her way to an interview, but Talia Green was about to do just that. Instead, she pulled out Dicko and typed, "On foot and late for an important press conference."

Dicko flashed the words: *Don't run. Pretend you are too important to be on time.*

*

Talia arrived at Hotel Rokku fifteen minutes late. She paused at the entrance and checked her reflection in the glass door. Surprisingly, she still looked like Maggie Foley...or at the very least Ellen Barkin's understudy. If she'd continued her panicked run over the five hilly blocks from her apartment, she may have only been ten minutes late, but she would've certainly been a sweaty mess.

Instead of a central lobby, the Hotel Rokku had a cascading series of mezzanines and koi ponds. Talia navigated them, walking up half-sets of stairs and crossing little arched bridges. At the third mezzanine, she saw a young woman standing near a brown metal door with a clipboard at her feet, sipping from a paper coffee cup. Talia strolled over. "I'm here for the press conference. For Crunch Pup."

The girl sneered at her. "You're late."

When sneered at, Talia Green would usually respond by backing down and slinking away, but Maggie Foley sneered back and said, "No, I'm not."

Coffee Girl stared at her. Outwardly, Maggie was calm and stoic, while inwardly Talia was freaking out. The girl studied the phony press credential (Ted's handiwork) jauntily pinned to the lapel of Maggie's blazer. The girl glanced at the clipboard at her feet and started to reach for it before she stopped and reached for the door instead. Talia stepped into a long hallway and suppressed the urge to pump her fist.

Her victory was short lived, however. The hallway was lined with unmarked doors. The press release Port found online hadn't given a room number, and her too-important-to-be-on-time routine wouldn't work if she turned around and asked for directions. She walked past door after door: all closed, all identical. She put a hand to her temple, immediately covering her finger tips in a mix of sweat and hairspray.

"Hey!"

Talia hung her head. A drop of sweat landed on the tip of her shoe. She ran the sleeve of her jacket across her brow and glanced over her shoulder.

"Can you believe those ghouls are firing up the promotion machine already? Jesus. The body's not even cold." Coffee Girl was on her phone, her back to Talia.

Talia turned and walked, quicker now, down the hallway. She saw it—a small card, no bigger than a business card, stuck to the wall next to a door. *CP Press Room.* Her hand grasped the door handle before she realized the rock-and-hard-place predicament she was in. If she opened that door, she would face a room full of real journalists who would surely recognize her as a fraud. If she didn't, Coffee Girl would notify security. She pushed slowly on the door handle until it clicked—loud enough, surely, for the room of journalists to hear. There was another click further down the hallway. She let go of the handle, turned toward the sound and away from the door.

Talia, although a Buster Bones fan, would not have recognized Crunch Pup if they sat next to her on the bus. She recognized an aging male rock star, though, when she saw one: clothes that were too young and too tight, dyed hair (usually black), bad posture (probably from the tight clothes), and jewelry that was either Satanic or Celtic. The three black-clad men slouching in the hallway fit the profile.

She walked toward them, allowing the click-clack of her heels to announce her arrival. She stopped about half-way there. She brushed one curling-iron-singed, sweat-dampened curl from her eyes and tried to look as smoldering and leggy as possible. "Hey, guys," she called. "Mind if I ask you a few questions?"

A raven-haired man of about forty, wearing skinny jeans and an inverted cross on a leather chain, changed his gaze from Talia's legs to her face. "The press conference is over, darling."

Talia Green would have apologized and walked away, but not Maggie Foley. "I was on another story. It couldn't be helped."

He narrowed his eyes at her. "So, you're from *Rolling Stone*, then?"

She could lie, but then the real *Rolling Stone* reporter could show and blow her cover. A door clicked open behind her and the murmur of voices rolled into the hallway. One of those voices probably belonged to the real *Rolling Stone* reporter. A drop of sweat trickled from her temple and onto her cheek. "Do you guys have a room here that we can go to?"

The three members of Crunch Pup walked toward her. The voices behind her grew louder. Talia stood her ground, smoldering as hard as she could. A sandy-haired man (the only one of them without a black dye-job) walked straight at her. Without breaking his stride, he hooked an arm around her elbow. "This way, quickly, before the vultures start to mob us, Miss um…?"

"It's *Ms.*, and it's Foley. Maggie Foley." She immediately regretted it. Surely an aging rocker had seen *Eddie and the Cruisers*. She searched his face for a flash of recognition. There was none.

"I'm impressed. I haven't met a Ms. in a long time. My name is Mark, but you can call me Ms. Lynn, if you'd like." He winked at her.

They took her, via a service elevator and two flights of stairs, to an unmarked, air-conditioned suite on what might have been the fourteenth floor. (Talia kept track, but wasn't sure if the hotel was superstitious enough to leave off the thirteenth floor.) Mark flung open the door to mini bar and said, "Can I get you a drink?"

She asked for what Maggie Foley would drink. "I'll have a Dewar's with a proper mixer."

"Got it." He nodded with admiration.

She brought out Dicko and typed in, "Interviewing a rock band and masquerading as a reporter from Rolling Stone."

It was a complicated task, so she expected a complicated series of instructions, but all she got was: *Don't break character.*

Mark handed her a glass. She thanked him and took a sip. She covered up her reaction to the straight whiskey blazing a hole in her esophagus with a fake cough. Apparently, to an aging rock star, a "proper mixer" was ice. She turned away, coughed again and then turned back with an '80s-era hair flip. She tossed Dicko on the table.

Dicko had created a kind of CGI skin and now looked like a high-end voice recorder, complete with flashing lights, a timer, sound and level displays, and a small "property of Rolling Stone" label that appeared to be torn on one corner. It was just an illusion, and if any one of them tried to pick it up or examine it, they would see that it was a phony, but she wasn't worried about that. Maggie Foley wasn't about to let anyone, rock star or not, touch her equipment. "I'm putting this conversation on the record." She pressed a little spot on the illusion that mimicked a record button. "Hope you don't mind." The level display moved in sync as she talked.

Chapter Six

Talia rode the T-Third as close to Deadman's Gulch as she could, which was still two very long blocks away. When she arrived, she greeted an effusive Butter, kicked her shoes off and requested band-aids for her '80s-style blisters. "The walking wounded?" Port looked up from his laptop. "There's a first aid kit in the big bathroom—second door on your left." He did not point.

Talia hobbled into the back. This was the first time she'd been to this part of the warehouse. She'd always used the bathroom next to the kitchen—the one referred to as *the small bathroom* which was a good size, complete with an industrial-sized steel toilet and a large claw-foot tub, ringed with an assortment of brightly colored rubber duckies. The big bathroom was nearly the size of her gym's locker room and was dominated by a glass-walled shower with a sofa-sized wooden bench against the dark blue tile that ran the length of the back wall. She found the band-aids in the medicine cabinet under an entire shelf devoted to diet pills—fat burners, carb blockers, and metabolism boosters. She grabbed two band-aids and walked back into the hall.

She stopped at a door that was marked by a framed picture of a Beatrix Potter-esque frog. Underneath the picture was a handwritten birth announcement: *Belisa Alma Cortés 7lbs 5oz.* Talia wanted to peek into the nursery but didn't dare. Belisa was what Darla referred to as a middle napper—she napped in the middle of the morning and the middle of the afternoon. "And," Port would joke, "she wakes up in the middle of the night." She smiled and imagined Port, the proud, sort-of uncle, hanging the little picture on the door but no, of course that didn't happen. Porter Nepal was as likely to enroll in a step-aerobics class as he was to use a hammer.

The back of the warehouse was set up differently than the front. Instead of an open concept, it had doors and rooms and a long hallway built with dark, wood-paneled walls that didn't quite reach the ceiling. Just past Belisa's room, a sepia-toned photograph of two men climbing a mountain hung on a wall. Talia leaned closer to read the caption: *Sherpa Tenzing Norgay and Sir Edmund Hillary climbing Mount Everest.* A sliver of paper stuck out from the bottom corner of the frame.

Talia looked behind her, but of course Port wouldn't be getting out of his chair to check on her. She lifted the picture off its nail and turned it over. A little card, the kind that came with bouquets of flowers, was taped to the back. She pushed the card open with her index finger, careful not to dislodge the tape. Inside was written: "To my own intrepid explorer. Here's to our next big adventure. JL." She put the picture back on its nail and limped down the hall to the office.

"So, what have you got for me?"

"Oh, did you want one, too?" Talia held up the band-aids. "Did you just walk here in '80s reporter shoes?"

Port laughed. "Yes. I saw those implements of torture, but I was talking about the press conference. Did you learn anything?"

"Maybe." Talia tossed Dicko on the desk much the way that Maggie had done at the Hotel Rokku. Port took out a pen and paper and pressed play.

Talia's Voice: So, for the transcript, can you start with your names and the instrument you play?
Male Voice: Devin Sullivan. I'm the drummer.
Male Voice: Gary Myers, I play bass.
Male Voice: Mark Lynn, I play poker...badly. Oh, and I play the guitar, too.

Talia smiled as Mark spoke.

Port laughed.

"What?"

"You didn't know their names, did you?"

Talia nodded and tried to stop smiling. "Shut up."

Talia: Thank you for talking to me. I know that this must be hard after losing...Buster.
Gary: You have no idea. He was like a brother to us.
Talia: Of course. I heard that recently, though, you guys were on the outs.
Devin: Listen you... (*unintelligible*). He was our friend, get that? He might be another dead rock star to you, someone to help you sell your shitty rag, but he was our friend.
Talia: I'm sorry. I....
Mark: Easy, Dev. Ms. Foley, who told you that we were on the outs with Buster?
Talia: Minnie Johnson.
Silence.
Devin: Oh. Well. We were not very nice to Minnie.
Gary: I was. I sent her a box of those egg tarts she likes from that bakery on Irving.
Mark: We're talking about back in the day, Gare. Were you nice to Minnie then?
Gary: Oh. No. None of us were. We thought she ruined him...and the band.

Devin: Poor Min. She was just in love, and what's wrong with love?
Gary: Nothing. I'm married. I got kids. I understand the love songs, now.
Devin: I've been married three times. I understand all the songs. Love, hate, Country, Western....
Laughter.
Mark: Look, I know that Buster became a huge star, and we're seen as a bit of an afterthought, but we've been given the unique opportunity to make a living, a pretty good one, doing what we love without being bothered too much. We never wanted Buster's life.
Devin: If we'd been the ones who got famous, I'd still be drinking. Or worse....
Gary: I wouldn't have gotten married or had my kids. My family is my life.
Mark: Yeah, and I wouldn't have my Honda Civic. I'd be driving an Escalade or a Lexus or something pimping like that. That'd be a nightmare.
Talia: (laughing) Fair enough. When was the last time you saw Buster?
Gary: Last...um...it was Thursday, right? He took us to Tommy's Joynt to tell us about his book.
Talia: He was writing a book?
Devin: Ah, shit.
Gary: Oops. Sorry. I let that cat out, eh?
Mark: It's okay, Gare. It'll be out soon enough. (*Pause*) Buster was writing a memoir. He brought the chapters he wrote about Crunch Pup for us to read, but we passed.
Devin: I told him I was going to get my copy from the book store...like everyone else.
Mark: Not me. I was planning on borrowing it from my local library.
Talia: You weren't curious to see what he wrote about you?

Devin: Shit. I was more curious about what he wrote about himself. This was the guy who did everything. Sex, drugs, sex, booze, sex, pills...more sex.
Gary: Yeah, man. His big confession must have been quite the bomb. What hasn't he confessed to already?
Talia: What are you talking about?
Gary: Oops. Oh man. I did it again.
Devin: Let's just say there are a lot of people who don't want this book to get out.
Talia: Like who?
Mark: Like Minnie. She didn't want her marriage getting dragged through the mud.
Devin: Mud wrestling is more like it.
Laughter.
Gary: Oh, Buster. Man, that guy.
Talia: What's with the mud wrestling? Did Buster like mud wrestling?
Devin: Who doesn't?
Gary: Germaphobes.
Laughter.
Knock on door.
Mark: Hold on. Yeah. Who is it?
Man's voice: Hey, guys. Mike Wave from Rolling Stone.
Sound of door closing.

Port whistled. "That sounded like a close call. Did you get away clean?"

Talia nodded. "The door to the adjoining room was open. I'd had it planned out since I first got there." Talia picked up Dicko. It had returned to its default screen—a blank text field under a large, cartoonish question mark. "I think Minnie was wrong about Crunch Pup hating Buster, don't you?"

"Maybe, if they were telling the truth."

"You don't really think they were lying. Do you?"

He looked over his notes, tapping his pen rhythmically on the paper. "Honestly, I think that loose-lipped act they put on was just that...an act. They knew they were on-the-record to *Rolling Stone.* Notice how they shifted suspicion to Minnie?"

"Yeah. I caught that." Talia tapped her fingers on the desk. "So, where should we start?"

"It's a puzzle, so we start with the missing piece." He held up his illegible notes. "Right at the beginning of the interview. Did you notice? Drums, bass, guitar. What's missing?"

She shrugged. "Keyboards? Cowbell?"

"Don't most bands have a manager? Managers usually attend press conferences, don't they?"

"I'm not sure. I didn't make it into the actual press conference." Talia shrugged. "I can do a web search, though."

"No need. Darla used to be a freelance music journalist. She'll know." Port then put two arms on the desk and, with an unnecessary amount of effort, pushed himself and his chair barely a half an inch backward and called, "Darla! Who is Crunch Pup's manager?"

"That's easy. The same as Buster's. A guy named Zone. Nigel Zone," Darla's voice came from the little bathroom along with the sounds of splashing and Belisa's laughter.

"He's probably online." Talia did a quick search. "Oh god. His Twitter name is DaZone!" She elongated the *oh* sound in *Zone* to demonstrate her contempt. "Listen to this." Talia tapped the screen and read aloud. "DaZone is going to get pissed at the Bird's Nest tomorrow night. Who's in?"

"I guess you're in, Miss Green. Now, let's see what this Zone character looks like." Port turned back to his computer screen. "Oh no."

"What? Is Zone ugly? Let me guess. Hair plugs and Botox?"

"No...well, actually, yes, that is an accurate assessment, but no, I just got an extremely terse message from Brad. Our client has just been arrested for the murder of her husband."

The side door banged open. It was Ted. He was carrying a laptop—a beat-up thing held together with duct tape and decorated with a faded radiation symbol. "Hey, Portentious. Did you hear about your cop buddy arresting your client?"

"Of course, *I* heard about it, but how did you hear about it? Did it already make the news?"

"You know I don't watch the televised news. Mind control." Ted tapped his temple. "But check this shit out." He held up the laptop "There's a—"

Darla entered the room, holding a smiling Belisa wrapped in a pink towel. Darla glared at Ted. "Oh, it's you." She stomped toward the nursery and slammed the door. Ted stood and stared down the hall.

"Ah, Ted? You said something about some shit we need to check?" Port said gently.

"Huh? Oh right. There's a video." Ted took a seat at the desk. "It's on the leak."

Port rested his head on his hand. "I've got a bad feeling about this."

"What's the Leak?" Talia said.

"*L-e-e-k*.com. One of those *E*s is a three, but I'm not telling which one." Ted typed at his keyboard with such fervor, he looked like the hacker version of Beethoven. "I'm not surprised you don't know it. It's a hacker site—by hackers for hackers. Nessie sightings, alien autopsies, the secluded location of an elderly woman named Genevieve Pickles who once went by the name of D.B. Cooper...you name it, The Leek's got it. Including, as of about forty minutes ago, a video of Minnie Johnson offing her husband."

"That doesn't mean anything." Port leaned back, put his arms behind his head, winced and then brought them down again. "There's probably a video on The Leek proving that Sasquatch is alive and well and living in the woods of Oregon."

Ted stared at Port before saying, "Sasquatch is a government conspiracy used to cover up the fact that all the marijuana harvested in the Pacific Northwest contains neurotoxins that were put there by the Forest Service. You'd know that if you bothered to read my zine." Ted bashed a couple of keys. "Now, I'm going to blow your mind and tell you that there was a surveillance camera at the recording studio the night Buster was killed." He pointed at one of the screens on the wall. "Get the popcorn ready, kids. This is a blockbuster."

The grainy black and white video flickered onto the screen. It showed a man lying on a couch, reading. He put down his book, stood, yawned and stretched. His black t-shirt lifted as he did, revealing his lanky, rocker physique. Buster Bones. Buster walked toward the camera but then turned to the right and sat in a chair that was almost out of frame, so all they could see of him was his hand, half of his arm and the right side of his head.

"Is this the only camera angle?" Port asked.

"Yep," Ted answered quickly. "Here. Lookie, lookie." He pointed at the screen.

Minnie, holding an umbrella, appeared in the center of the shot as she walked through a double glass door. She hooked the umbrella on her forearm, walked to the chair and leaned over her husband. All they could see was her shoulder and her long black hair as it cascaded over Buster.

"I can't really tell what's happening." Talia squinted up at the screen. "If that chair would turn just a few inches...."

"How long does this go on?" Port said.

"Exactly sixty seconds," Ted said, not taking his eyes off the screen.

"Exactly sixty seconds? That seems a bit...."

"Wait for it...There!" Ted pointed at the screen. "Watch Buster's hand."

Buster's hand slipped off the arm of the chair and hung motionless as Minnie stood and walked toward the door.

"That was horrible." Talia rubbed the goose bumps on her arms. "I'm almost glad that we couldn't see what was happening."

Port rested his chin on his thumb, hooking a question-mark shaped index finger around his cheekbone. "You have a point, Miss Green. We couldn't see what was happening. Yes, it looks bad for Minnie...but how bad? Can we play devil's advocate with this situation?"

Ted slapped his forehead. "Fine. Let's play devil's advocate. I say she did it. I say we just watched her do it. Now, let's play Chutes and Ladders because this case is closed, and we've got some time on our hands."

"Point taken, Ted." Port held up his hand. "But still, something isn't quite right. Minnie is four-eleven. How could she have the strength to murder a six-foot-tall man?"

"I was hoping you'd ask that. The Leek had this as well." Ted banged on the keyboard and clicked open a two-page document on another screen.

Port whistled. "Is that what I think it is?"

"That, my faux-fat friend, is the mother-fucking ME's report. Most of it, anyway."

The report was filled out with scrawled notes that rambled around the page, veering off answer lines and crawling up the margins. Port squinted at the screen. "Who called 911? Garrity? Gamera?"

Ted zoomed in on one spot of the document. "That's not a G. It's an S. It says security. I'm surprised at you. An ex-pig should have mad skills reading pig writing."

"Mad skills? They took those with the badge, I guess." Port shrugged and pointed at the screen. "Looks like they put time of death at approximately three a.m."

"Yeah. Yeah." Ted nodded. "Which jives exactly with the time stamp on the video,"

"I beg to differ. *Approximately* doesn't jive *exactly* with anything."

Ted swiped to another page of the report that featured a crude drawing of what looked like a bald Ken doll. A thick red line was drawn across the Ken doll's neck.

"It still jives. Check the cause of death. Ligature strangulation. And the murder weapon? It was one of his own necklaces—a leather strap he wore around his neck," Ted said.

"So?" Port shrugged.

"A lever," Ted said.

Port stared blankly at Ted.

Ted made a see-saw motion with his hands. "A lever. A lever, you maroon!" He sighed. "Even a ninety-pound weakling can exert a fuckton of pressure with a lever. Wrap the leather strap around, say the tip of an umbrella, and all it would take is a good, firm twist, and it's bye-bye Buster." Ted punctuated the lesson with a hand gesture and a guttural choking sound.

Talia tried to visualize what was hidden just off screen—Minnie, leaning down and slipping her umbrella between the cord and the skin of Buster's neck. "But why would he let her put that umbrella in the strap? It seems weird."

Port pointed at the screen. "And why sixty seconds?" The video was still frozen on Minnie, her hand reaching for the door while her husband lay dead on the chair behind her. "Don't you find it strange that it took Minnie exactly sixty seconds to kill her husband?"

Ted shrugged. "Coincidence."

"True enough, but this is Studio 9. A recording studio of some historical significance, correct?"

"Correct," Talia said. "When they were recording 'Walk of Love,' Minnie showed up at the studio every day, just to hang out. Crunch Pup was pissed." Talia might not have been a Crunch Pup fan, but every Buster Bones fan knew the Studio 9-Minnie saga.

"Yes. I remember that. It made the tabloids," Port said. "The comparisons to Yoko were abundant and scathing. So, if she'd been there before...."

Talia pointed at the freeze frame of Minnie's exit. "She would have known about the camera."

"Or...Or it might have been hidden inside a smoke alarm or a crack in the wall." Ted snapped his fingers in front of Talia's face. "Wake up, people! There are pinhole cameras hidden all over the place. Recording studios, mini-marts, taxi cabs, breakfast cereal...." Ted threw his arms up and crossed them on his chest, then uncrossed them and put his hands on his hips.

"So, where does this video leave our investigation?" Talia said.

"It leaves us with questions," Port said. "Which means we still have an investigation."

Chapter Seven

Talia hopped off the train and walked the half block to Studio 9. Makeshift memorials had cropped up all over the city at places that had even the smallest connection with Buster Bones, but here, at the place he died, there was nothing but a neat cobblestone path leading up to a plain brick building with steel and glass front doors. She heard music—a familiar tune. A fair-haired young man in a t-shirt with a large black star on the front stood in front of a single black candle, playing a guitar decorated with the Crunch Pup logo: an angular dog taking a bite out of a microphone. ("Black Star"! That was the song.)

She walked toward him, planning to ask him about his solitary vigil when a security guard stepped past her, snatched up the candle, held it behind his back and nodded wordlessly at the young man. Star Tee stared back at him for a long time before turning slowly on his heel and walking away. The security guard blew out the candle and tossed it into a pillar ashtray before entering the building.

The inside of Studio 9 matched its understated exterior: cream-colored walls, leather couches, and a dark wood floor. Talia scanned the lobby, half-hoping to find it filled with vaguely familiar members of semi-famous rock bands, hanging out and trading rock-star tips like where to get the best drugs or which city has the hottest groupies. No rock stars, just a woman on a couch typing into her phone and the security guard hunched over a standing desk in front of a pair of scuffed-brass elevator doors. He glanced up from what he was doing, tapped his pen on the desk and stared at Talia.

Talia looked around the lobby again, but this time she swiveled her head and let her mouth fall open. She pulled out Dicko and pretended to take a few photos like a gawking tourist would. The security guard looked back down at his computer. She typed "need to get information from security guard at recording studio" into Dicko.

Ask security guard to take your picture.

She strutted over to the security guard stand, ran one hand through her hair and smiled. "Hi."

"Afternoon, ma'am," he said, looking up at her briefly before turning his attention back to the desk. The desk had a wood and brass curved top that hid the desktop from view. Talia could hear his pen scratching on paper, but couldn't see what he was writing.

"Um...would you take my picture, so I can prove to my friends that I actually made it here?" She held out Dicko, assuming it would turn itself into a cellphone camera.

He smiled at her for the first time. "I sure can. Which button do I press, this one?"

"Um...." If it wasn't *the one,* hopefully it would be by the time he pressed it. "Yes, that's it."

Click.

"Can you take one more? Just in case...."

"Sure."

Click.

He handed Dicko back to her. "So, what do you think?"

She took the device and looked at the screen. Her image was replaced with a two-word command. *Walk away.*

"Eh. I hate all pictures of myself." Talia shrugged and shoved Dicko into her purse. "Thanks, though."

Once outside, Talia heard a sound she hadn't heard since she was a kid—the *ptoo-whrrrr-vrrrr* of a Polaroid camera spitting out a fresh photo—and it was coming from her purse. She took out Dicko. The screen had turned a faded blue. Was it broken? Maybe she could find a way to reboot it. Looking on the side for a button, she noticed the pattern in the image. It was a grid with words (one of them looked like *Tuesday*), but it was hard to read in the glare.

She looked around her. The tourists were out in the sun, strolling up Battery toward The Embarcadero and audaciously wearing t-shirts and shorts as if that sort of thing happened all the time on the usually foggy waterfront. Talia shaded her eyes. She was pale-skinned and, like most actresses, wrinkle-phobic, so she wasn't a big fan of the sun. Still, it was a welcome change after so many gray days.

"Miss Green?" Talia spun around. There was no one there. She looked at her palm. Dicko had morphed into what looked like an old-fashioned speakerphone—the kind Charlie had used to talk to his Angels. "I got the security schedule that you sent me."

"But I didn't send...oh." Of course! When the security guard pointed the "camera" at Talia, Dicko had snapped a photo of the contents of his desk and sent it to Port. "Does that photo help us?"

"More than I thought it would at first glance. Did you notice anything odd about that schedule?"

She shielded the screen with her palm, but as she did, the lighting on the screen changed, making the image easy to read even in the glare of the sun. On the left side, the names and shift-times of the security guards were written in pen. If the schedule were correct, the guy who took her picture was Joe, and he would be replaced by Pedro at four o'clock. On the far-right side, the names of the people who had reserved blocks of studio time were listed. One of the names leapt out at her. “Mark Lynn is going to be here at four-thirty.”

“Hmm? Oh yes. Good eye. More important, though, is what happens to the guard on duty after ten o’clock.”

“It says ‘keycard access only.’” Talia was thinking about what she was going to say to Mark. The last time she saw him, she was sprinting from his hotel room. She looked up at Studio 9’s facade. It didn’t seem as plain as it had before. Along the top of the building, she saw a line of small steel squares bolted to the brick, point side up. The same evidence of earthquake retrofitting could be seen on a lot of old brick buildings in San Francisco, but something about the sharp, neat pattern seemed more purposeful than practical.

Port was talking to her. “... implications of this raise some interesting questions, don’t you think?”

“Implications of what? I’m sorry, I can’t quite hear you. There was a train going by.”

“I was talking about the revelation that there is no security guard after ten.”

She stared at Dicko’s speakerphone illusion and thought about what Port just said. *“There is no security guard after ten.”*

“Miss Green? Are you still there?”

“Oh! Right. The security guard called 911 on the night Buster was killed, but if there was no security guard at the time of his murder, then who called 911?”

“Your guess is as good as mine. Maybe you can get the security guard to talk to you about that.”

She thought about the way he’d snatched the candle from Star Tee. He might have been momentarily charmed by her starry-eyed tourist routine, and fooled by Dicko’s camera disguise, but he wouldn’t give her information willingly. “Eh, I think it might be better to go back in a couple hours and try my luck with the next guard on duty.” She glanced at the schedule. “Pedro.”

*

The fireboat out by Pier 23 shot tall arcs of sun-lit water in all directions. Talia stopped along with a cluster of tourists to watch the spectacle. She remembered another time she'd walked along The Embarcadero. Instead of a sunlit fireboat, there had been shore-patrol helicopters and rescue boats with searchlights cutting through a foggy gloom. Later, she'd learned that a homeless mother had strapped her baby and her toddler into a stroller and pushed them into the icy water. Talia had avoided that portion of the waterfront after that, taking a longer route to work, through Washington Square Park and past a tree filled with wild parrots—the screeching birds making for a better soundtrack than the silent water.

Now, she walked along the water, past Pier 23, and toward Fisherman's Wharf, stopping in front of a building that was dominated by a cartoonish mural representing a gangster's life of crime from bank robbery to capture, trial, and execution. It covered the entire storefront, parts of the sidewalk, and the building next door. The centerpiece was a larger-than-life wooden cut-out of a hapless prisoner frying in an electric chair on the roof above a sign that read, *Grimey's Crime Museum.*

It felt strange walking in the front door. She hadn't done that since she'd shown up on her first day. The circular lobby looked the same. The same faux-bullet-ridden paint job. The same faded carpet. The walls were still covered with crime memorabilia, encased in theft-proof plexiglass. (Crime museum patrons were predictably sticky fingered. Someone had once stolen Talia's shoes while she was wearing them. She was corpsing at the time, so it made a small bit of sense, but not much.)

Talia walked around the room, trailing her fingers along the wall, touching the display boxes: hangman's nooses, makeshift prison weapons, rusty shackles. She paused at the bullet-riddled fedora that Clyde Barrow was supposedly wearing when he died. Grimey busted it out for pictures at the Christmas party every year. There was a framed photo above Grimey's desk of him wearing the hat, flanked by his favorite actresses, Lucy and Talia, as they struck glassy-eyed Charlie's Angel poses. Would it still be there, or had he taken it down after she quit?

There was a lump in her throat as she knocked on his office door. No answer. She opened the door slowly and peeked inside. Grimey wasn't there. Just the same old desk piled with odd, stoner knickknacks and stacks of papers. She smiled when she saw that the photo still hung on the wall next to a swirly poster for a Grateful Dead show at The Fillmore.

She closed the door and headed down into the caverns. The stinging, musty odor hit her halfway down the stairs. Had it always been this bad? She must have grown used to it. As she got to the bottom of the stairs, she felt like an intruder. She wasn't an employee anymore.

Someone screamed her name. She looked up to see Lucy running toward her. Lucy squealed and threw her arms around her. Talia squeezed back. Lucy smelled like roses and hairspray and the fabric of her dress rumpled oddly under Talia's hands. "What are you wearing, Loose?"

Lucy stood back, smiled and struck a pose. "Rayon!" Her dress was a strange iridescent purple offset with black buttons and strategically placed lace ruffles.

"Who are you? High-priced '90s call girl?"

"Better." Lucy turned and walked back into the dressing room.

"What could be better than that?" Talia said, following her.

"I'll give you a hint. I get to wear this as well." Lucy sat on the dressing table and held up a bandeau-type bikini that looked as though it were made from rhinestones and a space blanket.

"Get to?"

"I'm Pamela Smart!" Lucy shook the bikini at her, and the rhinestones glittered in the dressing mirror lights. "Remember that New Hampshire teacher who had her little boyfriend kill her husband?"

Talia nodded. Everyone knew who she was. The Pamela Smart case was a legend in New England. It was all about sex, murder, heavy metal, big hair, small New Hampshire towns, and bigger-city dreams. "Yeah, but...." Talia paused as she tried to figure out if she should finish her sentence with "Pamela's white" or "you're black" or just wait for the floor to open up and swallow her whole.

Thankfully, Lucy jumped in with, "I know! I told Grimey about color-blind casting and he went for it. Me and Nicole Kidman. Same role." She struck another pose, like the one in the photo on Grimey's office wall.

Talia opened a drawer, pushed aside a layer of old make-up brushes and grabbed a half-empty pint bottle of Jack. She took a small sip, and offered it to Lucy.

Lucy stared at the bottle as though it were a rat she'd just lit on fire. "Are you sure you want that? There must still be a bottle of your weird, flavored vodka around here some-where."

Talia laughed. "Lucy, can you keep a secret?"

"Maybe."

"I'm investigating the Buster Bones case."

"Buster freaking Bones?!" she yelled.

"Sh!" Talia held her finger to her lips and looked over her shoulder.

"Sorry," Lucy whispered. "You remember he came to the museum once, right?"

"He did? Oh yeah!" She'd pushed the whole incident out of her mind because it had happened on the day she'd called in sick with a debilitating post-Toby's-birthday-party hang-over.

"Yeah, Buster rolls into the museum with wife and kids...no nanny. Minnie gives everyone shade. Especially me. I was dressed in a hooker costume, so I got where she was coming from." Lucy looked down and pushed one of the lace embellishments on her dress flat, but it popped back up. "But for all the shade Minnie threw, Buster was nice to everyone: the box office, the actors, even Phil."

Talia laughed. No one was nice to Phil. He had a caustic personality that brought out the worst out in just about everyone who met him—even Midwesterners.

"He was nicest to Minnie." Lucy leaned toward her. "You know how famous dudes always let their wives do all the talking?"

Talia nodded. It was true. A lot of celebrities came to the crime museum, but they were usually D-list national celebrities and not A-list local ones like Buster Bones. The D-list guys she'd dealt with had all treated their wives and girlfriends like assistants.

Lucy gave a quick nod and then shook her head. "Yeah. Not Buster. He bought the tickets, e-tipped us at the end—well I might add—and Minnie just glided through, not lifting a finger. If she dropped a sippy cup, he picked it up for her. If the hair fell in her face, he pushed it out of the way. I was spying on them when they were in the snack bar; he opened her water bottle for her." Lucy leaned toward her. Talia could smell the rose and hairspray mix again. "Minnie had three kids with her. Two little ones and a newborn. And Buster didn't let her lift a finger. So, you have to wonder why she would off a guy like that."

"Lucy, do me favor. Don't tell anyone that I'm working this case."

"Cross my heart." Lucy dragged a finger in an X across the slick fabric of her dress.

Talia headed back up the stairs and into the lobby. Grimey, stocky and squat with a head of graying blonde curls, stood looking even squatter in a boxy tie-dye t-shirt near the door to his office. His brow was furrowed as his eyes shot daggers at her, but she could see that he was fighting a smile. "Hey, kiddo."

"Hey Grime. Still love me?" She gave him a hug and peck on the cheek. He smelled like WD-40 and patchouli.

"Just try and stop me. Hey! I heard you're on the Buster Bones case."

"Lucy texted you? Already?!"

"I keep my sources private." He tucked his phone in his pocket. "You know, you're fighting an uphill battle. I've been at this game a long time. It's always the wife. Always."

"Except when it's not."

Grimey hooked a thumb toward his office. "You want a drink? I've got some fancy booze that Toby sent me."

"Nah. I'm on the clock." She started to walk away, but turned back before she got to the door. "You know, I would've made a really good Pamela Smart."

"That's okay, kid. You've got a real live case...in the present. You don't need to dig around in the past with me anymore."

*

When she arrived at Studio 9, it was a little past four-thirty. Mark would already be upstairs in his studio. Talia jogged over to the security desk and tried to appear as harried, yet sexy, as possible. “Oh no! Did Mark go up already?”

The guard looked at his schedule and then at her. “Yes, I think he did. Sorry, Miss.”

“Damn. Did he ask about me? My name is Sloane Peterson. I’m his new assistant. I was supposed to be here ten minutes ago, and I really don’t want to get fired on my first day.” Talia leaned on the guard station and sighed.

He looked at her as if she were a small child who’d just lost her ice cream cone. “Oh no, I’m sure that won’t happen to you, Miss.”

“I hope not...” Talia pretended to read the name tag that was sewn above the breast pocket of his light tan shirt. “Pedro.”

When she said his name, he smiled. “Don’t worry, Miss Peterson, I’d be glad to....”

“Please, Pedro.” She put her hand on his arm—nothing too flirtatious, just a little tap to soften her interruption. “Call me Sloane.”

He smiled again. “Sloane. Of course.”

“Don’t worry, Sloane. I just got here,” a voice behind her said, emphasizing the word *Sloane*.

She turned around slowly.

“Sorry, Pedro. I snuck out the side door to grab some equipment from my car.” Mark grinned and handed her a guitar case that was much heavier than it looked.

Talia struggled to position the strap so it wouldn’t dig into her shoulder. While she was struggling, he tossed her a small, blue backpack. She managed to catch it, but it was also much heavier than it looked.

Once they were in the elevator, Talia reached out to press the floor, but pulled her hand back when she realized she didn’t know where they were going. Mark reached in front of her and pressed the button for the second floor. "So, what should I call you? Maggie or Sloane?"

Talia tried to disappear into the corner. "Oh, this is so embarrassing."

"Eh, don't be embarrassed. I'm just giving you shit." Mark smiled. "I'm impressed. Pedro was about to let you up, and he has literally turned away my own mother."

"Really?"

"Honest." He held up his palm. The earnest salute combined with his laid-back, rocker style reminded her of the leading men in the old movies she used to watch with her grandmother. "She tried to surprise me on my birthday, and he sent her away, and she was carrying a cake."

"I wasn't trying to... I mean.... Really? A cake?" Talia laughed.

"You laugh, but I'm serious. It had candles on it. Lit ones."

She laughed again. "Now you're teasing me."

He turned his upheld palm into an outstretched hand. "Here, let's start over...." The elevator door opened. Neither made a move to step out. "Hi, my name is Mark."

She took his hand. He squeezed lightly. She smiled and squeezed back. "Talia." The door closed. The elevator went back down to the ground floor. It picked up a janitor with his mop. He stood between them. Talia and Mark rode back up in silence, smiling at each other over a bucket of dirty water.

*

In the studio, Mark picked up a few scattered bottles and cans and dumped them into a blue recycling bin. "Excuse the mess. The Screaming Toads were in here before."

"Is that a band?"

"Sort of. They play about as well as they clean up after themselves." He opened a padlocked mini-fridge in the corner and tucked the key back in his pocket. "Can I get you a drink? I'm afraid I don't have any Scotch. Just wine."

"Even better." Talia sat on a low, black vinyl couch like the one Buster had been reading on in the surveillance video. A few books were piled on an end table between the couch and the wall.

"I hope Two Buck Chuck is to your liking, my lady." He sat next to her and placed a paper cup in her hand. His eyes were denim blue except for one yellow speck under the right pupil—an imperfection that was almost too perfect.

"Very much so." She turned away and looked straight ahead. Three black rolling chairs were laid out in front of a long panel of recording equipment that angled up to a window overlooking a series of small rooms filled with mic stands and musical instruments. A video camera was mounted on the left side of the wall above the window.

"That's not the chair."

"What chair?"

"*The* chair." Mark pointed solemnly at one of the rolling chairs. "That's not it. I don't know where it is. I guess the cops have it."

"Oh shit." Talia rubbed her arms. "I didn't know this was the studio that Buster...."

He nodded. "Yeah. Pedro offered to put me in a different room, but all my stuff is here and I feel like...I don't know. Like he's still here." He sighed and put his head in his hands. Talia put her hand on his shoulder. He exhaled slowly and looked up. "Hey, The Screaming Toads don't seem to mind it."

"I'm sorry I asked. I just meant...I thought it would still be sealed off with police tape."

"Is that what you thought? So, just when were you planning to go snooping around for the scene of the crime?"

She studied his expression. She couldn't tell if he was grilling her or flirting with her. She smiled. "I figured that you would give me a tour right after our drink."

He shook his head slowly. "And I bet I would, too. You seem to have a strange power over me, PI lady." He laughed and then stopped. "You *are* a PI, aren't you?"

"Something like that." She sipped her wine. "When did they reopen the studio?"

"I think it was right after they arrested Minnie."

"Wow. Case closed, huh? What do you think? Do you think Minnie did it?"

He took a deep breath and let it out before answering. "Yeah, I guess if she was caught on tape. I didn't watch the video, though. I don't think I ever could. Not in a lifetime."

"I watched it. It's not as...conclusive as you might think."

He eyes widened. "Really? You know...before I found out about the video, I thought it was someone else. In fact, I was sure it was someone else." He looked down at his hands. "Our manager. Nigel Zone. He's what we in the business call a real sleazeball." He looked up at her. "I guess you expect a certain amount of sleaze in this business, but Nigel is different. It's like he was born without a soul. We had a meeting about firing him right after he had that falling out with Buster."

Talia coughed and put her hand under her chin to catch the chardonnay she'd been sipping before it hit her dry-clean-only sweater. "Falling out? Why? About what?"

"About the party train pulling into the station. Buster wanted to make things work with Minnie and that meant quitting—drinking, drugs, women...all of it. Which meant Nigel would have to quit or start paying for his own drugs...and women. And Nigel didn't want to do either."

"So, did the rest of Crunch Pup have a hard time with it? With the party train coming into the station."

He leaned back and looked up at the ceiling. "Nah. For us, it derailed a long time ago. Which was good for me because, not only did it force me to grow up, it made me change the way I looked at myself as an artist."

"How so?" Talia pulled her knees up onto the couch, leaning toward him slightly.

"I realized that I'd had so many people around me telling me that I was good, that I never bothered to actually become good." He turned to face her. "You know what I mean?"

Talia nodded, but she didn't. Not many people in the acting business told her she was good. They mostly told her she was pretty or not pretty enough.

"You want to hear something I've been working on?"

"A new Crunch Pup song?"

"Nope." Mark stood up. "My own stuff." He walked over and sat in the chair that was not the chair that Buster Bones died in. "Believe it or not, I've had three solo albums in the past ten years." He pushed a few levers on the panel.

"I didn't know. Sorry."

"Don't be." Mark turned his chair toward her as the mellow, guitar-driven music filled the room. "Nobody knew. Nobody except a few deejays on adult contemporary radio...and my mom, of course." He winked.

Mark stopped talking as his own voice poured from the studio's sound system.

You struck me down/ to the floor/ to the place I've been before/ but I'm never going back/ Not now. Not now.

"Mark. This is really good."

"Really? It's not too adult contemporary?"

"Maybe a little bit." She looked in his eyes.

He walked over to her, took the cup out of her hand, and placed it on the table. He knelt in front of her and pulled her toward him. Talia slipped her feet off the couch so her knees wouldn't get in the way. Mark Lynn smiled before he kissed her. The kiss was soft and warm, but it was that sweet, vulnerable smile that tugged at her heart. She broke away. "I…I guess I should go."

"Or you could stay for the afternoon, drink cheap wine with me and make out some more."

"Good point." Talia sank back into his arms.

Chapter Eight

Talia walked into the warehouse, bent and rubbed Butter's head as the large dog curled in a backwards C-shape at her knees. When she looked up, Port was giving her a strange look. She already felt guilty—as though she'd somehow cheated on him by making out with Mark—so she gave him an even stranger look. "Good...morning."

"Good...morning. You're here early."

"I am?" Talia glanced at the clock—an old-fashioned cuckoo clock with duct tape covering the cuckoo's little door (probably put there by Darla to secure quiet for Belisa's naps). "Weird. I've never been early for a job before."

"I take that as a very high compliment."

"You should. You're a good boss," she said, pouring a cup of coffee. "You make me feel respected and—" she spotted a small silver and gray disc on the wall above the coffee maker. "What's this?"

"It's a camera, but it's not what you think."

"I think you're trying to figure out who's been stealing all your Equal packets." Talia deadpanned. "I admit it. It was me. I'm sorry. Everyone carries Splenda now, and I'm an old-fashioned girl."

"I'm not spying on you. I'm spying on me." Port's voice was strained. "It's Sombient."

"The sleeping pill? Do you take that?"

"No, I don't, but one of the well-documented side-effects of Sombient is sleep eating."

Talia brought her coffee in and sat down. "Yeah. I saw that on the news. Some lady ate her sister's wedding cake."

"My doctor told me that a normal man eats twenty-five hundred calories a day. I've calculated that I eat much less than that. My doctor said that if that were true, then I would be underweight, and as you can see, I'm not." Port waved a hand over his thin body. "So, I think I might be.... Oh, this is embarrassing." He looked away.

"It's okay." Talia reached across the desk and placed her hand on his.

He looked at the ceiling. "I think I might be getting up in the middle of the night and sneaking food." Port looked at her. "I have to do something. I can't keep...."

The door opened. "Whoa! Looks like I interrupted something pretty serious." Von pulled up a chair and sat between Talia and Port. "So, what are you guys talking about?" Butter came over and sat at his feet with her chin resting on his knee.

"Sombient," Port said.

"Oh yeah, that stuff is serious shit," Von nodded. "But if you're having trouble sleeping, you have to try Valisnore. It's kind of like a cross between a Valium and a sleep aid. I can get you guys a couple free samples if you want."

"No, thanks," Port said.

"Yes, please," Talia winked at Port. He smiled.

"I've got some Ativan. Would you like an Ativan?" Von glanced at Talia and then leaned in and whispered to Port, "Or a little weed laced with 'shrooms."

"I've said it before and I'll say it again. Yes, please!" Talia said, mostly to let Von know she could hear him, but also to make Port smile again.

"Now, Von." Port held up a hand. "It is one thing for a physically fit man like yourself to pop pills and whatnot, but it would be quite another if I were to partake. If I got carted off to the hospital, I might never get carted back."

"Huh? Oh! Right." Von winked overtly at Talia as if they were talking about the tooth fairy in front of a five-year old. "Because of the obesity."

"Well, Von...." Port glanced at the clock. "I don't mean to keep you from your duties, and I still need to get a full report of what happened at Studio 9 from Miss Green...."

"Yeah? You know, I recorded at Studio 9 once in the '80s." Von stood up and hooked a leash on a wiggly Butter. "I was playing bass in a ska band called Fergus Finger and the Upskirts."

"Ew." Talia said.

"Thank you." Von tipped an imaginary hat at her as he left with his furry charge.

Port coughed. "So, you...you talked to Mark Lynn?"

"Hmm? Oh yeah. He told me that Nigel Zone and Buster had a falling out. He'd gotten used to a certain lifestyle—partying with Buster. When Buster quit, Zone lashed out."

"Interesting. Providing, of course, that Mr. Lynn is telling the truth and not just trying to throw us off his own scent."

"Oh, I don't think he's doing that."

"Why not? Because he's cute?" Port's tone had an edge.

"Maybe?" she said sarcastically.

He sighed. "Great. I'll just call Detective Brad Nguyen and tell him we've eliminated Mark Lynn and all other cute men from the suspect list." Port pressed a button on his phone and tossed the phone on the desk.

"You're late, Porty," the voice on the phone said.

"What do you mean? You told me to call at nine, right Bradley?" He winked at Talia. She smiled.

"Right. Actually, we said ten, but..."

"Yes, but you must have known I meant nine."

"I did not know that, but it doesn't matter..."

Port leaned toward the phone and spoke softly into it. "Is this about Barstow?"

There was a pause. "I thought you said you weren't going to bring that up again."

"I thought *you* said you were going to give me my nine o'clock interview with my client."

"Yeah and I'd be doing that right now, if Minnie Johnson hadn't just made bail."

There was a knock on the door—two short raps followed by three bangs. Port waved at Talia to open the door.

Minnie stood on the front step, holding two babies about Belisa's age and flanked by three more kids, all dressed in miniature versions of faux-rocker wear. Even the younger one, a boxy little girl of about two or three, was wearing a beret and a Rolling Stones t-shirt. The other girl, who couldn't be more than seven, was wearing a mini-skirt and knee-high-boot combination that was too old for her. The oldest one, a boy of about nine or ten, was wearing a pair of red and black striped arm-warmers and a haunted expression that was *much* too old for him.

"Hello, family Johnson. My name is Porter Nepal, but you may call me Port. This is my assistant Miss Green, but you may call her Talia."

Minnie tapped the boy on the shoulder. He responded immediately. "Hello, Mr. Nepal, Miss Talia. My name is Vincent and I'm um...I'm pleased to meet you."

The older girl, who'd been carefully examining something on her shoe, looked up suddenly, as if she'd been given a cue. "Hello, Mr. Nepal, Miss Talia. My name is Miranda, and this is Joanne." She pointed at her little sister, who looked up at him, smiled mischievously, and shoved one finger up her nostril.

Minnie rolled her eyes. "And here we have Robert and Ruth." She bounced each baby on her hip in turn.

"I'm absolutely charmed to meet you all, but I've told you to call me Port, so please do. I'd also like you all to do one favor for me."

The children nodded, solemnly focused on him.

"I want you all—even you Joanne—to stop worrying about your mom. I promise you I am going to help her."

The front door swung open and Butter bounded into the room with a short, excited bark.

"Wow!" Vincent laughed. "That dog is really fat."

Port laughed. "The dog is fat? Is that all you've noticed, that the *dog* is fat?"

"Yes. This is the fattest dog I've ever seen." Vincent rubbed Butter's flabby side.

"Me too," Miranda said, throwing her arms around the dog's neck.

Joanne tried to hold Butter's wagging tail. "I kiss the dog-geeze butt." Butter turned and licked the little girl's face with such fervor that she nearly knocked her over.

"Okay kids, Uncle Von is going to have to walk Butter some more. We just came in to get the purple bags of power." Von plucked the little package of poopy bags from where he'd left them on the counter.

"Can we go with you?" Miranda said.

"S'okay with me, Princess." Von pointed a long finger at her nose until it hit, softly, with a silent beep. "But better ask your mom."

"Mom?!" Miranda and Vincent sang in unison.

"Take your sister with you, and keep a good effing eye on her, and don't...." The kids were out the door before she could finish her sentence.

Darla walked into the room with a yawning Belisa on her hip. She echoed the baby's yawn, and then stopped and stared at Minnie. Minnie stared back at her. Robert and Ruth looked at Belisa and immediately reached out, grasping at the air with their fists and leaning over their mother's forearms in a frantic attempt to get to the strange and exciting baby. Belisa replied by shoving Ninja Mouse in her mouth and promptly drooling on it.

Minnie nodded at Belisa. "Teething?"

Darla eyed Minnie.

Minnie leveled a stare at Darla. "You think I killed my husband." It was not quite a statement, but it wasn't a question either.

All three babies began fussing. Both mothers, still locked in a death stare, began softly bouncing them. Darla broke eye contact to look at the two babies being gently jostled into submission, then locked eyes with Minnie again and said, "Maybe."

Minnie sighed. "That's the best I can fucking hope for, I guess." Minnie plunked the twins on the rug and kicked a few toys toward them before taking a large step back.

Darla walked into the living room and stood in front of the play rug. She carefully placed Belisa on the rug, knelt, and offered her a series of toys but Belisa kept a tight grasp on Ninja Mouse. The three babies immediately started communicating with a system of arm flapping, hand clapping and squealing. Darla stood, keeping her eyes on Belisa.

Then Minnie did something Talia hadn't seen her do before. She smiled. "Ah. New mom?"

"Yeah."

"How old? Eight months?"

"Ten."

"My babies are the same age." Minnie nodded. "We all go through that nervous new mom shit. When I had Vincent, I didn't leave the house for three fucking months."

"If you don't count the driveway and doctor visits, I'm at ten months."

Talia gaped at Port. He nodded.

Minnie said, "Holy shit! That fucking baby needs to get her ass out of the house."

"Well, I take her out for fifteen minutes every afternoon, so she can get sun."

"She needs to be around other fucking babies." Minnie leaned down and looked closely at Belisa. Belisa responded by smiling at the stern-faced woman. "Cleft lip?"

"Yeah."

"Cleft palate, too?" Minnie stood up and looked at Darla.

"No, just the lip."

"My second child had the cleft palate, not the lip." Minnie opened her mouth and pointed inside, looking like a hungry bird for just a second before clamping her mouth shut.

"Hey, look at her go." Port pointed at Belisa who was crawling on her forearms like a chubby little Marine. She made an awkward attempt at chasing after Robert and Ruth as they crawled on their hands and knees off the play rug and toward the office area.

"Wow. I'm in big fucking trouble." Darla clasped her hand to her mouth.

"Oh yeah, they bring that out in you: the swearing. I used to have perfect fucking language before I had kids. Here." Minnie grabbed a card out of her diaper bag and handed it to Darla. "Call me. You'll take the baby to my house for a play date. Okay?"

Darla looked at her as if she had just suggested she tie Belisa into a burlap sack and toss her off the Bay Bridge, but then she looked over at Belisa, giggling and squealing with her new baby friends. She put the card in her pocket.

Minnie left Darla to hover over the babies and strode over to the desk. She stood next to Port's chair, and for someone as tiny as she was, managed to loom over him. "Now, about my case. What the fuck did you find out?"

"I found out a little more than I'm comfortable with, Mrs. Johnson." Port looked her in the eye. "They caught you on video."

Minnie calmly returned his gaze. "The video from the studio? I've seen that stupid shit. It's nothing."

"Then what were you doing in that video that took exactly sixty seconds?"

She broke eye contact. "That's private. It's none of your fucking concern."

"I want to help you, but you've got to help me." Port sighed. "Tell me what happened that night."

"I'll tell you what fucking happened. I didn't kill my fucking husband." Minnie placed a tiny hand on the desk and leaned closer to Port. "Every fucking night, before I go to sleep, I go to my kids' rooms, and I look at them until I see their little chests go up and down." Minnie patted her chest as demonstration. "That night, I checked on Buster, and when I left him, his chest was going up and down, so I went home. I went to sleep thinking my husband was still fucking alive."

"Minnie, why did you check on Buster? Did you think he might *not* be breathing?" Talia said.

Minnie shrugged. "I heard from a friend that he'd gone partying with that scuzzball, Nigel Zone. I wanted to see if he was on the fucking drugs again."

"Was he?" Port said.

Minnie looked down. "I think so. He was fucking passed out when I got there."

"And when he did them, what kind of drugs did Buster do?" Port said. "I'm sorry. I have to ask."

"All of them." Minnie's voice trembled slightly as she talked. "Look, I know a detective would have to be fucking crazy to take my case. That's why you are the only one who can prove that I'm not guilty because you are fucking crazy."

Port laughed. "You think I'm crazy?"

"You never leave your house," Minnie said. "People who never leave the fucking house are crazy."

Port flinched. Those words had to have stung. They stung Talia, and they weren't even directed at her. "But you can see, Mrs. Johnson, that I have my reasons for not leaving my house." Port raised his arms barely an inch from the massive armrests of his over-sized chair.

Minnie looked him up and down. "Yeah, and those reasons are bat-shit crazy."

"Hey, take it easy on him...." Talia began, not knowing exactly what she was going to say.

"It's quite all right, Talia." Port looked at Minnie as he spoke. "Mrs. Johnson is right. I am crazy, and luckily for her, I'm just crazy enough to believe her."

The door opened. "Hey oh! Last stop on the Dogwalk Express." Von held the door open as the dog and kids bounded into the room.

"We're having fun," Miranda said.

Vincent stood—shoulders back, feet together, head up—in front of his mother. "Yeah. We don't want to go home."

"Good. I like it when my kids have fun." Minnie walked to the play area and picked up Robert and Ruth. "Now, get in the effing car. It's time to go."

*

Not too long after the family left, Darla lifted Belisa off the mat. "Those rock star babies just wore you out, didn't they?"

Belisa blinked, yawned and then bonked her head onto her mother's shoulder.

When the nursery door shut with a soft click, Talia said, "So, Darla's...she's an agoraphobic?"

"Only since having the baby. We're quite a pair, aren't we?" Port lifted one finger off its perch on the arm of his chair to point in the direction of the nursery. "Did you know that I named Belisa?"

Talia shook her head.

"After Darla left Ted, I took her in. I refused to charge rent until she got her writing career back off the ground. In return, she wanted to name her baby after me." He laughed and shook his head. "But when she found out the sex, we agreed that Port is a terrible name for a girl, so I suggested a name from a play I read in college. 'The Love of Don Perlimplín and Belisa in the Garden.' Have you read it?"

"I've never even heard of it."

"It was written by Spanish poet named Federico García Lorca. It's about a young, impetuous woman named Belisa who marries a much older and much wealthier man." Port pushed up on one arm of his chair to straighten himself about an inch. "On their wedding night, she has sex with not one, but five other men. And do you know what Don Perlimplín did when he found out?"

Talia looked out toward the entry way, at the small window next to the door—so small, she couldn't see anything out of it but a square patch of blue the size of a potholder. "Did he kill her?"

"No. He fell deeply in love with her, more deeply in love then he had before, and then he died for her, teaching her about love and sacrifice."

"And that's the name you suggested for Darla's baby?"

Port laughed. "It's okay. She won't read the play until college. I'm sure I'll be dead by then."

Talia looked at him. "Dead? In eighteen years?"

"My body is not built for longevity, Talia."

She felt a warm, familiar tug in her chest when he said her first name. "I'm sure you won't die, Port."

"No, no. It's okay." He held up his hand. "It's like Lorca said, 'As I haven't worried to be born, I am not worried to die.'"

"I don't think I could've forgiven him like that, do you?" Talia put her elbow on the desk and leaned on her hand. "Buster, I mean. Not Pimple Ring."

"Perlimplín."

"Right."

"Have you ever been in love like that? Like Minnie and Buster?" Port looked into her eyes.

Talia returned his gaze. She opened her mouth to speak, but it was not an easy question to answer, considering the asker, and what had gone on with her and Mark in the studio, so she just smiled at him.

Port broke eye contact. "Yes. Well, enough about Spanish poets, true love, and fictional Belisas. We should get back to our real-life doomed lovers."

Chapter Nine

The Marina neighborhood was nearly destroyed in the 1989 earthquake, but had bounced back to become a playground for the rich, annoying and annoyingly rich. The Bird's Nest was at the epicenter of the annoying. Toby and Talia stood on the sidewalk and looked up at a small woodcut depicting a robin's nest filled neatly with pale blue eggs.

"Gross!" Toby said. "It's one of those bars that tries so hard to be cool, they don't even put up a real sign."

A car pulled up and dropped off two girls with long hair and short skirts. One of them squealed, "Ooh! This bar is so cool, it doesn't have a sign."

The other one was equally impressed. "So cool. Just like New York."

"Well, then go to New York," Talia whispered.

"Yeah, go to New York," Toby said loudly.

"Sh!" Talia said, but the girls were busy trying to convince the bouncer that they were on the list.

"If you're not on the list, you're not getting in. And you...." He tapped his clipboard for emphasis. "Are not on the list."

"Shit." Talia turned to Toby. "I didn't know we had to be on a list."

"List shmist." He eyed the bouncer, a large man with a long, beard. "The reason The Bobbsey Twins aren't getting in is because this place already has twenty other chicks who look just like them...and you too, but I bet that they don't have anyone in that bar who looks like me."

Toby strutted over to the bouncer and slipped lithely in front the girls, who protested with a sharp, synched "Hey!"

Toby put one elbow on the bouncer's shoulder while swatting blindly with his free hand at the girls behind him until they took a step back and out of his reach. Toby looked into the bouncer's eyes. "Hi. I'm gay."

The bouncer looked away, rubbed his beard in a slow, downward motion and then looked back into Toby's eyes. "I can see that. So am I."

Toby laughed in a way that was slightly breathier and much more flirtatious than his regular high-pitched cackle. "Am I on the list?"

The bouncer did not break eye contact to look at his clipboard. "You sure are."

Once inside, and away from the oddly coherent cries of "discriminative practices" and "prejudicial treatment" from the women who were still stomping in platform wedges on the sidewalk, they decided the best place to look for someone who referred to himself as "DaZone" would be the club's VIP room—a room in the back that was cordoned off with a red velvet rope and guarded by a stone-faced bouncer.

Talia pulled Dicko out of her purse typed in "need to sneak in to VIP room."

Buy a bottle of Dom Pérignon and flirt with the bouncer.

The bartender, with his slim-lapelled white tuxedo and bright blue, lilac-tipped fauxhawk, looked like an extra in a steam-punk remake of *Casino Royale*. Talia waved him over. "Excuse me, how much is a bottle of—"

Toby elbowed her and nodded at the bartender. "Bottle of Dom. Two glasses."

The bartender nodded and turned around.

"Sorry, Tea," Toby said. "You have to order the high-end shit with authority or they'll think you can't afford it."

"We can't," Talia said.

Toby smiled. "But your new boss can."

The bartender returned with the unopened champagne in a bucket of ice. He placed it next to him on the bar. He slid the bill toward her and rested both hands on the bar. Talia reached into her purse for the credit card Port had given her "for legitimate expenses." The champagne had been Dicko's idea, but could five hundred dollars for a bottle that she and Toby could down in less than twenty minutes really count as legitimate?

Just as she pulled out the card, a hand slid onto hers. "Put it on my tab, barkeep." She looked at the hand—stubby, pale and covered with dark, wiry hair—before looking up at its owner, who was also pale and stubby and covered in wiry hair. Some of it was on his head, but most of it was peeking out of the melon-colored shirt he wore unbuttoned past the third button.

"You got it, Mr. Zone." The bartender tapped the bar twice and walked away.

Talia pulled her hand out from under the clammy hand on the top of hers. Zone resisted and the friction created a sickening squeaking sound against the bar. "You don't need to do that," she said, shoving the card into her purse. "We can buy our own drinks."

Toby let out a short laugh—the cackle one, not the breathy one. "Don't listen to her. We love it when people buy us drinks. We'll be drinking in the VIP room, if you want to join us."

Zone eyed Toby and leered at Talia. "The bleedin' VIP room? Who do you and Cake Boy know that you're getting into the VIP room?"

"Oh, don't you worry, Herman's Hermit, we know people," Toby said.

The bartender returned with three glasses.

"Well?" Zone smirked and pointed at the VIP room. "Go right ahead. I'll wait here."

Toby grabbed the bottle. Talia grabbed the glasses and said, "Fine. You do that."

She smiled at the VIP bouncer as they approached. His gaze was directed at something about twenty feet behind them. Talia looked back at Zone. He crossed his arms, still smirking.

"VIP room only," Stoneyface droned.

"We're with Nigel Zone. He just bought this champagne." Talia held up the bottle.

"You can check with the bartender," Toby said.

Stoneyface eyed them coolly. He looked over at the bar. Zone was still smiling at them. Talia waved. Zone waved back.

Stoneyface pulled aside the velvet rope. "Go on in."

The VIP room was full of people who weren't doing much of anything except congratulating themselves for getting into the VIP room—which was exactly what Talia and Toby were doing when Zone made his entrance. As he did, the DJ turned off the generic, ambient house groove that was playing and put on a song by Sade.

"Who does this walking nose hair think he is that he gets a theme song played for his ass?" Toby whispered while smiling at Zone, who was currently slipping a small stack of bills into the DJ's tip jar.

"Yes, and apparently, it's 'Smooth Operator.' I think they played that at my prom."

"Cor! Did you say 'prom'? Wait, don't tell me..." Zone placed a ringed hand on his forehead. "I'm picturing a ripped taffeta dress and a crooked tiara in the back seat of the hire. Am I right?"

"How'd you guess?" Talia said flatly.

"Oh, it wasn't a guess, love. It was a fantasy." He ran a stubby finger along her arm, picked up her hand and kissed it. "What say we go make it a reality?" His grip tightened on her hand.

Talia yanked her hand away. "Not going to happen, Zone." It didn't matter what she said or did, Zone had targeted her. She just needed to get as much information from him while limiting physical contact. She shot Toby a look.

He nodded, and put one hand on Zone's shoulder. "Come here for a moment. I promise I won't bite." He pulled him aside and whispered something to him. Zone glanced at Talia, nodded and left.

"Toby, you didn't scare my suspect away, did you?"

"He'll be back. He's getting a bottle of Glenfiddich because I may have told him that...." Toby put one hand defensively over his head. "That expensive whiskey makes your panties drop."

Talia put her hands on her hips and stared at Toby. He put his hand down by his side. She smacked his head. "You know I don't like expensive whiskey, Tobe."

He rubbed his head and half-giggled and half-cackled. "Chill, Tea. You're not going to drink it."

"Good, because drinking whiskey is turning into a workplace hazard."

"Don't worry. As soon as he gets back. I'm going to challenge him to a good old-fashioned drinking contest. He's going to accept because he wants to show off for you, and he thinks he can beat me because I look like I don't eat carbs...and I don't."

"Much," Talia corrected.

*

"That book of Buster's has bleeding well painted me as a drunk, a playboy and a notorious womanizer, Vanilla Legs. But not in a good way. Not a good way at all." Zone hiccupped and burst into blubbery, drunken tears. Toby handed him a cocktail napkin. "Thank you, Fancy Pants." He had taken to calling them Fancy Pants and Vanilla Legs soon after slipping under the table.

"There's a good way of calling someone a drunk playboy?" Talia asked.

He blew his nose with a wet honk. "There is! He could've painted me as a rogue, a rascal, a roustabout, a gadabout, a rascabout. The kind of guy that women bleeding well want to sleep with and men want to party with." Zone let out a loud, mournful sigh, followed by an even louder, but less mournful, belch. "My reputation has been slipping as of late. This bar...." He pointed a finger at the world outside his hiding place. "This shithole that I plan on defiling with at least two different bodily fluids...."

Toby shrugged. "A man with no illusions."

"This shithole with its shitty V-I fucking P room represents the last place in this stinking town that will still bleeding well let me in the fucking front door. But even this place...even this pus palace will eighty-six me if that fucking book ever comes out."

"You read the book?" Talia said.

"Of course I read it. Buster was like a bloody brother to me. He didn't hide anything from good old Zoney."

"Did you ever fight with Buster?" Talia asked.

"Nah. Never. No. Wait." Zone belched and said, "We fought like a pack of wild dogs who'd been elected to the House of Commons."

"What did you fight about?"

"The fact that he used to be cool. Cor! I remember...an after-hours party at South by Southwest. Here's me and Buster, I'm snorting lines of coke off this model's ass while Buster—and I have no bleeding idea where he got the needle—is tattooing his own name on some rockabilly chick's tit when Iggy Pop, or some tosser who looked exactly like Iggy Pop, turns to us and says, 'I haven't seen anyone party like that since Ozzy Osbourne in '79.' Ozzy. Fucking. Osbourne. That happy little bastard partied so hard, he's not even *allowed* in Austin. Do you know what the worst part is?" Zone looked up at her. "No one will ever again compare my bleeding vast and impressive partying skills to Ozzy again."

"Everyone has to grow up sometime," Talia said, but there was no answer. She looked under the table. Zone was drooling on his chest hair. "Zone!" she yelled, startling him back to semi-consciousness. "You said *if* that book ever comes out. What did you mean by that? Is there a chance it won't come out?"

"Don't you know anything, Vancy Lakes?" he slurred. Talia considered correcting him but didn't want to break his train of thought while he was still conscious. "Minnie doesn't want that book to come out, and with Buster gone, that bitch holds the reins. Even if they throw her in bloody prison, no publisher would dare go against the team of lawyers in that bird's back pocket."

"Why wouldn't she want the book to come out?"

"Because it's bleeding chock-full of whores and mistresses, and wives and whores do not fucking mix." Zone made his point by throwing his index finger in the air, banging it sharply on the underside of the table. "Yow!" He sucked on the injured digit. "If Minnie were smart, she'd let that book come out. Her mortal enemies Crunch Pup come off like right bastards."

"So, Crunch Pup looks bad in the book, huh?" Talia said.

"Bad as bad bacon! There's a whole chapter called Bad Music and Egomaniacs." Zone burst into a fresh batch of tears. "But no one comes out worse than me. Buster painted me as a baboon with a coke habit. That's a direct quote. Bastard. You know what? I'm glad that bitch killed him. Good riddance to traitors, I say."

"Don't be sure about that. I heard that Minnie might be innocent," Talia said.

Zone perched his head on the booth between Toby's right thigh and Talia's left thigh. He gazed up at them. "She was caught on tape."

"I saw that tape. You can barely tell who it is. It could be anybody. Even a guy," Talia said.

"Even an ugly guy...with bad hair," Toby said with a hiccup.

"Oh, then it was probably Mark Lynn." Zone slumped back on to the floor.

Talia's heart sank at the implication, despite the unreliable source. "Why him?"

"Of all those Crunch cunts, he had the most to gain. What do you think is happening with the sales of those rubbish solo albums he had the balls to release?" He whistled wetly and pointed upwards, banging his finger again. "Bollocks!" He rubbed his finger. "Marky's cashing in on Buster's death. He either did it, or he'd like to shake the hand of the dirty-mouthed bitch who did."

"But they were friends," Talia said.

"Friends?!" Zone howled incredulously. "Buster didn't have friends. Just slime-covered stepping stones in his stream...his stream of piss."

Talia sat back. Toby leaned across the table and fumbled the bottle of Scotch toward him. He poured a shot and slammed it on the table in front of Talia. Talia took a small sip while Toby leaned under the table. "You know, Zoney, I heard that Minnie hates Crunch Pup. Maybe she'll release the book just to spite them."

"That would chaff their taints, wouldn't it? Cor! Can you imagine the enormous bit of coin that book will make now that Buster's buggered off?"

Talia put down her glass and looked under the table. "Who would stand to gain from that?"

Zone rested his elbow on Talia's thigh. "Minnie, I suppose."

"What about the publisher?" Talia pushed the elbow off her leg.

"Let's see if this really tastes like vanilla."

Talia felt something warm, wet and slug-like on her skin just above her knee. She yanked her legs up and hugged her knees to her chest. The quick maneuver caused Zone to fall, tongue first, onto the floor.

Toby leaned under the table. "He's passed out." Toby, stuck, held his hand out for help. Talia pulled until he popped out from under the table. He picked up her mostly full shot glass and drank it. "So, that Mark guy Zone was talking about...that's the guy you made out with at Studio 9, right?"

"Right."

"Damn. You might have been making out with a murderer." He looked at her wide-eyed and then hiccupped.

Chapter Ten

The first few notes of *Sketches of Spain* surprised Talia. As a kid, she'd spent hours looking through her father's vinyl collection, occasionally playing an album, but mostly she just imagined what they would sound like based on the cover artwork. Since then, she'd associated Miles Davis with the cover of *Bitches Brew*—an African couple standing on a beach, looking out on a stormy sea while a sweaty face loomed large in the foreground. Talia expected *Sketches of Spain* to be tribal, electric and sweaty, but it was soft and gentle like summer rain falling on cobblestone streets. She wondered if that was what the album cover looked like as she waited for the coffee to finish brewing.

"How do you like it?" Port called from the office.

"I love it."

"I'm glad. I had originally decided to play Cohen's *Various Positions*, but every time I do, I think about at how ham-handedly "Hallelujah" is used by every music supervisor in the movie and television...."

"Uh huh," Talia said, but couldn't hear his rant over the music, the noise of the kettle, and the clanking of the mugs as she whipped them out of the cupboard. Toby often complained that Talia made loud coffee. Talia would just shrug and say, "All the coffee shops I've worked at taught me to be quick, not quiet."

When she emerged from the kitchen, Port's rant had moved on to a sing-song recitation. "...And burn the corks. Chip the glasses and crack the plates."

Talia put two cups of coffee on the desk.

"Thank you, Bofur."

"Who's Bofur?"

"Just a dwarf who makes loud tea."

"Ah. I get it. I make loud coffee." She waved her cup at him. "You got to admit, though, I'm fast."

"I wasn't complaining." Port sipped his coffee. "Erm...I'm torn. I want to think Zone did it because he's...you know...."

"A scuzzbucket?"

"Right. But he almost has too much motive. I mean if he were going to murder Buster, I picture him going the violent, alcohol-fueled rampage route—running him over with a car, stabbing him with a broken bottle, throwing him off the Bay Bridge."

"But I think he also hated Minnie, so if he did it and framed her for it, then he basically...."

"Killed two birds with one stone?" He nodded. "Yes. Let's keep an eye on Mr. Zone, but right now..." He grasped the arm of his chair so he could lean forward and place his cup on the desk. "I'd really like to know more about what Buster wrote in that book, wouldn't you?"

She sighed. "I wish Crunch Pup had read it."

"If they did, I'm sure they have hard feelings about that Bad Music chapter Zone told...." He stopped and looked at her, eyebrows knitted. "What is it?"

"It's just...." She took a deep breath. "Zone thinks Mark Lynn did it. He thinks that Mark's solo albums would sell more if Buster Bones was dead."

"See, that sounds like adequate motive, but it falls apart when we look at it. How much would Buster's death really increase Mr. Lynn's album sales? Enough to kill?" He shrugged. "Probably not."

"I agree." Talia exhaled. "I talked to him about his music, and I honestly don't think that's why he does it."

"He hates money, eh? Typical rock star." Port put his coffee cup on the desk with a sharp *clang*. A few drops spilled. He wiped the coffee off the desk with a scrap of paper. Talia grabbed the scrap of paper, bunched it up, leaned back, and threw it toward the wastebasket.

Port shook his head. "So close."

"We need a larger basket."

Port opened his laptop. "Yes. I'm sure it's not quite regulation." He hit a few keys and a roughly sketched map appeared on one of the screens. "What do you think about my rendition of Buster's studio?"

"Eh, it's not bad." Talia pointed up at the sketch. "Except the security camera is more obvious. It's in plain sight."

Port clicked a few keys and stretched out the rectangle marked *camera*. "Let's fill in the rest. Tell me everything you remember."

Talia drummed her fingers on the desk and closed her eyes. "The lobby has double glass doors. Inside, there's a security guard stand in front of the elevator. On the second floor, Buster's studio is the second studio on the right. To the left is a glass-walled conference room, a utility closet, and then a unisex bathroom at the end of the hall near the stairwell. The door to the stairs is locked on the ground floor, but not on the second floor."

Port smiled at her. "It's like you're sending Morse code to the memory center of your brain."

She shrugged. "Actors have good memories...all those lines, you know?"

"So, our killer enters the building with a keycard, takes the elevator to the second floor, waits in the conference room and watches Buster's studio." Port peered at the screen of his laptop, fingers working the keyboard. "After Minnie leaves, he or she goes in, strangles Buster, and exits through the stairwell door." Port clicked a new expanded map on the screen and looked up. "Or does he? Would he be able to get out once he got downstairs? Or is the door locked on the inside as well?"

"I'm not sure," Talia said. "But I don't think he hid in that conference room. The glass goes all the way to the floor. Not a lot of places to hide."

Port edited the map to include the glass and a question mark on the first-floor stairwell door. "Maybe he hid in the utility closet." He moved his cursor over a rectangle marked *UC*. "Could a person fit in there? I mean a regular-sized person, of course, not a jumbo specimen like myself."

Talia glared at him. "Well, it was not exactly a plus-sized closet, but a person of average build could squeeze into it just fine. Besides, you're forgetting something. The killer would be on the video."

"Ah, but I'm not. The killer would have known about the camera, so he would have planned a way to get around it. Maybe he stole a key to the security room, so he could get in and tamper with the video." Port slapped his palm on the desk. "Yes, that must have been how he did it...or she."

"But wouldn't the police have noticed if the video was tampered with?"

"Good question. Let's call them and ask." He picked up his phone but didn't put it on speaker. "Bradley, I need to know if the Buster Bones video was tampered with. ...Right. But it might have been? ...So, what you are saying is.... So, there's a chance that it was? ...I'll take that as a maybe."

Talia could only hear one side of the conversation, but she could tell that Brad wasn't backing up Port's theory. She raised an eyebrow at him.

Port hung up and dropped the phone on the desk. "He said it might have been tampered with."

The side door slammed shut. "Tampering? That's my thing. What do you need tampered with?"

"The Studio 9 video. I think it was tampered with."

"Bullshit. That thing wasn't tampered with. I know tampering. I just said it's my thing." Ted postured dramatically, as though he'd been crowned King of Tampering.

Port waved his hand dismissively. "Did you get that studio schedule?"

"Right here, Portlandish." Ted waved a small stack of papers and then tossed them on the desk. "And you will never guess who was in the studio right before Buster got offed. The wussy guitarist from Crunch Pup. Mark Lynn."

Talia bristled at the word *wussy* and glared at Ted.

"Good work, Ted," Port said.

"Did I just hear the words *work* and *Ted* in the same sentence?" Darla stomped into the room holding an overstuffed diaper bag in one arm and Belisa—swinging slightly with each foot stomp while strapped in a portable car seat—in the other.

"You know, as a couple, you two have impeccable timing," Port said.

Ted tried to take the diaper bag from Darla, but she waved him off and let him grab the handle of the car seat instead. "I'll have you know, I'm helping out on Portly's dead-end case." Ted turned to Port. "You are paying me, right? I'll do it anyways...but you're going to pay me, right?"

"Of course."

"Really? Is he going to give you medical insurance, too?" Darla said.

"Medical insurance is a scam!" Ted waved his arms for emphasis. Belisa giggled at the motion. Ted looked down at Belisa. She smiled and sneezed at him. "Wait a minute. Are you going to the pediatrician? Don't let that bastard implant tracking chips into our baby. If he uses the word *vaccine*, run!"

"Shut up, Ted." She grabbed a tissue from a side pocket of her diaper bag and handed it to him. "I need a ride to our play date with Minnie."

"Really? I'd love to drive you ladies to the Bones mansion." He dabbed at Belisa's nose with the tissue, crumpled it then whipped it, underhand, against the wall. It floated into the basket. He raised his fist in victory.

"Not you, you lunatic." She pointed at Talia. "You."

*

Talia kept her hands on the ten-and-two position of the Saab's steering wheel as Darla had instructed. "I can't believe you let me drive."

"Just let me know when you're going to crash into something, so I can throw my body across my only child," Darla snapped from the backseat.

As brave as Darla had been to put Belisa into the car seat, when it had come time to actually get into the car, she ran into the house and barricaded herself and Belisa in her room. Ted had tried to talk her out for more than twenty minutes. Finally, Port shuffled slowly down the hall and leaned on the door. He reminded Darla that she had bought that car seat because it was the only one to test well in a seventy-mile-per-hour crash test and that the speed limit on the way to Sea Cliff wouldn't rise above thirty-five, so whatever happened, Belisa would surely survive the crash. Ted had reacted silently, with his hands in the air, as if he wanted to choke Port for mentioning the word *crash*, but that was when Darla had opened the door and Ted whispered to Talia, "I guess only crazy can talk down crazy."

Talia pulled off El Camino Del Mar and in front of Minnie's house. It was a Craftsman-style bungalow painted brick red with white trim. Its small front yard would not have stood out among the others in the neighborhood (which were decorated ostentatiously with Grecian statues and whimsical hedge sculptures) if it weren't for the hundreds of flowers, album covers and hand-written notes strewn all over the lawn.

They rang the doorbell. It played "Walk of Love." Talia expected to be greeted at the door by a maid or butler, but Minnie let them in. She'd traded her gold chains for a yarn necklace. Her hair was pulled up on the sides, braided with mathematical precision and secured with a plastic barrette—the kind drugstores sell in bulk packs. Her face was free of make-up except for two perfect swipes of pink blush.

Minnie stopped and pointed at a small room that was filled with flowers, boxes, mailbags and balloons. "Our fucking mail room now. Everyone I've ever fucking met has either sent me a package or shown up at my door with a crappy casserole. Fucking vultures!" She kicked a few packages that had spilled into the hall. She picked one of them up—a black box with no address or postage, tied-up with a pink ribbon—and placed it on a hall table. "Most of them anyway. I still have a few real friends."

Talia glanced at one of the packages Minnie had kicked. There was a crude black star drawn above the address label. "Minnie, have you seen a guy in a Black Star t-shirt hanging around here?"

"Just one fucking guy?" Minnie led them down the hall and into an enormous kitchen dominated by a long wooden table where the twins were seated in a double highchair.

"Uh yeah. Dirty blonde hair, tall, skinny...kind of creepy looking."

Minnie turned around. "That sounds like most of them. They knock on the door and fucking talk to me like I know them." Minnie shivered. "It's gross. I sent my older kids to stay with my parents. I don't want them to repeat the things that I say to those creepfucks."

Darla pointed an unmanicured finger at her. "You need to get a gun."

Talia spun around and stared at Darla.

"Get?" Minnie picked up the twins from a double highchair and winked at Darla. "What do you think I hold in my right hand when I open the door?"

Talia imagined Minnie tottering down the hall on her high heels to the door with a gun her hand. "Maybe you should just stop answering the door."

"Why? I like the fucking looks on their faces." Minnie widened her eyes and stuck her tongue out in an exaggerated pantomime of a surprised Buster Bones fan. Then she turned and pointed at a stainless-steel refrigerator covered in children's artwork. "Grab that pitcher of wine spritzers in there. The babies can play in the backyard while we get mom drunk."

"Great idea, Minnie. I haven't been mom drunk in months." Darla grabbed the pitcher with her free hand. "I haven't been drunk drunk in over a year." She bumped the refrigerator door shut with her hip and glared at Talia. "None for you. You're driving."

Talia and Minnie sat down at the well-worn patio set. Darla ran across the lawn to hover over Belisa as she crawled around the grass with the twins. Talia looked at Minnie, whose eyes were hidden beneath designer sunglasses. "I heard Buster was cheating on you."

Minnie took a long sip of her spritzer. "Who told you that?"

"Nigel Zone. He said he read it in Buster's book."

"Nigel fucking Zone is the biggest crap stain I ever met."

"I agree with that." Talia held up her glass of tap water. "In fact, I could drink to that."

Minnie smiled. "I'll drink to Nigel getting so fucking drunk that he gets his fucking dick caught in his own zipper."

"Deal." Talia raised her glass.

After a long silence, Minnie said, "I forgave him."

"For the affairs?"

"No. For the disrespect." Minnie turned full in her chair, so she was facing Talia. "But I'll tell you one fucking thing: not a fucking word about those sluts was going to make his fucking book. It was one of my conditions for forgiving."

"But Zone claimed the book was going to expose the affairs. Was he lying?"

"Nigel is a dog. He lies. He lied to my face about Buster's affairs, but he knew about them. He fucking participated, the dirtfucket."

Talia stifled a laugh in her glass. In the history of cursing, nobody had likely ever used the word "dirtfucket" before Minnie used it just now to describe Nigel Zone, but it was as precise as the braids in her hair.

Minnie turned her attention back to the twins who were crawling gleefully toward a wooden play structure that connected to a child-sized pirate ship with a rope bridge. She stood up and clapped her hands three times, yelling, "No, no, no! Not for babies." The twins stopped, looked up at her and then turned and crawled in the other direction, toward the sandbox where Darla was wiping sand off Belisa's hands.

Minnie sat down, leaned back and pointed at Darla. "I used to be like that."

Talia turned to see Darla trying in vain to get Belisa to drop a sun-bleached shovel in favor of a pre-sterilized toy from the diaper bag. "I don't believe you."

"Believe me. My kids were my fucking moon and stars. I spent all my time bending backward for them. That didn't leave much time for my husband. He gave his dick to other women because I was too tired for it. I went fucking months without so much as flashing the guy a little tit." Minnie swirled her glass. It was almost empty. "He had things to forgive me for, too. So you see why I didn't tell all that to Porter Nepal yesterday. I can't talk about my tits with some strange guy."

Talia laughed.

"Besides, he's crazy as a fucking loon."

"Yeah." Talia sighed. "I guess he is."

Minnie shrugged. "But we're all crazy, right? All these moms at school and on the playground tell me I have a potty mouth. So I tell them to fuck themselves. Who fucking cares? My kids don't. They're fucking rich." Minnie chuckled. "My fucking husband, god rest his soul, was the craziest one."

"Buster was crazy? How so?"

"He refused to grow up. On his forty-first birthday, I had to pick him up at the hospital. Surfing injury. At forty-one!" She tugged her sunglasses down and looked over the rims at Talia. "He was functionally crazy, though. You need someone who can buy you a nice house but also take you out fucking dancing or something."

Talia looked out at Minnie's fenced-in backyard with its partial view of the Golden Gate Bridge. "Minnie, what were you doing at the studio that night?"

Minnie leaned toward Talia. "I'll tell you, but you have to fucking promise that you won't tell anyone."

"But I have to tell Port."

"No, you don't. It won't help with your investigation. Just fucking promise."

"I fu...I promise."

"We were in couples counseling, you know that, right?"

Talia nodded, but she hadn't heard that bit of gossip. Out of the corner of her eye, she could see Darla walking toward them. Talia casually held up one finger to signal she should back off. Darla turned, and walked back toward the babies as they played in the sand box.

"Our shrink told us that we needed to re-learn how to love each other. He gave us homework. Most of it was bullshit but one of the exercises I liked. We were supposed to set aside one minute every day to hug each other. He told us to use a kitchen timer, or to sing the final *Jeopardy* song twice. You know it?"

Talia hummed the familiar tune.

"That's the one. We hugged for one minute every day, and it was nice. We didn't really need that fucking song, but it became kind of like...it was like our song." Minnie took a deep breath and let it out. "It was late, and we hadn't hugged yet. I had my mom come over and watch the kids. I drove to the studio and...Buster was alive, but he was passed out. I tried to put his hand on my back, so he could hug me back, but it just dropped like a wet fucking towel."

"His hand dropped?"

Minnie nodded and looked down. "That is what I was doing at the studio that night, hugging my fucking drugged-up husband and singing the *Jeopardy* song...by myself." She pulled a card out of her pocket and shoved it into Talia's hand. "This will help with your fucking investigation."

Talia turned the card over in her hand. It was black except for a blood-red bird stamped in the center. It read: "Red Robin Publishing. Linda Varela."

Chapter Eleven

"Oh, good. The detective. Have a seat." Linda Varela waved Talia into her office.

"Thank you, but I'm not really...I mean, yes, thank you." Talia moved a stapler off the only other chair in the room and sat down, tugging at her skirt as it rode up her thigh.

Linda sat on a pile of papers at the edge of her desk, loudly crumpling something that was underneath. She lifted one hip, so she could reach under and grab the noisemaker: an empty plastic cookie tray. She tossed it behind her without looking, and then started digging around her desk, twisting her torso back and forth, lifting stacks of papers and mumbling half-sentence questions to herself. "Now where is? What the? Oh, is this that? The hell is? Oh, I know what that...but what is?"

Talia looked around the office. The large window on the far wall looked out over a small, tranquil corner of Levi's Plaza where a willow hung over a stone path that encircled a little green hill like a moat. Except for a square vase filled with a neat row of irises up on a shelf, Linda's office was as disheveled as Linda herself with her untamed curls, pet-hair dappled yoga pants and red-framed glasses that sat, tilted slightly, at the end of her nose.

"Ah here it is." Linda held up a stack of papers triumphantly. "This is for you."

Talia took the document, felt the weight of the papers in her hands, rifled the edges with her fingertips. The title page, marred by coffee stains and what looked like a half a gummy bear, read, *Busted: Memoir of a Shooting Star*. "Is this?"

"Buster's book. It's no good to me now," Linda said, pushing her glasses back into place. "Maybe you'll find some use for it. It's just collecting dust around here."

Talia held it up, hoping the gummy bear would fall off, but it didn't. Normally, she wouldn't look down on someone else's mess, but the crime of using the life story of the biggest rock star in the country as a coaster warranted it.

Linda shrugged. "Keep it to yourself, though, unless you want to get a visit from Minnie's lawyers."

"So, they won't let you publish it?"

"They won't even let me talk about it. If they ask, you stole it."

"Fair enough." Talia put a hand on the script, as though the lawyers might burst into the room and try to take it from her. "So, I imagine that losing Buster's book was hard for you. It was predicted to be a huge bestseller."

"Our biggest bestseller ever. I was planning on buying a second home—someplace ostentatious like Dubai or Malibu." Linda sighed and looked out her window. "But it wasn't anywhere near as hard as it was losing Buster. He was a friend. I was in London on business when I heard. The absolute worst day of my life." She picked up a framed photograph from the shelf behind her and looked at it before handing it to Talia.

The photo showed Linda wearing a black cocktail dress, standing with her arm around Buster Bones. His hand was odd, though. Talia looked closer, her nose nearly touching the frame. There were hands around both sides of Linda's waist. Someone on the other side of Linda must have been cropped out of the shot. An ex-boyfriend? "So, you two were close?"

"Are you asking if we were lovers?" Linda smiled at her.

Talia smiled back. "Well, maybe not in those exact words, but sure. Were you?"

"No. I guess I can't say that, but we had a good working relationship." Linda said, twisting one of her curls around her finger. "He used to flirt with me. Harmless, really, but it made me feel...oh, I don't know. I don't want to sound too *Teen Cosmo*, but damn it, he made me feel special."

"Minnie told me that she made Buster sign something saying he wouldn't talk about his affairs in the book. Is that true?"

Linda leaned back on her hands, knocking a stack of papers onto the floor. "Minnie asked him verbally not to write about 'his fucking whores,' as she called them, but he had no choice. He wanted to write a completely honest book, and he did. Minnie might not like it, but that's too bad."

Talia sat up straight, her skirt riding up again. "You don't like Minnie very much, do you?"

"Eh. I'll say I didn't like their relationship. Buster's affairs put her in the position where she either had to dump him or stay with a guy who was cheating on her, and she didn't want to do either. But the person I got to know through talking to Buster, I liked her. You know, there's something he didn't put in the book. Minnie was his first." She widened her eyes and stuck out her tongue, making an unrestrained goofy face. "Can you believe it?"

Talia laughed. "My first was in high school, too."

"No." Linda shook her head, her curls bouncing around her face. "I mean first kiss, first date, his first anything. He was a nerd. He liked old punk music and playing Dungeons and Dragons, and that kind of thing was frowned upon in the Sunset. Everyone was supposed to be listening to slow jams and riding motorcycles. Minnie was the only girl to ever look at him and see something other than an outsider."

Talia leaned forward. "Do you think that Minnie killed Buster?"

She nodded slightly. "No."

Talia raised an eyebrow.

Linda shrugged. "I don't know. Maybe? I mean if you don't want to leave a guy, but you don't want to stay with him either, what do you do?"

"I guess you kill him." Talia looked down at the photograph. Buster's smile was even wider than Linda's, and she looked positively euphoric.

Linda leaned over and caught Talia's eye. She stared steadily over the rims of her red-framed glasses. "But you think she's innocent, don't you? Do you mind if I ask why?"

Talia took a deep breath and let it out slowly. She hadn't asked herself that question yet, but she knew the answer. "Because it would be crazy to believe her, and I do believe her...." She smiled and shrugged. "And I'm not crazy." She handed the photo back. "Linda, was there anyone else you can think of who didn't want the book published?"

"Oh, hell yes. Lots of people." Linda stretched to reach something in her top drawer, knocking two empty water bottles to the floor as she did. She managed to pull out a stack of envelopes. "At the top of the list is the person who sent me these death threats."

"Death threats? Do you know who wrote them?"

"I've got a good idea." Linda handed one of the letters to Talia.

Talia only needed to read the first sentence. "So do I."

*

"If you publish that book, I will bleeding well kill you."

"He actually wrote that? He wrote the word *bleeding*?"

Talia held the phone away from her ear and looked both ways before stepping into the crosswalk. When she'd first moved to San Francisco, there had been a story on the news about a woman who was hit by a Muni train while talking on her cell phone in an intersection. After that, Talia always put her phone down when she crossed the street.

"Are you still there?"

Talia didn't speak until both feet were on the sidewalk. "Zone goes through his whole repertoire—bleeding, bollocks, bloody...the C-word. He might as well have signed it."

"Do you know when the letters were sent? Specifically, were they sent before or after Buster's murder?"

"Linda got them yesterday...so probably right before or soon after depending on how fast the mail was."

"Well, that crosses Nigel Zone off our suspect list."

Talia stopped walking abruptly; a man bumped her shoulder with a curt "excuse me."

"Did I lose you again?"

"But I...I thought this would put Zone further up the list. In fact, I was hoping it would."

"It's just too obvious."

"Like the surveillance video." Talia put her hand on her hip and looked up at the sky—gray fog on gray clouds.

"Exactly. He must have known that a stack of death threats would call attention to his motive, and even Zone is smart enough to know that life in prison is worse than getting kicked out of a VIP room."

"Are you sure about that? He might have been blind drunk when he wrote them."

"So, Nigel Zone planned and executed a nearly perfect crime while sober and then fouled the whole thing up while drunk? Look, if he...." A delivery truck rumbled by. Talia held the phone tighter against her ear. "...months ago, but at the time he sent those letters, Buster's murder had either already happened or was being planned."

"Right, but is it possible that he didn't plan the murder? Maybe he just—" Someone pushed Talia's shoulder. She stumbled forward. A woman rushed past Talia without turning to look at her. Talia started walking again so she wouldn't get knocked to the ground. "Maybe he did it on a whim."

"Frame-ups are always planned. So, if this murder wasn't planned, then we only have one suspect."

"Minnie." The rush of late-morning sidewalk traffic rolled past an oddly-shaped glass building. Talia's footfalls echoed a tinny drumbeat as she walked by. "Oh hey! I've got something very cool." She opened her bag but then noticed a familiar frizzy-haired figure on the other side of the Embarcadero. "Port, Linda Varela is about a block behind me."

"Do you think she's following you?"

Talia watched as Linda trudged along the sidewalk, looking behind her several times. "No. It almost seems like she's worried about being followed...or being seen."

"So, what are you going to do?"

"I'm going to follow her."

Talia followed Linda until she stopped at a Muni stop. She typed "following someone waiting for a train" into Dicko.

Hide here and wait.

Dicko showed her a satellite map of the block. A yellow arrow pointed at a spot about twenty feet from Talia. She looked up and saw a six-foot-tall metal-framed advertisement for a Kylie Kismet concert. *Kylie* was written in glittery red letters with the words *San Jose* in black type underneath. Kylie herself was open-mouthed, holding a microphone and wearing a sequined dress with a slit up one side so high, it went all the way up her thigh, to her stomach and didn't stop until a full inch of underboob was showing.

Talia ducked behind the sign and peeked out. A dozen or so people were lined up at the Muni stop, most of them with their heads down, staring at phones, with a few craning their necks, watching for the train. She panicked for a second because she didn't see Linda. Then a man standing in front on the route map stepped out into the street, revealing Linda sitting on the ground behind the map.

Get ready.

Talia heard the train coming.

Wait for the mark to get on.

She took a deep breath. If she peeked out while Linda was looking over, she was sunk. She glanced at Dicko. It was in selfie mode, but it was twisted and distorted as though it were trying to take a picture of something to her right. She held it up and moved it until she could clearly see Linda standing up in anticipation of the F's arrival.

A few tourists walked past. "The people in this city are always taking selfies. Like everyone is their own private paparazzi."

Talia stuck her lips out and tilted her head in a selfie pose as she watched Linda. The doors opened.

Go now.

She couldn't go. Linda was still toward the end of the line and not on the train yet.

Go now.

Dicko had been right so far. She ran out from behind the sign. Another train was pulling up to a stop on her side of the street. It blocked Talia from Linda's view until she could get halfway across the street, but it also meant that she lost track of Linda. When she ran around the train, she looked but didn't see her.

She waved at the driver. She had to keep him from closing the door because if he opened the door after closing it, Linda might look up to see who the late-comer was. He put his hand on the door lever. She ran faster, knowing that if he shut the door while she was running through it, the high-pitched door alarm would go off, and everyone on the train would look up. She waved again. The driver nodded and moved his hand away from the lever.

She ran toward the back door, but then changed course quickly when she saw Linda was on a backwards-facing seat on the second car. Talia jumped on the front and hid behind a tall man with a hiker's backpack that loomed over his head.

Keep eyes on mark at all times.

To catch a glimpse of Linda—the shoulder of her jacket and a few frizzy curls—Talia had to peer between the crook of the hiker's elbow and his waist, which she hoped meant that Linda couldn't see her. The train was crowded enough that she probably couldn't, but Talia would need to be careful not to lose Linda in the crowd when she got off. The train pulled up to a familiar stop, and the glimpse of Linda changed from hair and shoulder to arm and waist to hip and thigh. Linda was getting off the train, and Talia knew where she was going.

Chapter Twelve

The tourists on The Embarcadero ran, hunched against the biting wind, into the souvenir shops. Talia had been standing long enough to see them walk out again, zipping up newly bought sweatshirts and ripping off the tags. She glanced out over the water. The bay made her uneasy on gray days when it was dark and choppy, so she turned back. The man she was waiting for hopped off a blue and yellow F-line streetcar. After he crossed the street and turned onto Lombard, she followed him, slowly. She needed to give him time to clock in.

As Talia stepped through the double glass doors, Pedro was opening the elevator for a strawberry blonde who, with her tight jeans, high-heeled boots and cropped fur jacket, looked like a supermodel from the '70s. Cheryl Tiegs stepped on the elevator, turned and glowered at Talia as the door slid shut. Talia frowned at the elevator doors but smiled as Pedro greeted her with a wave.

"Hi Pedro. Can you let me up? I left a cord up there. I don't want Mark to find out what a space case I am." She held up a blue backpack that looked exactly like the one Mark had shoved into her hands the other day. She covered the embroidered *San Francisco* with her hand so Pedro wouldn't figure out that she'd just bought it at the souvenir shop across the street.

"Of course, Miss Peterson. Go on up." He pressed a button on his desk, and the elevator door opened with a *ding*.

When the door opened on the second floor, Talia stepped out, looking around her. She flattened herself against the wall, tilted her head to the side and craned her neck so she could look into the studio without being seen. There were five people hanging out in there, but they were all seated, and she could only see the tops of their heads.

The top of Linda's head was easy to spot. Her curls bounced up and down in an erratic rhythm; she was either laughing or crying. She stood up and threw her head back, laughing riotously. The heads were turned toward her. Talia was mesmerized by the display herself. Linda could never be called polished, but with her wild hair, expressive eyes and animated laugh, she was striking. Talia was still staring, rapt, when she realized that Linda was walking toward the door.

Talia dashed across the hall to the bathroom. She put her hand on the door handle, but that was probably where Linda was going—she'd be trapped if she went in there. She switched her hand from the bathroom door handle to the closet door handle. She clicked the door open, slid in and then clicked it shut.

The closet door sealed tight. Talia stood in the blackness, breathing in the dusty, ammonia-tinged air, waiting for her eyes to adjust. After a moment, she could make out a mop and bucket. She looked down. Her purse was glowing. Her eyes hadn't adjusted. Dicko had turned itself into a flashlight—a muted orange color that was probably (hopefully) designed to keep the light from being seen outside of the closet.

She held up Dicko, and now she could make out more details of the small space she was hiding in: a bin of cleaning supplies, the ancient, well-folded copy of *Cheri* on a shelf next to a tower of toilet paper rolls. She felt a cough building in her chest. She wasn't claustrophobic, but she had once been in a stage play of Dracula where she'd spent the entire second act in a coffin. She'd had to use meditation and breathing techniques to get through it. She couldn't remember any of the techniques now because all she could think about was getting out of this closet before it killed her.

She held a hand over her mouth to muffle her sputtering cough. She opened the door and looked around. No one was there. She tried to step out, but something grabbed her purse and yanked. Panicked, coughing loudly now, she yanked back, but it was stuck. The openness of the hallway quieted her panic, and she was able to take a shallow, gasping breath, followed by a relaxed, deep one. She twisted so she could see where her purse was stuck and there, at about hip-height on the doorjamb, was a nail. She unhooked the strap. There was something else on the nail—a square of blue fabric. She tucked it into her purse and stepped out into the hall.

"Hello, Maggie."

She'd forgotten to recheck the hallway.

"Still sneaking around, eh?" Gary Myers had one arm around Cheryl Tiegs. She must be his wife. If she were his girlfriend, she wouldn't be staring at Talia with undisguised distrust.

"You caught me." Talia tried to laugh, but coughed instead. When she was in junior high, her bully, Marlene Durden, caught her in an empty hallway and gave her bargain-store outfit a spirited and unsolicited critique. (*That sweater looks like it came with a free bowl of soup, Talia.)* Gary's wife was looking at her clothes much in the way Marlene had then.

Talia looked down and tugged at her skirt. "I uh...came to apologize for the other day at The Hotel Rokku, but I lost my nerve. So, I uh...." She looked up.

Gary's wife rolled her eyes. "So you hid in the closet?"

"Yeah. I...I guess I...." Talia looked back down at her feet and tugged at her skirt again. It wouldn't budge. She looked up at Gary. "I'm really sorry."

Gary scowled at her. "And well you should be, you hyena." Gary's scowl broke into a smile. "Oh, come on. I'm just fucking with you. Don't be so serious. You're not the only rabid journalist who's been sniffing around us lately. You're just doing your job, right?"

"That's true."

Gary's wife sighed loudly. "I'm going to get some air, hon." She grabbed him by the face and shoved her tongue in his mouth with such force, it looked like it might come out the other side.

Talia used this as an opportunity to pretend to check her phone and typed, "Should I blow my own cover?" into Dicko.

Only if you have something to gain or if your cover is going to be blown for you.

She looked up. The couple broke apart with a wet, smacking sound.

"Hurry back, babe." Gary patted her butt as she walked away.

"I will." She swung the stairwell door open. Her high-heels echoed a *click-clack* down the stairs.

"Does she always take the stairs?"

"Kristen hasn't taken an elevator since she was pregnant. She likes to stay fit." Gary slapped his hip, indicating either the place Kristen liked to keep fit or where Gary most appreciated the fitness. "Hey...." He smirked, cocked his head to the side and waved a finger at her. "Always with the questions. Are you writing a story on stairs?"

Talia laughed and put Dicko back in her purse. "To be honest, Gary, I'm not a journalist. I'm a private eye."

Gary leaned toward her and whispered, "Are you trying to prove that Minnie's innocent?" She nodded. He put an arm on her shoulder and leaned in closer—so close, she could smell the leather of his jacket and see the millimeter of salt-and-pepper roots beneath his black dye-job. "She didn't kill Buster. No way."

"How do you know?"

"She might want Buster dead, but those kids are her world. She would never leave them orphans. Even if she thought she could get away with it. Which she obviously didn't. You know who I think did it?" He looked over his shoulder and then back at Talia. "One of her enemies."

"Minnie had enemies?"

Gary laughed and pointed at the stairwell door. "Did you notice how Kristen treated you?"

"I'm sure she's very nice."

Gary raised one eyebrow at her. His hair flopped over his eye. He pushed it out of the way and raised the eyebrow even higher. He shook his head. "She's not. Let me tell you, though, that was the freaking welcome wagon compared to how Minnie treated any woman who got close to Buster."

Talia took a step back and to the side so she wouldn't get caught with Gary's arm around her when Kristen came back. "I should get going."

"Good idea." He laughed.

Talia glanced into the studio as she walked past it to the elevator. She recognized Devin but no one else. She turned around. Gary was opening the men's room door. "Hey, Gary!"

He paused in the doorway. "Maggie?"

"Are you here recording a new Crunch Pup record?"

He shook his head. "No, just an impromptu, informal wake for our friend Buster."

*

When she stepped off the elevator, she saw that Pedro was looking down at something on his desk, frowning. "Something wrong, Pedro?"

"Oh no, Miss. I just found out they're going to bring back the third shift. It's no good for me. I can't sleep when the sun is out...even if I pull down the shades." He tapped the top of his head. "My brain can't be fooled."

"I'm the same way," Talia lied. She could fall asleep on a sunny day at noon, and she wouldn't even have to be that tired.

"But I shouldn't complain." He looked over his shoulder. "The bosses here know what's best."

"I'm sure they want to beef up security after...you know...." She leaned closer to him. He did not lean away. "The tragedy."

He raised his eyebrows. "Buster Bones? Nah. A third-shift guard wouldn't have stopped that because it was Minnie. She came and went as she pleased. They can't blame the keycards on that."

"What do you mean?"

"People around here are complaining about keycards. There are too many out there. People are giving them to their friends...having late night parties in the studios...." He smiled at her and then looked away. "Entertaining females."

"So, is that why they're adding a third shift—to crack down on the sex parties?"

"Maybe, but to tell you the truth, I think it was the paramedics. They couldn't get in, to save Buster, you know. They had to call the building management for the door code."

"There's a door code?"

"There's a door code for the main entrance, Miss." He pointed to the main door. Talia looked over at the glass and brass door. For the first time, she noticed that it was covered by two cameras, one on each side. "The keycards are for the side entrance." He didn't point, but Talia assumed the side entrance could be found at the end of the dark hallway directly behind her. She resisted the urge to turn her head and, instead, faked a coughing fit. "Are you okay, Miss Peterson?"

"Ye-hess. Is the-hair a bubbler around he-here?" She meant to say water fountain, not bubbler. Talia Green from Maine said bubbler; California girl Sloane Peterson said water fountain.

"I don't think so, Miss, but there's a drinking fountain right down that hall." This time, he pointed.

She coughed down the hall until she got to the drinking fountain. She took a few sips and looked around, still coughing. *Cough.* The side door was painted metal with a rectangular glass window. *Cough.* There was a keycard reader on one side. *Cough.* No cameras.

She tried the door—unlocked. She pushed it open as slowly as she could, hoping it wasn't hooked up to an alarm. Thankfully, it wasn't, but the bottom of the door scraped against the floor with a screech so loud, it might as well have been. She stopped, barely daring to breathe, until she heard Pedro talking to Kristen. She was telling him not to let anyone up who wasn't on the guest list. His tone was apologetic but casual. She held her breath and pushed the door the rest of the way, quicker this time, and it barely made a sound, proving that the rule of pulling off band-aids also applied to noisy doors.

She stepped out and let go of the door. She took in the scene. At her feet, twenty or so cigarettes littered the ground near a large rock. She connected the dots, but it was too late.

She kicked her leg out behind her, the door banged into her ankle, but it didn't shut. She kept her foot in the door as she bent and picked up the rock. She slid it between the doorjamb and the door. She exhaled and rubbed her mildly-injured ankle, looking up. No cameras.

She pulled out Dicko and snapped a few pictures. *Snap.* The left side of the alley was littered with debris (a few cans, a jacket that may have been used as a toilet) and closed off by an olive-green PG&E shed. *Snap.* In the middle of the alley there was an abandoned Buster memorial between two dumpsters. *Snap.* Hidden in a doorway next to the dumpsters was a shopping carriage filled with bottles and cans—the kind homeless people rattled over to the recycling center early on weekday mornings. *Snap.* The right side of the alley opened out to the cobblestone walk. No cameras.

"They won't let us in." The voice hit like a car crash, shocking Talia into dropping Dicko. It clattered on the ground and skidded across the pavement. She snatched it up.

"Bummer. Is it crunched?" It was Star Tee. He was standing next to the dumpster, but he hadn't been there when she'd taken the picture of it.

She turned Dicko over. Thankfully, it was unharmed—not even a scratch. "No. It's good."

He laughed—loud and gravelly. "Wow! What kind of phone is that? I want one."

She put her hand on the door, her instincts telling her not to stay and interview the strange man who had materialized out of nowhere, but instead she asked, "What did you mean, 'they won't let us in'?"

"You were there. You saw the guard take my candle." He looked at her, his deep-set eyes and sunken cheeks giving him a haunted-skeleton look. "We just want to mourn Buster, but they won't let us in. But me? I was here before."

"Before what? Before the murder?"

He licked his bottom lip and stared at her.

She tightened her grip on the door knob.

"I know stuff," he said.

"What stuff?"

"Minnie didn't do it."

"Who did?"

He smiled at her. "The imposter."

She backed toward the door. "Who's the imposter?"

He put a finger to his lips and jumped toward her. She pushed the door open, it scraped again. She heard footsteps running in the direction of the street. She looked out. He was gone. Her heart was beating fast as she shut the door and walked back.

Pedro smiled at Talia. "Are you better now, Miss Peterson?"

"Allergies." Talia waved at the invisible, offending pollen.

He stopped smiling and raised both eyebrows at her. "Maybe you shouldn't be going outside then, Miss."

Of course, he'd heard the door and connected it to what Kristen had said to him. As the blush covered her cheeks, she assessed the damage—he'd only caught her snooping around. She just needed to come up with a passable story, but all she could think to say was "Shit. You caught me."

He wagged a finger at her. "It's not good for you."

She nodded and looked down, trying to decide if she should make an excuse to check Dicko or just make a run for it.

"I quit a few years ago, myself."

She looked up. "You...you quit smoking? Was it hard?"

"The hardest thing I ever did." He put a hand on her forearm and looked in her eyes. "That's why I'll never take it up again."

Chapter Thirteen

Talia lined up three Equals in her hand, tore off the tops and dumped them in her coffee. She picked up Port's cup and walked into the office. Port was holding the scrap of fabric under the light of his desk lamp, examining it. "The fabric seems rather inexpensive," he said.

"Yeah. It reminds me of the material they used to make our dance team costumes out of."

"Dance team?" He smiled at her. "I'd had you pegged as a cheerleader."

"I wasn't cool enough for that." Talia handed Port his coffee.

"Thanks, Bofur."

She clunked her own coffee on the desk. "You're welcome, Bombur."

"Hey! You do know *The Hobbit*."

"Told you I wasn't cool." She grabbed the manuscripts from the printer and plunked his copy in front of him.

They mostly read silently, but occasionally, one of them read a fascinating or salacious passage aloud. The first couple of chapters detailed Buster's dismal childhood: his overbearing father, his mother's death when he was just a teen, being bullied at school. The only bright spots were the music classes he took in the back room of a record store and meeting Minnie. After that, it devolved into a cascade of sex and astounding tales of intoxication. Zone's story about partying like Ozzy in Austin was in there, as well as a story about Zone passing out in and *soiling* the bed of an underaged groupie that Talia and Port both agreed was, on its own, adequate motive for murder.

There was surprisingly little about the music except for a chapter called Bad Music and Egomaniacs, which included a passage about the Crunch Pup break-up: *My head was so far up my own ass, I thought mine was the only opinion that mattered. The other guys, they valued their own opinions, they thought they were right, but they were willing to compromise. I wasn't. The result was crap music and that was my fault, not theirs.*

By the time they'd finished, it was dark outside, and they'd switched from coffee to Dewar's. Port flipped through his pages. "Did you read anything about a Doc Gray?"

She shook her head.

"Strange." Port held up his portion of the manuscript. "I found just one sentence about him. Quote, Doc Gray left after last call, but Nigel and I stayed, snorting coke and playing liar's dice with the bar staff, unquote. That's it. Nothing else about the guy anywhere."

"Oh yeah. That does sound familiar. Wait a minute...snorting coke?"

"Yes, Miss Green. Back in the '80s it was popular to put this white substance up one's nose."

She tossed a pen at him. He twisted his upper body out of the path of the pen. Talia smiled. She hadn't seen him move that fast, not even the day he'd rescued her from the raft. "I know what coke is, Port. It's just that I didn't notice much else about drugs in here. Just lots of booze. Didn't Devin say something about drugs during the interview at the Rokku?"

"I think you're right. I have the transcript." He opened his laptop. "Here it is. He said that Buster was all about: 'Sex, drugs, sex, booze, sex, pills...more sex.' There was plenty of booze and sex in here." He tapped the manuscript.

The side door slammed shut. "What are you two doing? Planning my birthday?"

Port flipped over his manuscript. "Ted, can you keep a secret?"

"Secrecy is literally my middle name, Portugal." He nodded earnestly.

Port flipped the manuscript over.

Ted picked it up, read the title page and whistled elaborately. "Has Darla seen this?"

"She's hiding in the back," Talia said. "She said it's too much and too soon for her grieving heart to bear."

Ted nodded knowingly and looked down the hall.

"Hey, in the Rokku interview they also talked about mud wrestling." Port had turned his attention back to the computer screen. "Wasn't there a mention of a mud wrestler in here?"

"Yes!" Talia flipped through her manuscript until she found the page. "There's not much, but he talks about mud wrestling night at a place called The Platinum Club and meeting someone he describes as 'an exotic dancer with short dark hair, smallish tits and a muscle butt.'"

"A stripper with short hair and small tits?" Ted looked over her shoulder. "She should be easy to spot." He looked at Port. "Want us to check it out?"

"I think Miss Green can handle it on her own."

"It's no problem. I need the money."

Port shot Talia a look. She shrugged. Ted could tag along with her to the strip club. She might even find a use for him.

"Shit." Ted snapped. His fingers seemed too long for the act of snapping and they folded over each other in the attempt. "I can't drive. The Interceptor is out of commission."

"Interceptor? Is that a car?" Talia said.

"Interceptors are those three-wheeled cars that the meter maids tool around in. I bought one at auction a couple years back," Ted said. "It's a thing of beauty."

"A broken thing of beauty, so you should take the Legs moped." Port pointed to the far end of the living room where, as far as Talia knew, there had never been a moped.

"There's a moped?" Talia thought about the long walk in her Ellen Barkin heels.

"To be honest," Port said. "It's been so long since I've been small enough to get on a moped, I forgot all about it."

"Come with me, Nancy Drew. I'll show you to the secret passage." Ted sprinted over to an old tapestry that depicted a faded mountain with a goat perched on its peak at the end of the living room. Talia followed him. Ted pushed it to one side, revealing a red button. He pressed it with a flourish. A motor whirred and a large section of the wall rolled upward, revealing a dark, cavernous garage.

"When you said 'secret passage,' I pictured a laboratory or a dungeon or a pile of treasure being guarded by a dragon or something cool like that," Talia said.

He turned on the lights. "What are you talking about? This garage is cool. It's bigger than my apartment...and my apartment is a warehouse."

The garage was large enough for a fleet of cars, but only housed a forklift, a dark-green sedan and a beige van with a handicapped placard hanging from the rearview mirror. Talia peered into the van's back window. All the seats had been removed and replaced with a king-sized mattress made up with red and gold sheets.

"That's Port's end game," Ted said.

"End game?"

"A couple years ago, Port got me, Darla and Brad together. He bought us a huge spread from the Indian place on Third, and then he said that his weight was going to kill him one day, maybe soon, and when that happened, we were to collect his body with that." He pointed at the forklift. "And put it in this." He tapped the van with a morbid laugh. "You got to love Portland. That guy is committed to his own special brand of crazy." He shook his head as he walked over to something covered with a dingy tarp. "Now let's go. The strippers are getting cold." He pulled back the tarp to reveal a shiny red Vespa.

*

A nearly naked blonde woman approached them as they sat down at a chrome-trimmed wooden table at the back of the club. "Hi, I'm Honey. I'm looking for a party." She put her hands under her zeppelin-shaped boobs and pushed them up—first the left and then the right, as though she were about to detach and then juggle them.

"Actually, I'm in the mood for a brunette." Talia turned to Ted and put her hand on his knee. "How about you, babe?"

"Um, yes, of course...uh...kitten. Eh, take a hike Honey...if that is your real name."

They had worked out their cover beforehand (a couple looking for three-way action), but her performance clearly flustered Ted. She giggled, nestled her head onto his shoulder and ran her hand further up his leg. "Now Sweetums, let's not be rude." She looked up at Honey. "Maybe you could bring us a friend. My man here likes curvy blondes, obviously, but sporty tomboys drive me wild. You know anyone like that?"

Honey smiled. "Oh darling. You are going to love my friend Lulu."

"Does she have small tits?" Ted said. "I like a big rack, like the magnificent shelf of abba-zabas that you're sporting." He put his arm around Talia and squeezed. "But snookums here likes 'em small and pert."

"That's our Lulu." Honey laughed as she walked away. She sashayed past a man in a dusty work jacket. He reached out a bulbous hand with black-stained fingers and slapped the white skin of her exposed ass. She turned and flashed the man an enormous smile.

When Lulu arrived, they offered her a hundred dollars to sit and talk with them for twenty minutes. Talia tried to casually bring up the subject of Buster. "You must meet so many famous people here."

Lulu was unexpectedly forthcoming, though. "Sure do! Would you believe that I dated Buster Bones?" She ran a hand through her short, dark hair and leaned one well-toned arm over the back of her chair.

Talia and Ted acted shocked.

"For real! In fact, I was just saying that I'm glad they got his wife on tape doing it because the last time I saw him, I threatened to kill him."

"Holy crap!" Talia said.

Ted was even blunter. "Shit. It can't be that easy. Can it?"

"Oh, I'm easy." Lulu winked at Ted.

"I'm sure you are, lovely Lolita." Ted lowered his voice and looked over his shoulder. "Excuse me for asking, but did you...you know, kill him?"

Talia held onto the chrome edge of the table, and she and Ted leaned toward Lulu.

"What? No. His bitch wife did." Lulu lowered her voice. "Wait. Didn't she?"

"Oh, of course." Talia leaned back. "It's all over the news. She was caught on tape."

"True. Still, let me play devil's advocate for one second. She was caught on tape. Dead to rights. The bitch is going up the river." Ted paused and smoothed his mustache. "Video can be altered, though. I mean, I just saw a movie where the Bay Bridge blew up, but if we walk out of this club, stand on our tippy toes and look down the hill, there it is—clear as fucking day with nary a scratch."

"I saw that movie!" Lulu said.

"Me too," Talia lied. "But Ted, sweetie, if that video was altered and Minnie didn't do it, then who did?"

"I bet I know." Lulu tapped her index finger twice on the table like a gavel. "His latest whore. Kylie Kismet."

"The frou-frou singer? Wasn't she claiming to be a ...you know...?" Ted cupped a hand around his face and slunk down in his chair. "...a virgin?" He mouthed the word *virgin* more than he said it, as if he were swearing in church.

"Virgin, my ass. The slut was having an affair with Buster. He dumped me for her."

"He didn't dump you for his wife?"

Lulu stared at her, wide-eyed. "No. Why would he do that?"

"Don't be a dum-dum, sweet punch." Ted planted a kiss on Talia's temple. "Men don't leave strippers for their wives."

Talia nodded. "Of course, they dump them for frou-frou singers."

"Slutty frou-frou singers," Lulu's voice cracked.

Talia reached out and grabbed her hand. "That must have been awful for you. I'll bet the jerk brought the whore in here and paraded her in front of you."

Lulu sniffed. "Oh, no. He wouldn't even admit that he was seeing her."

Talia handed her a cocktail napkin. "So, how did you know that he was...you know...."

"Banging the trollop?" Ted said.

"He told me." Lulu pointed at the three men approaching the table.

"Hey look! It's the *Creem* reporter," Devin yelled. His arm was around a man in his early forties with sharply angled cheekbones and a platinum blonde dye-job.

"Was that it? *Creem*? I thought that rag went the way of the keytar." Gary laughed and gave Talia a quick wink.

"What's a keytar?" Lulu asked.

"Luscious Lulu!" Gary kissed the top of Lulu's head. "I've missed you like the deserts miss the rain."

Devin grabbed a chair and pulled it over to their table. "Tell me, what are you and your boy toy doing here?" He pointed two fingers at Ted and Talia.

"I prefer *man* toy." Ted brushed imaginary dust off his shoulder. "And I'm doing the same thing you're doing, Night Ranger. Waiting for the mud wrestling."

"Oh, then you'll be waiting a while," Lulu said. "They found some kind of virus in the mud."

Ted nodded. "Probably the bubonic plague, planted there by government agents trying to take down the porn industry. It's all over the Internet...the real Internet anyway."

"I believe it. They're always hassling us." Lulu glowered.

"Don't you two look cozy?" Mark said. Talia sunk in her chair and looked up. He was smiling at her. Somehow that made it worse, but Talia smiled back. Mark grabbed a chair and sat next to her. "I hope you didn't say too much, Lulu. Maggie here is a private eye."

Gary picked up a soggy drink coaster and whipped it at Mark. "Way to rat her out, you uncouth dink."

"I knew it!" Lulu squealed.

"You did?" Talia laughed.

"No, but I think it's exciting. Like that movie I saw."

"Where the Bay Bridge exploded?" Ted said.

"Yeah. That one."

"It's okay, Lulu," Gary said. "She had us fooled as well. We thought she was from *Rolling Stone*."

"That was it." Devin snapped his fingers.

"Nice." Ted offered Talia his fist to bump. She accepted with a shrug.

"Your own damn fault. You should know by now that *Rolling Stone* never sends hot chicks to interview the golden oldies. If they had sent this guy..." The blonde man pointed at Ted. "Then I could see it. Now...." He pulled a bottle of expensive-looking booze from his jacket pocket and put it down on the table. "Let's get this party started." He waved at a topless waitress. She nodded once and hurried off.

"Maggie, may I introduce Doc Gray, our bartender for this evening." Mark gestured toward the blonde man. "Doc, this is Miss Maggie Foley and...her...." Mark gestured at Ted and raised his eyebrows.

"Man toy." Ted reached out and shook Doc Gray's hand. "The name's Pirate Mace."

The waitress arrived with a large bottle of sparkling water and seven glasses. Gary tossed a stack of bills on her tray. Doc Gray immediately set about filling six of the glasses with golden-colored liquor. He plunked two generous portions in front of Talia and Ted.

"Oh, hey man, we'd love to join your little party." Ted slowly pushed the glass away. "Talia has to drive us back, and if I get too drunk, I just might fall off the back of the moped."

"You can ride with us." Gary pointed in the direction of the door. "We've got the limo tonight."

"We're still rock stars." Devin filled his glass with sparkling water.

"Rock-ish stars," Mark corrected him.

"Rockfish stars? Is that what we are?" Doc Gray laughed and pushed Ted's glass back toward him. "Please, I insist. Doctor's orders."

"Oh! I've got a great idea." Lulu bounced up and down in her chair like a child who'd been offered double dessert. "You can throw your moped in my apartment. I live right across the alley."

Talia fixed Ted with a stare that was meant to convey, "*It is a bad idea to leave the company Vespa in the hands of a stripper.*"

Ted returned Talia's stare, nodded and then downed his drink. "Keep 'em coming, barkeep."

Talia sighed and lifted her own glass. She took a large sip, barely noticing the absence of a mixer. As she brought the glass down, the rim of another glass clinked against it.

"Cheers, Maggie." Mark smiled at her and ran a hand through his wavy hair.

"You know, you can call me Talia."

"I thought Maggie Foley was your professional name?" Mark looked into her eyes. Talia looked at Ted. He was locked in a discussion with Devin and Gary about old rock clubs that closed and how everything was better before "They" took over. Mark brushed one finger along her cheek, bringing her attention back to him.

"Hmm? No, it's just a name I got from a movie, *Eddie and....*"

"*...the Cruisers.*" Mark leaned in, his arm pressing gently against hers. "I saw that movie a million times when I was a kid. It was one of the reasons I wanted to get into the music business."

"You knew?"

"The whole time. So, tell me, Talia...." He looked around and leaned closer. "How is the investigation going?"

Talia took a deep breath and let it out, slowly. "Well, we found out who was in the studio right before Buster."

Mark leaned away, picked up his drink, sipped and then paused, looking in his glass. "You know what sucks?" He sipped again. "It sucks that every time Buster and I crossed paths at the studio, he would always—no matter what, no matter how drunk he was or what they were saying about us in the press—he would always stop and ask about how my album was going. He listened to all my music. He didn't have to. I didn't listen to his." He tapped the rim of his glass with his index finger. "That night, my album wasn't going well. I knew Buster was coming in, and I didn't want him to ask me about it. So, I ducked out early." He looked into her eyes. "I missed out on saying good-bye to my best friend because I was in a bad mood and wanted to pout."

Talia put her hand over his.

"Oh, oh! Something is happening here. Lovebirds." Gary pointed his glass at them.

"Leave them be, Gary." Doc Gray sighed. "They look so happy. Happiness is a good thing." He downed his drink.

Devin grabbed the bottle, put his arm around Doc Gray's shoulders and poured him another shot. Devin leaned over the table and whispered to Talia, "You know it's bad when the sober guy is pouring a drink for you."

"Hey, I heard that." Doc Gray clapped a hand on Devin's shoulder and pulled him back so he could throw his arms around him. Devin completed the hug with a few manly slaps on his friend's back. "God, I love these crazy bastards!" Doc Gray yelled, raising his glass in the air. "A toast. To a crappy boss, an infuriating patient, and the best god-damned friend a man ever had. Buster Bones."

"To Buster." They all raised their glasses.

*

A few hours later, Talia was drunk—not swaying-in-a-spinning-room drunk, but just drunk enough so that everything looked fuzzy. Mark had wandered off somewhere, Ted and Gary were at the stage serenading Lulu with obscure

Beatles songs, and Devin had bowed out hours before. Doc Gray and Talia were alone at the table.

Talia sipped her drink and then slid the glass across the table so she wouldn't be tempted to pick it back up. "I'm sorry about your friend."

Doc Gray looked at her and smiled even as his ice-blue eyes filled with tears. "I've never lost a patient before."

"But it wasn't your fault." Talia put her hand on his arm.

He patted her hand. "Thank you for saying that, but I'm starting to think that if I'd been a better doctor, he'd be like our boy, Dev. Clean, sober and alive."

"I have a great doctor and I'm not sober." Talia pointed at her glass as proof.

"I never wanted to be a doctor. I wanted to be a rock star but, alas, no talent." He held up his hands and stared at them as if willing them to either be better at playing guitar or taking care of patients.

Mark stumbled over and swayed drunkenly behind Doc Gray's chair. He slurred something that sounded like, "Sip dools? I'm drunkle!" then tried to walk away, but his sweatshirt was caught on the back of the chair.

Doc Gray rolled his eyes. "I suppose I could save this patient by making sure he doesn't fall and crack his skull open on the way to the men's room."

Mark made a desperate, drunken attempt at escaping his chair trap, but the chair tipped, sending Mark stumbling, face-first, toward the floor. Doc Gray caught him by the arm before he hit the ground. "I'll be sending you a bill for this one, Marky."

Talia watched the two men stumble away.

"What's wrong, sweetie?" Lulu was standing over her with two drinks. She handed one to Talia. "Your new boyfriend too drunk to fuck?"

Talia accepted the drink, but placed it on the table. "You...uh...you said we could leave the Vespa at your place?"

Lulu grabbed Talia's hand, pulling her out of her seat. "Follow me."

Talia walked with her, but when she paused to look for Ted, Lulu dropped her hand and bounced ahead. Talia stood on her tiptoes and scanned the dim bar but only saw grunting, bulbous-handed men and twirling girls. A large man walked past her to the bar. When he was out of her sightline, she spotted Ted and Gary. They were leaning against a high circular stage, lost in a loud, drunken debate while an enthusiastic pole dancer spun above them, her plastic high-heels whirring past the tops of their heads. Talia walked quickly toward them.

"...falling for Lennon's bullshit pseudo-intellectualism and artsy-fartsy crap. McCartney was the real genius," Gary slurred.

"McCartney wasn't fit to wipe Lennon's bunghole!" Ted slurred.

Talia looked around. Lulu was standing by a back exit, waving at her. Talia held up one finger and then waved at Ted, signaling him to follow her.

Ted waved back, but not in a "Yes, I see what you are trying to say" kind of way but in a "Hello, how are you?" kind of way. Talia waved again. This time, Ted got it and pointed at the front door. Talia nodded and hurried out the back.

The back door opened into a small, dark alley. The air outside was cool. Talia looked toward Broadway but could only see a billowing wall of fog, rolling up the hill. "Lulu?"

"Over here, doll." Lulu was standing in front of a one-story building near where the alley dead-ended against a steep, rocky cliff. She struggled with her keys. "This is the place...if I can ever get in."

"I'll go get the Vespa." Talia headed around the corner to where the moped was parked in front of the club. "Shit." She didn't have the key.

"Meeeeee-chelle! My belle! Meeeeee-chelle! My belle!" Gary and Ted were walking out the front door, arm in arm, crooning like a couple of cartoon drunks.

Talia put her hands on her hips. "Do you have the key?"

"Yesh. It's in one of my pockets, try to guess which one." Ted thrust his pelvis toward her.

"Keys!"

"Oh, now, will you look at that." Gary gazed down the hill. They all turned and looked. They couldn't see the bay anymore, and despite what Ted had asserted earlier, could only see a small corner of the Bay Bridge; the rest was engulfed in fluffy, white fog. The wind picked up, and they watched as the fog breezed past them and toward the bright lights of the bars and strip clubs of Broadway.

"See that there." Ted pointed at a streetlight that was surrounded by a swirling, fine mist. "That almost makes up for this city's horrendous lack of snow."

"You mean you like snow?" Gary leaned toward Ted, stumbled a bit and put one hand on Ted's shoulder to steady himself.

"I'm from Buffalo. Man, I used to love to stand on the streets and watch the lights of the city shine off the falling snow." He pointed at the streetlight. "It was kind of like this, only colder and better."

"So, if you love snow so much, why did you leave the wilds of Buffalokes?"

Ted grinned. "Because I'm a freak, Gare Bear, and there is nowhere like San Francisco to fly your freak flag."

"I'm a freak too!" Gary threw his arms open.

Ted tried to hug him, but ended up hugging the empty space next to him. Talia grabbed the back of his t-shirt before he fell. "Okay, I hate to break up the bromance." Talia held her other hand, palm up, in front of Ted's nose. "But keys keys keys!"

"Fuck the keys! Help me out, Gare." Ted picked up the front end of the Vespa. Gary grabbed the back end, and they shuffled toward the alley.

"It's over here." Talia ran ahead.

The door was open just a crack. Talia rapped softly on it. Ted and Gary came up behind her. "Meeeee-chelle, my belle!" They pushed the door open and dropped the Vespa on the floor with a crash. They stared at the young woman lying in the middle of the floor, her head bent at an odd angle and her eyes fixed on a spot on the wall. Something black was wrapped around her neck.

Talia rushed over to her and ripped the black material (a pair of stockings?) from Lulu's throat, revealing a deep red mark. "Help me!"

"I...I know CPR." Gary knelt next to her. "Get her flat. Lean her head back."

Talia tilted Lulu's head back and whispered, "Oh god, oh god, oh god...."

Gary straddled Lulu's waist and started compressing her chest. "One, two, three. One, two, three."

Talia pressed two fingers on Lulu's neck, just under her jawline. She felt Lulu's body react limply to Gary's frantic revival attempts, but nothing else. The world that had been going in and out of focus since her last drink suddenly became clear. "I don't think that's going to help."

"Oh god." Gary fell off Lulu's torso and buried his face in his hands.

"We should look for clues." Talia struggled to stand up on shaky legs, but then sat back down. She took in the scene. The apartment consisted of one large square room. Each wall was painted a different color—one pink, one red, one purple and one white. A narrow plywood wardrobe hung open, revealing a few stripper costumes: doctor, construction worker...what was that one? Jazz dancer? Prince? Scattered everywhere, the day bed, the red plastic chair, the floor, were bits of string, feathers and rhinestones. She picked one up and realized that it was an outfit—an entire outfit that didn't even fill the palm of her hand.

"Why would anyone...." Ted sunk down until his elbows were on his knees. He hung his head in his hands.

"Maybe we got too close and someone...." Talia couldn't finish that sentence. She thought of Mark blowing her cover. Who else had heard him say that she was a private eye? "God, this is my fault. If I hadn't...." She choked back a sob and looked at Lulu, not daring to touch her now.

There was an empty glass on the floor next to her. It was from the club. She reached out to pick it up when Gary said, "Hey guys...someone killed Lulu."

Talia looked up at the ceiling. A water stain shaped liked Asia spread from behind an art deco lighting fixture. She looked back at Gary. "We know that."

"What if the killer is still here?" Gary pointed toward a narrow door on the pink wall that looked like it might lead to a closet or bathroom.

A radiating heat grew in Talia's chest, as if someone had lit a fire under her ribcage. She sprang to her feet and raced out of the apartment. As she ran through the alley, she turned and gestured at Ted and Gary to hurry. She wasn't surprised to be in the lead, but she didn't want them to die just because they were too drunk to outrun a killer. When she turned back, the word *Security* in white letters dominated her field of vision. She tried to stop but couldn't and ran into the chest of a large man. She looked up. He didn't look amused, or angry, or any emotion at all.

Gary and Ted careened around the corner. One of them kicked over a novena candle from the small Buster memorial that ran along the wall of the Platinum Club. The thick glass hit the concrete with a gritty crunch and rolled across the sidewalk.

"Hello, big man." Ted leaned on his knees, breathing heavily. "We're going to stand in your giant shadow while I report a murder to our local police." He pulled his cellphone from his pocket.

The security guard glanced at Gary and then back at Ted. "Murder?"

"A girl who worked here, Lulu." Talia's hand shook as she pointed back toward the alley. "She was killed in her apartment."

The bouncer stared at Talia, his face still flat and emotionless. A single tear crept out of his eye and rolled down his cheek. He threw his face into his hands and wept loudly. Gary wrapped his arms as far as he could around the weeping giant. The bouncer wiped at his eyes and sniffed. "She was my favorite, Gary."

"Mine too, Bob."

Chapter Fourteen

Detective Nguyen shoved his hands in the pockets of his long gray coat. "I thought you idiots were detectives. What are you doing messing up my crime scene?"

"In our defense, mon Capitaine, we're extremely drunk." Ted put his hand to his head and held a wavering salute.

Talia elbowed Ted, but he held his salute. Her fingerprints were all over the murder weapon and Lulu's body. She imagined calling her mother, trying to explain why she'd been arrested for killing a stripper. (She couldn't picture her mother's exact reaction but it would involve a lot of crying and I-told-you-sos.)

Brad pulled one hand out of his pocket, reached out with his index finger and pushed Ted's hand back down. "And I'm jealous. Go home, sleep it off and tell Port he'd better call me...but not too early. I'll be digging through this mess all night." He turned around and ducked under the length of police tape a young uniformed officer was stretching out behind him. Brad glared at him. "Am I in your way, Officer Lew?"

"Sorry, Detective Nguyen." The young man held the tape aside. Brad walked past it and into the alley toward Lulu's apartment.

*

Back at the warehouse, Talia fell into her chair and put her head on the desk. "Oh, Port. We fucked up."

Port reached into his desk drawer and retrieved a bottle of Dewar's.

Ted sat on the arm of Port's chair. "No, we didn't. We kicked ass."

"Well then, the truth will probably be found somewhere between 'fucked up' and 'kicked ass.'" Port picked up his phone. "I'll see what Brad has to say."

Talia looked up. "He said you should call him in the morning."

"Ah...I see. He'll be expecting me to call him now, then." He put the call on speaker and tossed the phone on the desk.

"What do you want, Nepal? I'm not in the mood."

"I can tell. What do you got?"

"I've got a dead girl, no suspects, and no breakfast because the falafel place is closed. Oh, and your so-called detectives messed up my crime scene."

Talia put her head back down on the desk but then looked up and said, "Oh! Ask him about the glass."

Port pushed the phone toward her. She leaned on her elbows and bent her head toward it. "Did you check the prints from the glass yet?"

"What's that? What glass?"

"There was a glass. A rocks glass. From the club, beside the...beside Lulu."

Silence. Then Brad's voice, muffled, "Hey, you! Stop what you're doing and go search the dumpsters in the area for a rocks glass. It'll look just like the ones they have in the club, and don't lie to me and tell me you've never been in there because I am not in the mood."

Port smiled at Talia. "I think we helped."

"Port." Brad's voice again. Hushed. "Listen, I do have something. This one. There's something about it. No sign of a struggle, and it was too.... I don't know. Neat? I don't think this is our killer's first murder. I'm just praying to God it's the last."

*

Talia woke to Oscar's nose in her face, sniffing at her eyelid. The combination of cold nose and prickly whiskers made her swat him away. "Back off, Ozzie." Why didn't Oscar go bother Mom? Mom was always up early.

She opened her eyes. Butter sniffed again. Talia squinted against the onslaught of dog nose.

"Who's Ozzie? Ex-boyfriend?" Ted asked.

Talia squinted up at him. His hair was wet, and he held two cups of coffee. "Ex-beagle. Is one of those coffees for me?"

"It can be." He held out a cup, coyly.

She accepted it and took a large sip. It was black. She swallowed with a grimace. "When did I fall asleep?"

"Hopefully before Darla woke up because when my woman found out how close I came to death last night, she took me to her room and rocked my world. Up high, Buffy." Ted held up a hand for a high-five. Talia shook her head.

"Congratulations, Ted." Port sat in his giant chair. Had he slept there or at all? "But let's get back to the case. It is all the more important we solve it now that we have two bodies."

Talia hung her head and stared at the ground. She thought about how Lulu bounced away from her when she last saw her. Lulu's voice lilted through her head. *Over here, doll!* She looked up. "Let's do this thing."

"Good. Let's start with this flowchart I made this morning." Port flicked on one of the big screens to reveal a crude but detailed chart that, using text boxes and stick-figure avatars, appeared to reconstruct the scene of Lulu's murder. One of the stick figures looked like Talia, even down to her blue sweater and the green barrette in her hair. In the right corner, Port had listed the suspects—Minnie Johnson, Mark Lynn, Devin Sullivan, Gary Myers, Doctor Robert Gray, and Linda Varela.

"That is craptacular, Porta Potty." Ted pointed at the screen with his coffee cup. "It's an insult to PowerPoint."

"That's because I did it in Paint."

"Disgusting." Ted shook his head. "Still, I'm proud of you for putting Minnie at the top of the list. She did Buster and then she did his mistress. Case closed. But who is this Linda character?"

"Buster's publisher," Port said. "She's got an alibi for Buster's killing. She was speaking about celebrity authors as part of the European Publishers Convention at the London Convention Center at the time. Here's a verified picture." Port clicked a few keys and sent a picture of Linda to one of the screens. It was an unflattering shot of her: mouth open, one eye half-closed, hair pulled into a tight bun except for two errant tendrils escaping in different directions like frizzy antennae.

"She's hot," Ted said. "No way a woman this hot killed anybody."

Port rested his face in his hands, sighed and rubbed his temples. "Yes. That's becoming a popular alibi around here, but I haven't been able to get a hold of her yet to get an alibi for last night, and she's been acting suspicious enough that we think she might be involved."

Ted twirled his mustache at him. "Suspicious how?"

"Well, she had a pretty strange relationship with Buster," Talia said. She brought her cup to her lips, looked down at the bitter brew and then put the cup on the coffee table. "She acted like she was being followed and then attended a pretty suspicious meeting at Studio 9 with Devin, Gary and a few other people."

"News flash! Everyone always acts like they're being followed because they always are. And all meetings are suspicious. Even this one." Ted twirled his index finger, implicating all three of them.

The familiar sound of Belisa's come-and-get-me cry resounded through the baby monitor. "Ho!" He ran toward the nursery. "How's my girl? Are you glad to see Daddy? Of course, you...oh, shit. Hey, I know you guys are out there listening. You can turn off the monitor now."

Talia got up and turned off the monitor. She stopped at the arm of Port's chair and leaned down, whispering, "What's that about?"

He widened his eyes at her. "Darla has gone shopping with her mom and has left Ted in charge of Belisa."

"That's huge!"

Port leaned toward her. "Yes, I'm cautiously optimistic that this is the beginning of..." Port was so much more attractive than usual this morning. It was startling and made it hard to pay attention to what he was saying. What was it? The gold rings in his brown eyes were brighter, maybe. Or maybe her subconscious was cleverly trying to derail the sleeping-with-a-murder-suspect train which, after last night, was dangerously close to pulling into the station. But no, he was more attractive. His usual dark but slightly ashen complexion was definitely brighter, with a deep red blush on his cheeks, like a little kid who'd just been playing in the snow.

Ted walked out holding Belisa. "Here." He kissed the baby on her chubby cheek and held her out with one hand to Port. "Take my awesome baby for a minute while I find where Darla hides the baby food."

“The diabolical woman keeps it hidden in plain sight—top shelf of the refrigerator.” Port reached out for Belisa as she reached out for him. He grabbed her with his right hand and then cradled her in the crook of his left arm. She was a little too big for the seat, but Port didn’t seem to notice, and the baby didn’t seem to mind. “So, where were we? Oh, yes. Our suspect list. I’m going to do this.” He clicked at his laptop with his free hand and marked a red M and then a black O with a question mark next to Linda’s name. “She has the motive, but we don’t know if she had the opportunity as of yet.”

“Bullshit! Linda the Hottie might have had motive to kill Buster, but why would she kill Lulu?” Ted grabbed Belisa and plunked her into the highchair.

“Ah! Because...straps!” Port said and continued once Ted strapped the baby into the chair. “Because we don’t know how yet, but this murder is clearly linked to Buster’s murder.”

“So,” Talia said. “Whoever has a motive for Buster’s murder has motive for Lulu’s?”

“Exactly. In Minnie’s case, she has clear motive for both murders.” He put an M next to her name. “And when I called Minnie earlier this morning, she said her alibi is, and I’m quoting, ‘I was home with my fucking kids.’” He wrote an O without a question mark. “Gary Myers was with you at the time of the murder, but he has the same motive all members of Crunch Pup have, so....” Another M.

“I refuse to believe my cuddly Gare Bear is a cold-blooded murderer, and she feels the same way about her boyfriend.”

“Not my boyfriend, Ted.”

“Bullshit! I saw the way that bruiser looked at me when we were pretending to be a couple of red-blooded pervs out prowling for trim. Daddy was pretending to prowl for trim, wasn’t he? Yes, he was!” That last part was directed at Belisa, who responded by clapping, and as she did, drops of green glop flew into the air. "Whoa!" Ted wiped at the counter with his sleeve.

Port shifted his weight onto his left elbow so he could lean forward and point with his right hand. "There's towels in the drawer." Still leaning on his elbow, he hit a few keys on his laptop. "Devin had the same motive, but this morning, I found a blind-item gossip story about him that said he was at an AA meeting in Daly City during the time of the murder."

"I believe it," Ted said. "If I had to witness our drunken debauchery last night, I'd need a meeting too."

"Yeah, but," Talia picked up her coffee and sipped, forgetting how vile it was. "Aren't those meetings supposed be anonymous?" She stood up and walked to the kitchen.

"Ah! Yes, but celebrity stories often prove to be too tempting for some people to resist, especially one of this magnitude."

"What do you mean?" She grabbed three Equals, ripped the tops off and dumped them in her coffee.

"According to the blind item, Devin talked about Buster's death, and he gave his old friend credit for helping him become sober. I guess he used to drive him to meetings."

"That's nice, but maybe..." Talia opened the refrigerator, and pushed aside the low-fat milk to get to the skim milk. "Maybe Devin planted that story to establish an alibi." Talia poured the milk into her coffee and took a sip. It was cold.

"I thought the same thing, so I called one of my old CIs who was known to attend that particular meeting. He didn't comment on what was said, of course, but he verified that Devin was there for the entire time." Port paused, his cursor over Doc Gray's name. "Doctor Gray, however, is a bigger mystery. We know he had opportunity, but what about motive? For either killing."

Talia sat at her seat at the desk. "Well, he was barely mentioned in Buster's book. Maybe he's pissed about that."

Port nodded. "Or maybe Buster knew something that would get his medical license revoked."

"Of course Buster knew something—him and about forty other people knew something. Doc Gray is a rock and roll doctor. He injects all those guys with uppers, downers, shots of adrenaline right in the ass...." Ted whirled the spoon in the air above Belisa's head. "Here comes the drone strike."

"You know what's weird?" Talia pointed up at the stick figure that was supposed to be Doc Gray but looked like a cross between Sammy Hagar and a yeti. "When I talked to Doc Gray, he said he blamed himself for Buster's death."

"That is weird." Port scratched his jaw. "Why would he blame himself for Buster's murder? It's not like he died on the operating table."

"He said he feels bad that he didn't insist on sobriety."

"Again...bullshit! He's a rock 'n' roll doctor. He doesn't care about sobriety. That pusher was pouring me drinks all night. I think he was purposefully trying to get me drunk."

"No, Ted. You were purposefully trying to get yourself drunk." Talia scanned the suspect list. "Speaking of drunks, why isn't Nigel Zone up there?"

"Ah! I took the liberty of tracking DaZone's tweets." Port tapped a few keys on his laptop. "Now, we know, based on the 911 call, that Lulu was murdered right around one-thirty. A little before midnight, Nigel tweeted that he was about to go out and show the ladies his quote bleeding beautiful naked arse unquote. A little after one, he was in the VIP room of the Bird's Nest, 'naked as a bleeding jaybird,' and at one-fifteen, he was getting kicked out of the Bird's Nest because, apparently, they can't handle his mojo."

"But just because Nigel tweeted that he was in the Marina doesn't mean he was there," Talia said.

"Sure, but if some jerk drops his pants," Ted said, "you can bet bedknobs to broomsticks that some other jerk is going to take a picture of dat ass and post it on the Internet."

"Aha! Look at this." Port clicked a photo up to one of the big screens that showed a...sickly lion? But he didn't have eyes or a nose.

Talia stared at it in growing horror and then looked away. "Oh, good lord!"

"Holy balls! Is that Zone's ass?" Ted covered Belisa's eyes. She laughed wildly and hiccupped.

"In all its glory. Captured at the Bird's Nest and posted on Twitter at exactly one-fifteen by someone who goes by the name @Bilfboner." Port rubbed his chin with the backs of his fingers. "Do you think Zone could get from the Marina to North Beach in ten minutes?"

Ted nodded. "Hells yeah, you'd just shoot right up Bay to Columbus. There'd hardly be any traffic at that time of night."

Talia closed her eyes and tapped her fingers on the desk. "But Lulu's apartment was at the end of the dead-end alley. Zone would've had to walk past us while we were standing there talking about the fog and Buffalo."

Port put a map up on one of the screens. "Could he have turned on Vallejo, gone through the backyard of this apartment building, and then climbed down the cliff behind Lulu's apartment?"

Talia looked at the map. "I don't see Zone climbing that cliff. It's pretty steep."

Port nodded. "Agreed. I think whoever did it was already in the apartment, lying in wait."

Talia studied the list. All the names either had an M or an O next to it and, in the case of Minnie, Mark and Doc Gray, both. A slick, oily feeling sunk deep into her bones. How had she gone from answering a Craig's List ad to hanging out with suspected murderers at murder scenes? She rubbed her eyes with her fingertips.

"Hey, guys? Does this...is this supposed to happen?" Ted lifted Belisa out of the chair. The calm look on her face was out of place with the green mush covering her body.

Chapter Fifteen

"Am I dreaming? Is this real? Where are the surviving members of Skynyrd?" Toby held on to the back of the Vespa seat and looked around him. "They're usually around here somewhere when I'm having a really good dream."

"Will you be quiet? I knew I should have waited until after the stakeout to tell you that."

"Maybe if we were in a car instead of crammed onto this damned scooter like a couple of middle-schoolers. I don't even have a cup-holder for my coffee." He held up his cup. The barista had scrawled Tony on the side. "Where am I supposed to put this when we finally move off the sidewalk?"

"Put it between your legs, like I do."

"Not likely. If anything happened to this crotch, half of the Castro would be disappointed." He blew through the hole on the lid and took a careful sip. "Next stakeout, we're taking the Blue Meanie."

"Why? I'm comfortable." Talia leaned her elbow on the handlebar and looked out at the sparse midday crowd on the waterfront. The Vespa was hidden on the dock behind a larger-than-life-sized clown sculpture that was too creepy to be arty and too arty to be ironic. They could see up Lombard Street, past the entrance to Studio 9, to where it dead-ended against a cliff. "Besides, I had to get the Vespa out of impound today, and it wasn't exactly going to fit in the Meanie's trunk."

"Impound? Sounds expensive. What did that cost you? A low-cut shirt and a fake phone number?" He smiled.

"Don't be a jerk." She poked him until he edged away from her. "Port has a friend on the force."

Toby scooched back onto his portion of the seat. "Those are nice to have. Cops always get the best drugs. Cops and doctors." He blew on his coffee and took a careful sip. "How about I just do a top-of-the-hour blind item?"

"Toby!" Talia grabbed him by the collar of his well-pressed Iron Maiden t-shirt. "You can't tell anyone this."

"Talia, the biggest virgin since Mary has been..." A group of women dressed in office attire walked by. Toby lowered his near-shout to a whisper. "...knocking boots with the biggest, most testosterone-packed rock star in the world, and I can't even do a blind item about it? That's just cruel."

"It is not cruel. I'm asking you to help me in a murder investigation. People investigating a murder generally.... Oh shit. There he is." Talia started up the Vespa. Toby leapt off the back and started to run down the sidewalk. "Where are you going?!"

He threw his coffee cup in a garbage can and ran toward her, then climbed on and put his hands around her waist. "Sorry."

Mark pulled a parking ticket off his car, crumpled it up and shoved it in his pocket. Talia had wanted to feed the meter, but Toby said it would be bad stakeout form and, worse, might call attention to their already shaky position behind the creepy clown. When Mark finally pulled out onto The Embarcadero, Talia followed.

When she slowed for a yellow light, Toby yelled, "Speed through it Tea Bag! It's yellow, not red!" When she sped up to pass a DPT truck, Toby yelled again. "Slow down! This isn't a race." Talia tried to shut him up by elbowing him in the chest, but he yelled louder. "Pay attention to the road! I'm too pretty to die."

They left the tourist-congested Embarcadero for the upscale shops and Golden Gate views of The Marina, which they soon traded for the eucalyptus groves and brick-and-cream military buildings of The Presidio. Toby held on to her waist as they soared down steep grades and careened around the curves, clinging to the edges of the cliffs that hovered high above Baker Beach.

"Where the hell is he going?" Toby yelled over the Vespa's buzzy whirr.

Mark made a familiar left off El Camino Del Mar. Talia slowed down.

"You're going to lose him."

"No, I'm not." Talia pulled over. "I know where he's going."

Instead of turning, she pulled the Vespa up onto the wide median across from Minnie's street and stashed it behind a squat palm tree that was just the right width to conceal it. "We lost him. Told you." Toby stepped out from behind the tree. Talia pulled him back and pointed at a Honda parked near Minnie's house. Only part of the hood and half of the windshield was visible, but they could see Mark as he sat in the front seat. He got out of the car and walked toward Minnie's driveway. Toby grabbed a pair of binoculars from his messenger bag.

"You brought binoculars?"

"Duh. You said it was a stakeout."

Talia grabbed the binoculars and focused them on Minnie's doorstep.

"What's he doing?" Toby said.

"He's ringing the bell," Talia said. The door opened, and then slammed shut. Mark rang the bell again...and again.

Finally, the door opened. Minnie stood in the doorway, her arms folded across her chest.

"What's happening? Let me see."

"Hold on."

Mark held up a black box about the size of a child's shoe box. Minnie took it, and they both walked into the house.

"Here." She handed Toby the binoculars.

"Thanks for nothing. Next time, you bring your own." Toby sat, put the binoculars on his lap and looked around. "I'm not surprised Minnie chose to live here. This hood is kind of like where she's from in The Sunset...only a little ritzier. Her parents still own a hardware store out in the avenues."

"I didn't know that." She was quiet for a while, watching the door, and then she said, "Toby, do you think Minnie killed Buster?"

He shook his head, "No. I think your new boyfriend did."

She smacked him.

"Ow! Sorry. I don't know who did it, but I think she's being set up as scapebitch again, just like when Crunch Pup broke up."

Talia laughed. "What do you mean 'scapebitch'?"

"How much do you know about Buster's time with Crunch Pup?"

"Not much."

"Come into my office." Toby patted the seat of the Vespa. "Come on. You watch and I'll talk."

Talia sat, keeping her eyes on the door.

"Once upon a time, Buster Bones was in a young surf punk band named Crunch Pup. They had a freshman album with one hit and a sophomore album with three hits—three top-forty hits. One of them, 'Rough Ride,' was a top ten hit. If they kept it up, didn't burn out or find religion, their third album was sure to be a huge hit. A rarity in the rock world.

They'd be up there with Led Zeppelin and Radiohead and to a lesser degree The Beasties."

"Wait, I'm lost. What does this have to do with Radiohead?"

"Pay attention. Okay, let's rewind. When Crunch Pup formed, Buster was still going by the name Craig Johnson and attending Lowell High School. He met a girl named Minerva Wong. She and Craig were quite the item."

Talia sighed. "I already know all that, Toby."

Toby patted her knee. "Did you know that after graduation, Minnie dumped Buster so she could concentrate on getting an MBA?"

"No. Minnie has an MBA? She doesn't seem the type."

"Oh, she's not. When I first started at WSHK, I sat in on an interview with Minnie where she said that her parents wanted all that crap for her, but she didn't really find her calling until she started popping babies out of her twat—her words, not mine."

"Did twat make it on air?"

"Course not. I had that filthy-mouth on a seven second delay with my finger poised above the kill switch." Toby held up a curved index finger in her sightline. She slapped it away.

"After she graduated, she got back together with Buster. They started taking long walks around Lake Merced. And then, on one of those walks, Buster proposed to Minnie, and she said yes. This was around the time when Crunch Pup was getting ready to start work on that third album."

"The Radiohead album."

"Ah! It learns." Toby put his arm around her and squeezed. "So, they go into Studio 9, and the first song that Buster brings them is a love song called 'Walk of Love.'"

"Oh, I love that song!"

"Yes. You and every other twelve to fifty-five-year-old woman in the country. But here was Crunch Pup, poised to pull the rock throne out from under Led Zep, and Buster was writing love songs that Paul McCartney would find a bit sappy. They rejected the song, which, to Buster, meant that they rejected Minnie. The band imploded. They broke up before the album was finished, and 'Walk of Love,' as you know, was put out on a Buster Bones solo album." He paused. "So, what does that tell you?"

"It tells me Minnie made Buster Bones who he is.... I mean was." Talia looked at Toby.

"That's adorable. It should tell you that when Crunch Pup was poised for super-stardom, Buster took it all away because of Minnie. Now...." Toby pointed at the door. "How do you think that little meeting is going in there?"

There was a scream. Talia grabbed the binoculars from Toby. She scanned Minnie's house. The door was wide open. "I don't see Mark."

"I don't either, but there's Minnie. In the driveway."

Talia scanned the driveway until she saw Minnie, fuming, standing with her hands on her hips. She followed Minnie's sightline. She was looking at her son, Vincent, as he stood returning her gaze. Vincent tilted his head, and the light hit something on his ear. "Damn! He's a little young for that."

"What is it? Let me see." Toby grabbed at the binoculars.

Talia twisted out of his reach. "Vincent got his ear pierced."

"Just like his old man," Mark said.

Talia dropped the binoculars. They hit the grass. Mark picked them up and said, "Can I join the stakeout?"

"I wish you could, but there's no room." Toby shrugged and moved around on the seat, an inch one way and an inch the other, to show how cramped he was.

For years, Talia's second most embarrassing moment had been the time the acting agency sent her on a job that required her to wear a Petunia Pig costume at a frat party, and her ex-boyfriend showed up with a date. That had barely edged out the time she'd gotten her period on a field trip to Strawbery Banke, and everyone called her Strawberry Pants for the rest of Junior High. This moment was not more embarrassing than that, but it had just edged out Petunia Pig for second place. She looked at the binoculars for a long time before finally taking them and looking up at Mark. "How long have you known?"

"That you two were following me? I guess since Studio 9." He smiled. The sun hit his eyes, and they glinted like Vincent's earring. "How could I miss a hot blonde on a cherry red Vespa?"

"Ahem." Toby raised his arm above his head and pointed at himself.

"Sorry, I meant two hot blondes."

"Mark, this is my friend Toby."

"Wait. You're not Toby the Flaming Rock God, are you?"

"The one and only." Toby bowed from his seat.

"I'm a big fan."

"Likewise." Toby held his hand out. Mark shook it.

Mark turned to Talia. "Will I have the pleasure of being tailed by you for the rest of the day, or is the stakeout over?"

Toby stood up. "We're just trying to rule everyone out, you understand, Mr. Lynn. Don't you?"

Mark laughed. "I understand that you watch a lot of detective shows."

"What's in the box, Mr. Lynn?"

"I can't tell you that, Detective Rock God, but I can tell you it was a present for Minnie that has nothing to do with your investigation." He handed the binoculars back to Talia. "I'm leaving now. You can follow me, if you'd like. I've got some Two Buck Chuck in the fridge."

Talia shook her head.

"One of these days I'm going to take you on a real date, Sloane Peterson...if that is your real name."

Talia watched him turn and look back four times as he walked to his car.

"Tea? Why does he think you're Ferris Bueller's girlfriend?"

"It's a long story." She rocked the scooter off its center stand. "Tobe, remember when I got that job at that pizza place off-campus?"

"The one where you had to spin the dough in the air? Of course, I remember that. I was one of the people you dropped dough on."

"I'm starting to feel like that. Like I'm dropping dough all over the place." She put both hands under the Vespa's seat.

Toby grabbed the handlebars. "Yeah, but by the end of the first week you were catching the dough and pulling off spins and pirouettes as well. You were like the Brian Boitano of pizza." He helped her pull the Vespa off the median. "Give yourself a break, Tea. This is still your first week."

"Yeah, but I'm not making pizza."

When they pulled out onto the street, tires screeched from somewhere behind them. Toby's hands tensed around her waist. Talia braked and looked over her shoulder. The road curved about a block away. She could hear the car but couldn't see it.

"People always drive like maniacs in rich neighborhoods. Come on, girl." Toby tapped her hip. "Let's get back to the wrong side of the tracks where people are more civilized."

Talia sped out of Sea Cliff. When the road twisted into the Presidio, they heard the screeching again. Toby gripped Talia's waist. She slowed. The road curved and led them up a steep hill. At the top of the hill, there was another curve, and they were on the cliff above Baker Beach again. She heard the squealing tires again, coming up behind them. She tightened her grip on the handlebars. She wasn't sure if she should squeeze the gas or the brake, so she did neither, coasting around the curve.

The car sped up and cut around them on the right, driving up onto the grassy shoulder. At the apex of the curve, it cut sideways toward the Vespa, pushing them toward oncoming traffic. Talia screamed. She swerved hard to avoid a minivan and careened toward the cliff. A line of white-capped waves marked the end of their trajectory. Her brain registered that she should hit the brakes, but before the message made it to her hand, the Vespa slammed into the guardrail. Toby screamed just as Talia tumbled over the handlebars and down the cliff.

Talia squeezed her eyes shut, bracing herself for the long, screaming fall that would end with her painful death in the wind-swept ocean below. Something (a tree branch?) hit her chest, knocking the air out of her lungs. She opened her eyes. The pavement rushed toward a very specific spot on her forehead—a spot that suddenly felt soft and vulnerable. She threw out her arms. They hit the ground with a slap.

The wind was knocked out of her. She gasped and sucked in a breath. Once she could breathe normally, she sat up and looked around. She'd landed on the narrow beach trail that couldn't be seen from the road because of a row of short, stiff-needled pine trees. The cliff dropped off a few feet from where she'd landed. She watched the waves crash against the rocks at the shore.

"Tea! Are you dead?"

"No." She stood up and looked around but didn't see Toby.

"Good. Then come help my ass down."

Talia tilted her head back and saw Toby directly above her, perched on a branch of a tree. He clutched the twisted trunk of the tree with one hand and reached down to Talia with the other. She stood on her toes and stretched her arm out but couldn't reach. She tried to get closer to the tree, but it was growing out of the side of the cliff. Talia put one foot in the dirt as high up the cliff as she could and raised both hands towards Toby. He reached down, grabbed her hands and jumped, landing with a thump. The dirt crumbled under his feet and he started to slide toward the pavement. Talia grabbed his shoulders. Toby threw his arms around her waist and squeezed. "Oh, thank god I'm still alive!"

Talia squeezed back. "Are you sure, Tobe? Maybe you're dead. Do you see Skynyrd anywhere around here?"

"Shut up. Those rednecks wouldn't be caught dead in this liberal, homo-loving town."

*

Talia thrust her road-rash ravaged elbows at Port.

"I'm relieved you weren't more seriously hurt. Did you get a good look at the car that did this to you?"

Talia shrugged and walked to the kitchen. "It happened too fast, and I think Toby's eyes were closed the whole time," she said, pouring a cup of coffee. "I think it was silver...or blue."

"That's not much to go on."

"That's what Brad said, but he's looking into it."

Darla walked into the kitchen with Belisa on her hip. "What happened?" She grabbed Talia's arm and yanked it upward so she could inspect her elbow.

"A car cut us off in the Presidio. Luckily, the ground broke my fall."

"Fucking tourists. I don't like the look of that." Darla let go of her arm. "I'm getting the first-aid kit."

"No need. Brad took us to the ER just in case. I'm fine, Darla."

Darla shifted Belisa from one hip to the other. "And how's your friend?"

"Toby? Not a scratch. He complained a lot, though." Talia grabbed a large cookie off a plate next to the coffee pot. After being dropped off a cliff, she figured she deserved a treat.

Darla shook her head and issued a warning look. Talia looked into the living room. Port was tapping at his keyboard. She took a bite out of the cookie and leaned toward Darla.

"Don't eat those," Darla whispered. "They're all peanut butter, butter, and cream. Just one has a half-a-day's calories." Talia spit the cookie into her hand. Darla lowered her voice even more. "I made those because you-know-who is getting skinny. I tell him they're low fat."

"What are you two whispering about? Not me, I hope."

"I was telling Talia about the sex I had with Ted. It was crazy hot," Darla said loudly.

"Good god, woman! There's an innocent child present."

Darla laughed.

Talia threw out the offending bite of cookie. That was why he was so attractive lately. Darla was fattening him up. Talia sat at the desk and watched Darla as she got ready to leave the warehouse with Belisa. No panicking. No locking herself in her room. She just picked up a diaper bag, hitched the baby up on her hip and walked out the door.

Chapter Sixteen

Toby was supposed to be home at exactly six o'clock. She looked out the window a few minutes before six. Toby was standing on the sidewalk, but why wasn't he coming up? He turned. It wasn't Toby but a blonde, thin homeless man selling copies of *Curbside.* Toby would be pissed if he knew Talia had mistaken him for a homeless person, but it was his own fault for growing his hair long and never wearing anything but concert t-shirts and second-hand jeans with bright orange stitching.

Talia sat on the couch and turned on the television. The cat jumped up and curled up next to her, leaning against her thigh and purring loudly. She put one hand on his rumbling side. He'd been more affectionate since she started bringing him into her room at night. Kirk used to sleep with Toby, but Talia needed the company because of the nightmares.

She was still having the same one she always had with the dark water and the giant with the tire iron, but lately there was a new one. She was floating in a darkness so black and thick, she could feel it pressing against her shoulders. She fell deep into it, deeper and deeper until she felt as though it would go on forever, and then she stopped. The blackness in front of her wasn't blackness, but a blackboard. She picked up a piece of chalk and wrote the words *Talia was here*. She always woke with the same horrible feeling that she'd just dreamt about her own death.

"...the Platinum Club murder is somehow connected to...." She jumped, startling Kirk, who leapt onto the remote, changing the channel to Jeopardy. "the Daily Double. How much will you...." Talia pushed the cat off the remote and switched back, quickly. Her mouth dropped open. It was Lulu. Alive. She was talking to a reporter.

"Juliet was a good girl. She didn't deserve this." It wasn't Lulu, but her mother. She looked a lot like her daughter, only older—but not much. She couldn't be more than forty. She looked into the camera and wiped at her tears, saying, "Please. Find who did this. I want justice for my little girl." Talia grabbed a tissue and pushed at her own tears.

Talia wanted to hear more from Lulu's mother. What had Lulu been like as a child? Did she want to be something besides a stripper, like a secretary or an actress? But the anchor moved on to the next story. Another reporter was questioning "folks on the street" about their thoughts on Minnie's guilt. A man in a Crunch Pup t-shirt didn't wait for her to ask a question before yelling, "Hang the witch!"

Talia was about to change the channel when she saw a familiar face in the crowd. A man she'd seen before. The reporter pointed her microphone at him and asked, "How about you, sir? Do you think Minnie is guilty?"

Star Tee smiled and looked into the camera for a long time before saying, "Minnie will be freed. She is meant for other things. Things that will make this whole damn monkey house scream and rattle their cages with horror."

"What are the 'other things' that Minnie Johnson is meant for? Can you tell us?"

He just smiled, held up his fist, and then splayed out his fingers like a star—a common hand-gesture at Crunch Pup shows. He stared into the camera as the reporter turned away from him. The camera focused on the reporter until only half of Star Tee's face was in the shot. He kept staring into the camera with one crazed eye. Talia stared back. She was barely aware of what the reporter was saying. A few words broke through: "Buster's fans," "holding a vigil," "toxicology report..."

She tore her gaze from Star Tee's eye and watched the reporter. Had they released the toxicology report? The reporter opened her mouth and screamed. Talia jumped. It wasn't a scream. It was a trumpet blast from the Blue Meanie's horn. The reporter kept talking, but Talia couldn't hear because of the French national anthem being played out below. By the time it finished, they'd cut to a commercial.

She looked out the window. A blue Mini Cooper with a bumper sticker that read "Clapton is not God, but he is a god" was parked in front of the building. Toby rolled down the window and hit the horn again. Talia rolled her eyes. She would have to sit through the first four bars of the French national anthem before she could speak. When he'd first had the expensive custom horn installed, Talia had asked him why he'd chosen it when he was, in fact, not French. Toby never answered her; he just ranted about her inadequate knowledge of The Beatles.

When the horn was finally quiet, Talia yelled, "You're late!"

"No, I'm not. Our clocks are ten minutes fast. Remember?"

Talia shut the window without answering him because of course he was right. She'd set them like that on purpose so she would get places on time. She grabbed her purse and ran out the door.

Out on the sidewalk, Talia stopped and looked down. Toby's doppelganger had abandoned his makeshift newsstand—an overturned milk crate next to a paper cup and a stack of *Curbsides*. Talia got in the Meanie, buckled her seatbelt and turned to Toby. "Here's the game plan. I'll pretend to be your producer. We interview Kylie and ask her about her affair with Buster."

"That's great, if we want to get Kylie to *not* talk about her steamy little affair with Buster Bones. First, we go back stage, you look hot, and I strut my stuff like Justin Timberlake. Kylie falls madly in love with our fabulousness. We take her to a bar and party one of her tits off. Then we go to a second bar and party her other tit off. Then, she tells us everything."

*

Toby parked next to a van with the words *KGAY Party Bus* painted on the side in rainbow colors. Talia climbed out and followed Toby to the back of the van. "What do you think of the name Roz Doyle? Do you think I'd be believable as a radio producer?"

Without looking at her, he reached into the van's cargo area. "I think you're totally believable as an intern." He handed her a large shopping bag. "Give these bumper stickers out to those tween girls over there so they can plaster them on their closet doors or something."

"Oh, so I'm...."

"Handing out bumper stickers, yes."

"Okay, but when are we going to talk strategy?"

"We already talked it, sugarplum. The Justin Timberlake tits-off drink-fest, or did you forget?" Toby tweaked her nose.

"I thought you were kidding."

"I don't kid about drinking with pop stars." Toby sat down next to his producer, Karen, at a folding table set up next to the van.

Karen smiled and waved at Talia and then started counting down from five. On one, she pointed at Toby, and he switched to his on-air persona, which was a lot like his off-air persona only more flamboyant. "Hey pop tarts! This is

Toby the Flaming Rock God coming at you live from the Mecca of all things pink, sparkly and virginal—The Kylie Kismet concert. And guess what? My number one fag hag, Teabag, is going to be here with me all night, handing out bumper stickers. Are you ready to party your tits off, Teabag?"

Talia switched to her actress personality, which was much like her regular personality, only more confident. "Are you allowed to say *tits* on the radio, Toby?"

"I don't know, can you say *tits* on the radio, lovely producer Karen?"

Karen shook her head. "Absolutely not. Now will you two please stop saying *tits*?"

The small crowd that had gathered cheered and whooped. Talia gave them all bumper stickers. There was more whooping.

"I'm not sure...maybe...." Talia began.

After an hour of whooping, banter and bumper stickers, Karen, who was known for never staying anywhere longer than she absolutely had to, called an end to the pre-concert show. "Well, I'm going to turn into a frigging pumpkin."

Toby bowed at her. "And I'm going to turn into a very drunk, very gay, and devastatingly handsome man." He grabbed Talia by the arm and ushered her toward the backstage entrance.

The security guard recognized Toby and waved them in. "Thanks, Roland." Toby leaned against the backstage entrance and pulled out his cell phone. "Hold on a sec. I got to get my soundtrack ready." Toby swiped through his phone, not looking up. "My entrance music needs to let everyone—roadies, groupies, entourage, drug dealers, everyone—that a bona fide Rock God has entered their midst. I'm thinking "Children of the Revolution" by T Rex, but I'm not sure. Do you think a deep cut like that would be lost on these bimbos?"

"Nah, it'll be tight," Roland said, giving the evil eye to a group of girls trying to slip past him.

"I trust your judgment, Roland. Let me just get it cued up and...." Toby held up his phone as the sound of classic guitar rock blared from the speaker.

They strutted into a long hallway lined with hangers-on, sycophants and groupies. They must have looked the part because the throng parted to let them by as the little phone blasted out an anthem to the scenesters.

But you won't fool the children of the revolution/ No you won't fool the children of the revolution. No no no!

Toby leaned on Talia, as though he were a little drunk, even though he wasn't. Talia leaned back. Her character, a model named Diamond, would also be slightly drunk. Toby waved and smiled at the crowd that was forming around them. Toby pointed dramatically at a young man who was dressed only in hot pants and suspenders. "Hey, bitch. Are you coming to my party?"

"Um, well...of course, bitch."

Toby beamed and spread his arms out. "My subjects!" Someone put a glass of champagne in his hand.

An authoritative voice called from behind them. "Hey, princesses!" They turned slowly. His imposing size and stance indicated that he was a security guard, but instead of a t-shirt, he was sporting a black suit and an ear piece. He looked like secret service, only larger.

"Uhhhh..." Talia began. Toby elbowed her.

"I beg your pardon." Toby sipped casually from his newly acquired glass of champagne. "I'm not a princess. I'm a queen."

Secret Service looked him up and down. "Come with me." He turned and started to walk back the way they had come in. They followed him, but after a few steps, he spun around so fast that Talia nearly bumped into his chest. He pointed a thick finger at Toby. "Lose the theme song, Ally McBeal."

Toby turned off the music. The scenesters groaned. They'd wasted their excitement and energy on a couple roustabouts who were about to get rousted. A hand reached out of the crowd and took back the glass of champagne.

"Damn," Toby whispered.

Talia quickly typed "getting hassled by security" into Dicko.

Hot Pants turned to a girl dressed from head to toe in pink feathers and said, "I can't believe I fell for that bitch."

Toby started to follow Secret Service. Talia glanced at Dicko and held him back. "We're not going anywhere until you tell us where you are taking us."

"To the VIP lounge."

The crowd gasped so loudly it almost sounded like a cheer.

"Apparently, you queens are fabulous," he said flatly, "and Miss Kismet wants to party with you."

The gasp turned into a real cheer. Someone pressed a piece of paper in Talia's hand. She twisted around to see who it was. The back-up dancer.

Toby raised an eyebrow at her. "Hmm. Not what I expected."

Someone placed a fresh glass of champagne in Toby's hand. Someone else tapped Talia's shoulder. "Hey, can you give that number to the Queen for me?"

Toby smiled, looked into her eyes, plucked the paper from her hand and sang, "No, no you can't fool the children of the revolution."

"No singing."

"Sorry, sir." Toby grabbed Talia by the hand, and they followed Secret Service into the arena's inner sanctum.

*

The sycophants in the VIP room were not nearly as fabulous as the ones in the hall. They were also older, richer and much less sycophantic. Kylie's concert was broadcast live on monitors, but no one watched it, even when she sang her hit song, "Baby Touch," while riding a pale-pink mechanical unicorn that farted fireworks. Instead, they just drank free beer, ate free cold appetizers, and acted entitled and unimpressed.

They were still acting like they didn't care when Kylie made her big entrance flanked by sweaty back-up dancers and followed by a mousy-looking girl carrying a clipboard. Toby was the first to say anything to her. "Kylie! You were amazing tonight. Will you have my gay babies?"

In a green tutu, coconut bra, fairy wings and high ponytail fastened with a giant baby pacifier, Kylie looked like she'd just stepped out of her video for "Crazy Lumps." She moved her gaze to where Toby and Talia were standing, looked them over and then whispered something to one of the back-up dancers. The dancer looked around until Kylie pointed in Toby and Talia's direction. The dancer whispered something to Kylie and then they both laughed.

"Toby, they are literally pointing and laughing at us."

"Oh god. This is like Rush Week all over again."

Kylie strutted toward them. "What are you two doing here?"

Talia's throat went dry while the rest of her was anything but—even her eyeballs felt sweaty. "Uh...actually...."

"Actually," Toby leaned one arm on her shoulder. "We came to party your tits off."

Kylie laughed again. The back-up dancers joined in. The Ivy League sycophants looked over briefly, as though they were wondering what the joke was before remembering that they weren't supposed to care. "Well then, we need to get the fuck away from this tool box," Kylie said. "Do you guys know any good bars?"

"I know of two in the area," Toby said.

"Hooray!" Kylie jumped up and down; her fairy wings flapped as she did. "It's Iris's twenty-first birthday." She pointed at the mousy girl with the clipboard. "We need to get her cosmically drunk." Iris smiled shyly at them.

A young man wearing an argyle sweater over a checked shirt that was buttoned to the top and secured with a necktie walked in the door and put a hand on Kylie's shoulder. "If you're drinking, Kylie, you need to keep it under three drinks. Don't forget."

Chapter Seventeen

The crowd at The Brouge Room was sparse, quiet and either unaware of or unimpressed by Kylie's presence. "A bottle of Kristal, please." Kylie leaned so far over the bar, Talia was afraid she might topple into the ice bin. Benji grabbed her belt loop and gently pulled her back onto her stool. She put her arm around him and planted a kiss on his cheek. "Don't worry, Benji. These lushes will drink most of it." She walked two extravagantly manicured nails around the knot of his tie. "And you'll have a little glass, won't you?"

Benji smiled and nodded. Kylie handed him a glass, then turned to Talia and whispered, "I've got him wrapped around my pinky."

"Is he your boyfriend?"

"My doctor." Kylie clinked glasses with Talia.

A third glass joined their cheers. It was Benji's. "And I'm only trying to keep you healthy, Kylie. You could try making it easier."

After the bottle was drained, Toby stood arm and arm with Jordy and Jules, announced that The Brouge Room was played out, and told everyone to follow him to a better bar. The bartender, a man of about sixty in a crisp blue apron, didn't look up from the glass he was washing to say, "Thanks, then. Come again."

*

The Nightingale was a karaoke bar with an underdressed, overly loud crowd that appeared only to serve Crown Royal and schnapps.

"Here. Drink this." Toby handed Talia a glass.

"What is it?"

"They call it a Long Island Iced Tea, but I'm pretty sure it's Crown and Coke."

As the drinks flowed, the little group grew drunker and louder. As sober as she claimed to be, Kylie was the loudest. When she found out about Toby's Flaming Rock God alter ego, she insisted he sing a Queen song and then insisted on singing with him. Toby belted out "I Want It All" with one of the country's biggest pop stars with a surprising amount of confidence. When Iris softly sang a meek rendition of "Girls Just Want to Have Fun," Kylie jumped in and sang back-up. The small crowd cheered. Iris held her glasses to her face as she bowed.

The KJ, a heavily tattooed woman in a frilly rockabilly dress, pulled Talia aside and pointed up at Kylie. "I like her. She's the coolest rock star we've had in here. Most of them are real jerks."

"Do you get a lot of rock stars in here?"

"Sure do. Rock stars love to slum. A month or so ago Buster Bones came in with her."

"Kylie was here with Buster?"

"Didn't you notice the memorial?" The KJ pointed toward the corner at an old telephone booth filled with candles, flowers and pictures of Buster. "He didn't sing, though. I wish he had. Kylie sang."

Talia asked what song Kylie had sung and signed up for it herself, hoping Kylie would join in, but she didn't. When Talia got to the chorus, Jordy and Jules grabbed Toby and dragged him to the dance floor. She craned her neck to see where Kylie was but couldn't see her. During the second verse, Toby and Jordy stopped dancing and started flirting. Jules stomped back to the bar when the flirting turned to making out.

When Talia got to the second chorus, a familiar voice joined in. "Another one bites the dust." Kylie winked at her as she sang. "And another one gone, another one gone." Talia nearly dropped her microphone, but caught it before it hit the ground. The KJ gave Talia a thumbs-up as the crowd cheered for Kylie. "Another one bites the dust."

Kylie put her arm around Talia as they walked off the tiny stage. The pop star smelled like Scotch and flowery perfume. "Thanks for the back-up." Talia meant to lean against the bar, but fell against it.

"No worries." Kylie fell against the bar next to her. "That's my favorite song...used to be anyway."

"Um...Kylie? I was wondering...have you been here before? To this bar, I mean."

"Yeah. Once." Kylie looked at the phone-booth Buster memorial. Where the phone would've been, there was a poster of Buster. It was the iconic shot from his "Walk of Love" video, with his heavily lined green eyes focused on the camera and black hair framing his pale face.

"You know what? Men suck." Kylie picked up a cocktail napkin, crumpled it up and threw it. It floated slowly to the floor. She sighed. "I was so hard-core in love with this guy." She turned to Talia. "I'm talking true love, Talia, and then one day, he dumped me. Me! America's freaking princess. He said he was in love with his wife. Can you believe that shit? How does anyone dump this?" Kylie ran her hands over her torso. "And the really sad thing is that...that...." Kylie's blue, professionally lined eyes misted over. "That bitch of a wife, the bitch who he dumped me for, murdered the love of my life in his recording studio."

"I'm...I'm so sorry."

Kylie threw her arms around Talia and sobbed. Talia patted her back and handed her a cocktail napkin. "Here, don't mess up your make-up."

"Thanks." Kylie dabbed at her eyes. "You know...." She picked up her drink and took a sip. "I think I've finally met someone new."

Talia nodded and smiled, even though the word *finally* sounded a bit strange considering that Buster hadn't even been buried yet.

"That was a great duet, ladies." Benji stood in front of them, holding a pint glass filled with something brown and fizzy.

"That was all Talia." Kylie put her drink down so she could give Talia a little round of applause.

"Oh stop." Talia waved her off and then turned to Benji. "Are you going to sing?"

"I don't sing. I warble...and not in public." He put his glass on the bar next to Kylie's. "Unless, of course, I've had a few drinks, but I can't drink much if I want to keep up with this whirlwind." He put an arm around Kylie's shoulder. She eased an arm around his waist.

"He takes care of me." Kylie shrugged and smiled.

"Not an easy task." He picked up his glass and took a sip. His expression darkened. He looked at Kylie. "This isn't my drink."

"I didn't ask for it. The bartender just made it for me, Benji." Kylie stuck out her lower lip. "Don't be mad."

"I'm not mad. I just can't help you if you keep fighting me." He bent down and kissed her forehead. "I'm going back to the hotel. I'll see you in the morning." He walked toward the door.

Kylie looked at Talia. "I'm a jerk, right?"

"Uh...no, you're not a...."

"No. I'm a jerk. I have diabetes. He's just trying to keep me safe."

"You're right." Talia nodded. "You're a jerk."

"I'm going after him." Kylie picked up her drink and sipped.

"Go!" Talia waved her away from the bar.

"Liquid courage." Kylie put the drink on the bar and ran toward the door.

Talia stood and looked around for Toby. She'd just spotted him in a booth with Jules and Jordy when she heard tires screeching followed by a scream. Her mind flashed to the moment when she'd found Lulu's body. She stood, frozen.

Someone ran past her. She looked up. It was Iris. She followed her out of the door. There, in the middle of the dark empty street, Kylie lay in a crumpled heap. Talia looked for cars and ran across the street to the faded, double yellow line. She could hear someone running in the other direction. Kylie was bent, sobbing, over Benji's lifeless body. Blood trickled from the corner of his mouth, and his legs splayed at sickeningly odd angles. Talia put two fingers on his neck, but couldn't feel anything, so she held her hand under his nose. Talia felt the whispery scratches of Kylie's hair as it brushed her wrist with each heaving sob, but no air. Talia edged her fingers closer, almost shoving them up his nostrils. She felt the faint in and out of breath.

She patted her pocket for Dicko, but it was in her purse back at the bar. She heard Toby, standing behind her, calling for an ambulance.

Jordy dropped down to his knees and loosened Benji's tie. "They say to loosen tight clothing. We also need to keep him warm. Does anyone have a coat?"

"He can have mine." The KJ handed Jordy a cherry-red dress coat with white bric-a-brac trim. Jordy was tucking the material around Benji's arms when Talia heard a fast-approaching car. She snapped her head up to see headlights coming at them.

"Oh shit," Toby said. "I'll direct traffic."

But Jules was already there, waving the car into the other lane. The car slowed as it moved past the spectacle. The bartender waited for the car to clear before crossing the road. He'd brought the purses Talia and Kylie had left at the bar and handed them both to Talia. Someone was running toward them from up the street. It was Iris, out of breath and struggling to hold her glasses to her face. "I couldn't see the license plate, but I saw the car. It was a silver Lexus."

Chapter Eighteen

The sun streamed through the passenger side window as Toby pulled onto the freeway. Talia snapped her visor down and flipped it to the side. They didn't talk much for the first few miles, but when Talia found a Kylie Kismet song on the radio, they both sang along.

Stupid heart, my stupid heart. I don't know what to do. You call it off before we start. But all I want is you. And your stupid heart.

"I think he's going to be okay." Toby checked over his shoulder before changing lanes. "I mean, Kylie said he's out of the woods, right?"

"Yeah, but I don't think he'll be leaving that hospital for a long time. I just hope he leaves on his own two feet." Talia looked out the window, watching the other cars slip by as Toby sped past them.

"Yeah. And I hope he got the license plate of the bitch that hit him." He made another lane change, this one a little quicker and more dramatic, as though he were punctuating his point.

"If it had one. If Iris didn't see the number, it might mean that there wasn't one to see."

Toby jerked the wheel and swerved into a lane where traffic was moving slower than he was. He stomped on the brake. Talia pitched forward, clutching her coffee cup. A few drops flew out of the hole on the lid and onto the floor.

"Whoa, watch the caffeine, Tobe." She took a sip and then stared at the road ahead of them.

"I am sorry to be blunt, Tea, but murderers seem to be following you around." Toby glanced in the rearview mirror. "Literally."

"Shit." She tapped her fingers against the armrest. "I was just thinking the same thing, and I'm starting to worry that...."

"That you might be next?"

"I hadn't thought about that. I was going to say I was starting to worry that I might not catch the killer before he, or she, kills again."

"Or *they*. It could be a group thing." Toby checked his side mirror.

"This is murder, Tobe. Not brunch."

Toby looked quickly over his shoulder and pulled the wheel. The Blue Meanie slid into the lane. Without looking over his shoulder, Toby pulled the wheel again and the car skidded across two lanes, tires screeching.

Talia yelped, catching her coffee just before it tumbled onto the floor. "Are you trying to kill us?"

"Nope," he answered flatly, looking in the rearview mirror. "I'm trying to shake the car that's been tailing our ass."

"What?" Talia twisted around as far as her seatbelt would allow. She could just barely see the silver Lexus a few cars back. "I can't see the driver." She put her hand on the seatbelt release. Toby put his right hand on top of hers.

"I wouldn't do that if I were you, Teabag."

"Why not?"

"Because I'm about to pull some Dukes of Hazzard moves right now."

"In the Meanie?!"

Toby glanced over his shoulder and then pulled the wheel to the right. The car swerved across the next lane, the next lane and then into the next lane over. Toby glanced over his shoulder, accelerated and jerked the wheel. The Blue Meanie careened toward the median. Toby jerked the wheel again and they slid off the freeway and onto the exit ramp.

"Toby! That was awesome."

"I know." He slapped the steering wheel in celebration. "I'm so Bo Duke. Uh oh."

"What?"

He pointed at the rearview mirror. "To quote Elton John, the bitch is back."

She looked behind them. The silver Lexus was right on their tail. "I'm calling the cops."

"I hope they hurry. I used up all my Bo Duke moves getting off the exit."

"Don't panic." The Lexus started to pass them, but instead of fully passing them, it veered, clipping their bumper. Toby swerved violently.

"I'm panicking!" Toby stepped on the accelerator, speeding through a red light. Talia looked in the side mirror. The Lexus was stuck at the light behind another car.

"*Take a hard right at the next intersection*," a smooth, female voice said.

"Who said that?" Toby looked around, startled.

"Dicko." Talia held it up for him to see. The screen looked like an intricate GPS navigation system.

"Is that from the future?"

Talia swiped at the screen. On the upper right corner, she saw two little cars moving along a red stretch of the freeway. The cops. They were on their way, but they were stuck in traffic. Dicko must have called them.

"Brake, quickly."

Toby slammed on the brakes. He hadn't been paying attention to the slowing traffic in front of him and came within an inch of hitting a beer delivery truck. The sound of tires spinning on asphalt squealed from behind them.

"Accelerate and pass slow traffic on the right."

Toby started to turn to the right and then hit the brakes again. "The right?! That's the fucking sidewalk."

"Pass slow traffic on the right."

Talia looked behind them. The Lexus was edging to the left, attempting to pass the cars between them. "Do it, Toby!"

"Oh Jesus." Toby pulled up onto the sidewalk, yelling, "Out of my way, pedestrians!"

There weren't any pedestrians. The sidewalk was clear except for a mailbox on the corner. The Mini Cooper managed to squeak by the mailbox, but then came the sickening screech of metal hitting metal. Talia cringed and checked the side mirror. The Lexus had torn the mailbox from its foundation and was dragging it through intersection. The mailbox bounced on the asphalt. Sparks skittered along the road and under cars.

Toby looked behind them. "Maybe that'll slow their ass down."

The Lexus swerved, crashing up onto the curb and shaking the mailbox loose with a loud *clang*.

"They're still coming after us," Talia said.

"Oh, hell's bells. I do not want to die in the South Bay."

"Turn left now."

"What left? There's no left. Just a hedge!"

"Turn left now."

Toby turned the wheel hard, and the car crashed through a row of hedges. The sound of the branches scraping against the windows turned Talia's stomach. She gripped the armrest and braced for the worst. She heard a line of sirens pass on the road behind them. Toby swerved to avoid a tree, and the windshield was covered in something white and loud. Talia saw a beak. They'd driven through a flock of birds.

"Watch for geese."

"Oh, now you fucking tell me?"

"Stop the car."

Toby stepped on the brake. The car squished to a stop as though they were driving through a bouncy house.

"Get out of the car." It was a man's voice speaking through a megaphone. Toby put his hand on the door handle.

"Stay in the car. Roll down the window."

Toby looked at Talia. She shrugged. "It's been right so far." They looked down at the little device. The futuristic GPS was gone, replaced with a realistic badge.

"Okay, bitch. I think I can take it from here." Toby grabbed Dicko and rolled down the window.

The man with the megaphone turned out to be a boy with the megaphone. The teenager inched his way toward the open window. "Guh-get out of the car, sir."

Toby leaned out the window and casually flashed his virtual badge. "United States Fish and Wildlife Service, hotshot."

"Fish and Wildlife?" The young man peered in the window to get a closer look at the "badge." Toby flashed it again.

"That's what I said. Officer Duke Lucas. Are you hard of hearing?" The boy dropped his megaphone. As he was picking it up, Toby leaned over and whispered, "How was that?"

"Very butch," Talia said flatly.

"Exactly what I was going for." Toby turned back to the boy, who had now successfully retrieved his megaphone. "Now then, are we done here?"

"Done? Well, I was just...sir...wondering...why...."

"Wondering what, Sunshine? Spit it out."

"I was wondering why you were driving on the golf course."

Toby nearly broke character. "Golf course?"

Talia looked behind them and saw a golf cart with the words *Minnow Bay Golf Course Security* printed on the hood.

"Golf course...right." Toby looked at Talia. A golf ball hit the hood of the car with a *plunk*.

Talia leaned over Toby and stuck her head out his window. "Sorry about that, but we're investigating a band of rogue geese who've been disturbing the mating area of the Tasmanian spotted booby owl."

Toby elbowed her off his lap. "That's...that's right. I just used this vehicle to scare a few of the more blatant culprits away, and in doing so, I just saved the lives of countless...dotted booby owls. I'm doing God's work here. You don't want to get in the way of that, do you? You don't want to impede God's work, do you?"

The kid brought the megaphone up to his mouth, started to speak, and then brought it down. "Um, no sir. I guess not."

"Good." Toby flashed the virtual badge again. "Because you wouldn't want to get a citation from the Fish and Wildlife, a federal agency, would you?"

"No, this is just a part-time job."

"Take off, then. I'll let you know if we need you."

He took off. They sat back, staring out the windshield. It was a bright, sunny afternoon on the golf course. A flock of geese flew in the distance.

"I just impersonated a federal agent, didn't I?"

"Maybe." Talia said, scratching lightly at a particularly itchy patch of road rash on her elbow. "Is Fish and Wildlife a federal agency?"

"Ask Dicko."

"Shit."

"What?"

She held up Dicko. "The Lexus got away."

"Shit." Another ball hit the hood with a *plunk*.

*

At Deadman's Gulch, Toby parked the car slant-wise, somehow managing to take up enough space for three cars with the compact Mini Cooper. Talia put her hand on the door handle. "Okay then. I'll see you later."

Toby opened his door and hopped out. "If you think I'm going to blow a chance to lay my eyes on your crazy boss, you've got another thing coming." He slammed his door shut.

"Fine, but there's not much to see."

Inside, though, there was a lot to see and smell and hear. There was a strong aroma of curry, candles and...something else...honey, maybe? Chime-and-bell-heavy music played softly beneath the boisterous voices coming from the kitchen that was, for some reason, hidden behind a gold and cornflower-blue curtain. The desk had been covered with an orange and red tablecloth and two neat lines of elaborately etched silver serving dishes. Butter had strategically placed herself beneath a chair, presumably waiting for treats to fall from above. A petite woman of about sixty carried a triangle-shaped serving dish out of the kitchen. She had a bright white streak shooting through her dark hair and eyes like Port's.

"Oh, thank goodness, you're safe. Port!" The woman called toward the kitchen. "The kids are here, and they don't look any worse for wear."

"Talia?" The curtain snapped open. "Are you okay?" Port shuffled slowly out of the kitchen, leaving the curtain open to reveal counters littered with spice jars and an errant chair in front of a sink filled with odd clay pots. He dried his hands on a kitchen towel.

There was something about the scene—the concern in his eyes, the possibility that Port had washed dishes, the way he was standing on his own two feet like a normal person—that made her want to hug him and put her head on his shoulder, but instead she said, "I'm fine."

"I got an alert from Dicko, and I thought...." Port put one hand out and leaned against the wall, returning to his usual slump. "Are you sure you're okay?"

"I'm sure." Talia glanced over at the woman who was standing in the entryway, holding a serving dish and smiling at her.

"Please forgive me." Port shuffled toward the table and lowered himself into the largest of the chairs at the impromptu dining table. "This is my mother, Rupa Nepal. Mother, this is my brilliant assistant, Talia, and her sidekick, Toby." He winked at Toby when he said *sidekick*.

Belisa howled. Darla carried the post-bath, bunny-bathrobe clad baby into the kitchen. "Oh, what an adorable baby," Toby said. "She looks like she's going to a party at The Grotto."

"Hey, Starsky and Hutch. Nice to see you guys in one piece." Darla hitched Belisa up on her hip and the bunny ears jiggled.

"Darla, let me help you." Rupa put down her platter and ran over to her, grabbing the baby and kissing her cheeks. "Who is the most beautiful baby? It's Belisa!" Belisa flapped her arms and laughed.

Darla put an arm around Rupa. "I see how it is. You just flew out here to spoil my baby."

"That's part of it, but also," Rupa glanced at Port. "I wanted to be sure my son was eating. You see, Darla. You never stop worrying about them."

Darla pushed a wet lock of hair from Belisa's forehead. "I'm beginning to figure that out. Come. Time for your nap, *mija*." She pried the baby from Rupa's grasp.

"So soon?" Rupa frowned. "But you'll be joining us for dinner, won't you? There's so much!"

"I'd love to, but I was actually hoping you would watch Belisa for me." Darla smiled. "I have a date."

"A date?!" Port said. "Who is this scoundrel?"

The side door banged open. Ted walked in. Darla smiled at him. "Did you bring me a flower?"

Ted pulled something from behind his back. It stuck momentarily on the tails of the red-trimmed black tuxedo jacket he was wearing over his usual t-shirt and black jeans, but he managed to present it with a shaky flourish. "It's a basil plant. You always complain about how hard it is to keep basil fresh in the fridge."

"Well, you two lovebirds aren't staying. How about you two?" Rupa turned hopefully to Talia and Toby.

"I don't know.... We don't want to intrude." Talia did want to intrude, so she hoped Rupa would insist, and thankfully, she did.

*

While they lay the last dish on the table, Port's neighbor Irina showed up with paint splotches in her hair, ceramic dust under her fingernails, and with what she called "a bold little Malbec and a salacious Sangiovese." There were pickled potatoes, naan seasoned with a couple leaves from Darla's romantic basil plant, curried pumpkin-vine tips and a spicy dish that Rupa called Jwanu chicken.

Toby scooped a huge helping onto his plate. "Me. I ja wanna chicken."

Rupa smiled and raised her fork in victory and then turned to Port. "So, what is this big case that is so important that you had to risk the lives of these poor kids?"

"Well, I wouldn't say he risked our..." Talia said.

"I would. My whole life flashed before my eyes. I had to come out to my father all over again." Toby put his hand on Rupa's arm. "It was horrible."

Rupa nodded in sympathy and patted his hand.

"It's the Buster Bones case," Port said and then to Toby, "And I'm very sorry."

Toby waved it off. "De nada."

"You know, I met him once," Irina said. "It was at Ocean Beach."

"He used to surf there," Toby said.

"That's exactly what he was doing. Surfing. Well, not exactly. When I saw him, he was fighting." Irina's accent changed the soft *G* in *fighting* and *surfing* to a *K* sound.

"With his wife?" Toby asked.

"No, no. See, this is how it happened. It was three years ago, I remember because I was up for a fellowship, and I didn't get it. I was despondent because I thought it was something I needed. So, I went to Ocean Beach so I could...." Irina sighed and looked at the ceiling. "Oh, I don't know. I felt that I needed to stand in front of nature's terrible power and feel insignificant and unimportant."

"Oh! I so get that." Toby nodded at Irina, turned toward Talia, widened his eyes and shook his head slowly. He did not get it. Talia stifled a laugh.

Rupa shot them a look and then nodded at Irina. "Go on, dear. You were saying...the insignificant power of nature."

"Terrible. The terrible power of nature," Irina corrected. "Ocean Beach is a volatile place. The epicenter of the 1906 earthquake was right off the shore. Now, the undertow drowns swimmers. The waves *crush* the surfers." At the word *crush* she brought her hand down on the table with a loud *bang*. Toby jumped. Butter looked up briefly from her nap. "It's strange that a place so beautiful and full of life could at the same time bring such death and destruction."

"So...you saw Buster there?" Talia asked.

Irina picked up her glass, took a long sip and then slowly placed the glass back down. "I saw something in the water. Something black. I thought it was a seal, but then I realized, no, it was a surfer. Then...*swoosh*...another surfer cut in front of him. The first surfer fell with an incredible force. I thought he would surely drown. I waded out to try to...oh I don't know what I was going to do. I'm a terrible swimmer. There were not many opportunities to learn to swim in communist Czechoslovakia. Still, I pushed on against the force of the waves, and he came up out of the water in front of me. This man—gray-green eyes, like a sea during a squall, and black hair like midnight rain. I gasped. I don't pay too much attention to popular music, but I knew Buster Bones. He was the most famous man in this town, yes?"

They nodded in rapt agreement. Even Butter left her post at Port's feet to put her chin on Irina's lap.

"He was even more striking up close. I've been married for twenty-five years to a man I love so much, and right then, I wanted nothing more than for him to grab me, kiss me, roughly but passionately, and then just walk away without saying one word. Do you know what I mean?"

"Yes." Talia, Toby and Rupa said at the same time. The table burst into laughter.

"He didn't kiss me, but he looked at me, with those stormy eyes...well, he knew. He knew I had waded out to save him, and he was...I don't know...more than grateful—touched? At that moment, the other surfer rushed past us, creating a wave that nearly knocked me off my feet. Buster grabbed me before I fell. His grasp was firm, but soft as well.

Then another surfer rushed past and knocked Buster over. He let go of me so he wouldn't drag me down with him."

"A third surfer appeared out of nowhere. I looked in his face. He was smiling just as he rammed his surfboard into my upper thigh. I went down. Under the water, I didn't know the way up or down. I thought I would die there. Buster pulled me out of the water with great force. It was brutal and terrifying and joyous. And, just as I realized that I was going to live, I felt like I was being born all over again."

"We hooked arms and waded to the shore. Once we were safely on land, he looked in my eyes and pushed a lock of wet hair from my forehead. Now, in any other man, this action would seem brazen but with him...it was nice. Tender." Irina's eyes softened; even her accent seemed softer. "He didn't speak. He just pulled me close and hugged me. Hugged me—as if we weren't strangers who met in the rough surf of the Pacific but old lovers. I wanted to stay in his arms forever. But then one of the surfers called out, telling us to leave. They were standing on the beach, not too far from where we were."

"Buster told me to go. I did go, but slowly. As I walked up the sand, I heard him argue with the men. He told them that it wasn't their beach. They laughed and said it was. As if anything so wild and terrible could ever be owned by something as simple as a human being. Buster said, 'One of these days, you're going to kill someone.' And they laughed. I'll never forget the sound of that laughter. It was colder than the ocean." Irina looked at Toby. She grasped his hand. "I want you to know that I like you. I don't want to insult you."

"Okay, I like you too." Toby reached out with his free hand and flicked the nearly empty bottle so that the nail of his middle finger hit the glass with a *ping*. "I think you've had a little too much of the grape, but I like you, Irina."

"I think the surfers, the ones Buster argued with, I think they were gay."

"A gay surf gang?" Port said.

Toby dropped Irina's hand. "Holy shit!" He turned to Rupa. "Pardon my filthy mouth."

"Perfectly all right," Rupa said.

"Holy shit! Sorry, but I've heard about those guys. We did a story on them at the station once. They call themselves the Surf Pinks. You know, kind of like the Pink Ladies, only they rule the beach instead of Rydell High. They've been accused of bullying other surfers. On the morning we did the story, we got a caller who claimed that he'd nearly been drowned by a couple members of the Pinks."

"Do you think the caller was legit?" Port asked.

"Maybe. Those guys are badass." Toby sipped his wine. "I mean, they have to be, though. Can you imagine being gay and thrown into all that crazy cut-throat competition that goes on between Ocean Beach surfers? I think they banded together, initially, out of necessity, but it got out of hand."

"Port, do you think these surf pinkies could be connected to poor Buster's demise?" Rupa said.

Toby shot Talia a look as she struggled not to laugh out loud at Rupa's ability to make the possibility of a gang murder sound almost adorable. She glanced over at Port. He was smiling at her. Rupa poked Port in the arm. "Well? Do you?"

"I think it's worth looking into, but for now, we've got such a lovely little evening on our hands." Port raised his glass, looking around the table. "Let's not spoil it."

"Fine. I just have one question for Toby," Rupa said.

"Ask away."

"Who are the Pink Ladies, and where is Rydell High?"

"That's two questions, Roop."

Chapter Nineteen

The next morning, Talia couldn't sleep and assumed Port couldn't either, so she showed up a few hours early. The *crunch crunch* of the gravel under her feet and the distant foghorn reminded her of the second time she'd been there—for the interview. She looked down and watched her shoes disturb the white stones; a few were flecked with brightly colored paint. She looked up just in time to avoid walking into what looked like a taco truck with an SFPD logo on its side parked in front of Port's door.

She peered around the truck and saw Brad Nguyen standing on the front step of the warehouse. His hand grasped the doorknob, but he stood there for a long time until the door opened from the inside. Brad stepped back to make room for the woman who'd opened it.

"Brad! What are you doing sneaking around at this hour?"

"Rupa, come here and give me a hug, you sexy thing."

"Smooth talker." Rupa gave him a quick hug and a kiss on his cheek.

Brad held the door open. "Join me for coffee."

"I'm sorry. I'm on my way to the airport. My chariot awaits."

Talia craned her head around the bulk of the police truck and saw Ted opening the passenger-side door of Darla's Saab. He waved at Rupa and hooked an impatient thumb toward the open door as the door-is-ajar alarm persisted with a *beep beep beep*.

Rupa waved Ted off and turned to Brad. "I just flew in for the day. You know, to check in on my boy."

"How's he doing?"

"Too skinny and too sad, but maybe he will be a little less skinny. I brought a suitcase full of ingredients and left a freezer full of food."

"Get a move on, woman!" Ted yelled, slapping the roof of the car. He looked over at Talia. "Hey Blondie, guess who has two thumbs and got busy last night." He held up his two thumbs and waggled them.

Rupa turned and waved at her. Talia walked over, the *beep beep beep* of the door alarm competing with the *crunch crunch* of the gravel.

Rupa smiled and held her arms out. Talia smiled and hugged her. Rupa pulled away, put her hands on Talia's shoulders and pivoted her toward Brad. "Brad, have you met Talia?"

"Unfortunately, yes."

"I messed up his crime scene."

"Oh pssh! He should be so lucky." Rupa gave Talia's shoulder a squeeze

The horn honked.

"Keep your shirt on, Mason. I'm coming." Rupa hurried to the car and hopped into the passenger side. She waved one hand out of her window as Ted drove away.

Brad turned to Talia. "I have something for you."

He walked to the back of the police truck and unlocked the cargo door. It clanged loudly. The floor of the wagon was littered with zip-tie handcuffs. "Tsk. Look at that. Someone must have gotten a surprise when they arrived at 850 Bryant last night. Never put a drunk in zip cuffs, Talia. Drunks are notoriously slippery."

"I'll remember that.... Hey! That's my Vespa."

Brad slapped the side of the truck. "That's why I commissioned ol' Robo Wagon here, so you wouldn't have to stand in line at impound again. I had one of our mechanics put the side mirror back on, but I want to secure it, just in case. Other than that—barely a scratch on it. How about you?"

Talia held up her elbows. "Not too bad."

Brad examined the road rash that had already begun healing. "Not bad at all. You got lucky. Any better recollection of the car that did this?"

She nodded. "I'm almost positive it was a silver Lexus. The same car responsible for putting Kylie Kismet's doctor, Benji Cohen, in the hospital."

"That hit and run in San Jose? I know about that." Brad grabbed a handle on the inside of the door, put one foot up on the tailgate and pulled himself into the back of the truck.

"I don't have a license plate number, but do you think...?"

"Working on it." He rocked the Vespa off its kickstand and wheeled it to the tailgate. Talia grabbed the handlebars, and they lowered it to the ground.

Together, they wheeled the Vespa inside. The warehouse was quiet, dark and smelled of brewed coffee. "I guess Port is asleep," Brad said. "That's what a good, home-cooked meal will do for you."

Talia pointed into the kitchen, "Then who made the coffee?"

"The housekeeper." Brad pushed the Vespa through the living room. "You didn't think Port made his own coffee, did you?"

They opened the secret passage door, and wheeled the Vespa into the garage. Talia looked at the van and rubbed the gooseflesh on her arms.

"So, you heard about Port's end game, eh?" Brad said.

"How did you guess?"

Brad pulled open a drawer in a large, red tool chest. "Because it's warm in here, kid, and you're shivering." He held up a wrench. "Here's the one."

Talia sighed. "What was he like...before?"

Brad bent down, clacked the wrench around the bolt on the Vespa's side mirror and pulled a few times. He looked up and smiled. "You would've liked him. He was a hopeless romantic. I'll tell you a story about that if you like." Brad put the wrench back in the tool chest. "Not in the garage of insanity, though. Let's sit in the parlor—like civilized folk." He walked to the passage door, turned and waited for her.

She put her hand on the side mirror and tried to twist it. It budged slightly. She opened the drawer, grabbed the wrench, tightened the bolt a few more turns and handed the wrench to Brad on her way through the door.

*

Seated on the couch with their coffee cups in hand, Brad began his story. "Back in the day, Port and his partner, Julia Lake, were dating in secret. They didn't tell anyone. Not even me. I knew something was up, though, so I asked Port to meet me at Annie's—this old cop and lawyer bar across from the courthouse. It only took two Dewar's, the way Annie poured them, to get Port to spill. Port had this goofy smile whenever he talked about Julia, so I just asked him point blank if he was banging her, and the goofy smile turned into a shit-eating grin. He told me that the worst thing about dating in secret was that they couldn't ride in together. Can you beat that?" Brad laughed. "Port wanted to chariot his lady to the station like Prince Charming, but Julia insisted on taking the bus."

"She didn't drive?"

"Julia told me once that if she had a car, she'd forget to move it for the street sweeper, and it would end up costing her too much in tickets. She was a cop who worried about tickets. You got to love that." He took a sip of his coffee and leaned back. "I drove past her, once. She was waiting for the 38." He laughed and looked at Talia. "Now that's commitment. It's one thing to take Muni to work. It's quite another to take the 38."

Talia smiled. She'd taken that line many times herself. The last time she did, she got stuck between a woman holding a bag full of live fish and a man who smelled like a bag full of dead fish.

"So, there's Julia, standing there, and I'm just about to stop and offer her a ride, when I notice that the top of the bus stop is covered in pink daisies. There must have been hundreds of them. Julia was staring up at them. She had this smile.... It was such a private smile that I would've felt like I was intruding if I pulled over, so I kept driving."

"Port did that?"

"He must have, the old son of a bitch." He looked down at his feet. "You know, I told Port about that smile because I thought it would make him feel better, but...well, by then...."

A door opened at the other end of the warehouse. Butter bounded down the hallway and greeted Brad, shoving her nose in his crotch. He pushed the dog head from between his legs and gave her ears a scratch. Butter yawned and lay down at their feet.

Port emerged from the hallway, lumbering and breathing heavily. When Port saw Brad and Talia, he jumped. A little jump, but still, it was not the slow jump of the fat man he pretended to be but the quick jump of the thin former cop he really was.

"Good morning, Porty," Brad said. "Want me to whip you up an omelet?"

"No," Port said, still breathing heavy. "I'm skipping breakfast today. I ate too much at my mother's semi-annual fatten-up-the-fat-guy dinner party."

"Sounds nice," Brad said.

"It was." Talia smiled.

Brad raised his eyebrows at her and then said, "I'm sorry I wasn't invited."

"You know my mom hates you."

"Bullshit, that woman thinks the sun rises and falls with me. You, however, are a horrible son. Your mother goes through all this trouble to fatten you up and you go and skip the most important meal of the day."

"One of my daily injustices is that my mother is constantly trying to put more weight on her morbidly tubby son. And people say that I'm crazy." Port shuffled toward the living room, all signs of accidental spryness gone. He plopped into the oversized chair across from them, looked at Talia and pointed at Brad. "This guy knew me back when I was a looker, believe it or not."

"It's true." Brad smiled at her. "I could barely keep my hands off him, and I'm straight."

"Did you ever think, while we were on the force together, that I would turn into this monstrosity you see before you?"

"Nope. Still don't. I'm pretty sure it's just an illusion." Brad winked at Talia and then said, "Think about it. If you were really a big fat monstrosity, would this beautiful woman look at you the way she does?"

"I don't know what you're talking about." Port glanced at Talia and then quickly looked away.

Talia realized the tight spot Brad had just smiled and winked her into. If she disagreed with him, it meant telling Port that his perception of himself was correct: he was fat, incredibly so, but she loved him anyway. If she agreed with him, she would be admitting that she wouldn't be attracted to

Port if he were fat. If she did nothing but wait for an earthquake, or for someone to change the subject, she would still have to admit to herself that she was not the person Port saw. He saw an attractive woman who was falling for him despite his weight—a woman who looked past all his fat to see the real him. What would he think of her if he found out who she really was: a shallow person who was attracted to a possible murderer just because he was good looking?

Brad was talking about the armored car heist: "...found one of the middle men. It was that muscle head you told me about."

"The Krav Maga instructor?" Port said.

"Yeah, him. He's been crying like a baby and singing like a bird ever since we nabbed him. We're closing in on the guy at the top now."

Port raised an eyebrow at him. "That'll be a nice feather in your belt."

"I hope so. My belt is featherless." Brad pointed at his waist. "But getting back to what I asked before...."

"Hey," Talia said. "Did that glass ever turn up? The one from the Platinum Club crime scene?"

"Of course not. The perp took it with him."

"The perp took it?"

"That's what perps do. That's why we call them perps and not total sweethearts," Brad said. "But I'll tell you something. It was strange. The tights we found in the vic's apartment? They were all a brand you'd buy at one of those fetish stores in SoMa, but the tights we found around her neck were expensive numbers imported from France. They come in a fancy little black and pink box."

Talia looked up at Port when Brad said the words *black and pink box*. He raised his eyebrows and then looked away.

"Aha! So, here's how I interpret that little look you two just shared." Brad pointed at each of them in turn. "You two didn't know about the tights, but you know about something else, and I want to know what it is."

Port nodded at Talia. She turned to Brad. "I saw a pink and black box at Minnie's. I got the idea that someone special had given it to her."

"There. That wasn't so hard, was it?"

"There's more." Talia glanced at Port. "I saw Mark Lynn hand Minnie a black box the other day, but that was after Lulu's murder."

"Oh yeah? Maybe Lynn is Minnie's underwear pusher. That would be...." He stopped, looked at Port's face and then pointed at Talia. "You didn't tell Port about Lynn and his mysterious box, did you?"

Talia avoided Port's eye. "Not yet, but I was going to tell him."

Port shrugged. "See, Bradley? Perfectly reasonable explanation."

"Right. I'll make a deal with you, Porty. You give me all the evidence you've been hoarding, and I will give you the unnamed piece of evidence behind curtain number one." He tapped at a folded paper sticking out of his breast pocket.

Port rolled his eyes. "Here's what I know. That is your grocery list. I also know that you checked out our evidence board as soon as you walked in the door."

Brad walked over to the bulletin board behind the desk and lifted the scrap of blue fabric without unpinning it. "This? This is your evidence? It's probably nothing. Where'd you find it?"

"Studio 9. Talia found it in the utility closet."

"Huh. Wonder why our guys didn't find this first?"

"Because my girl is better than your guys." Port stared at Brad. "It's yours. Take it."

Brad unpinned the scrap of fabric from the bulletin board and put it in his pants pocket. He took the piece of paper out of his shirt pocket and dropped it onto Port's lap before walking to the door. He grasped the doorknob. "Hey, aren't you going to look at that paper? That's quality evidence right there."

Port kept his eyes on Brad. "I don't need to look at it to know what's on it. Some trendy vegetable that the girls at the gym told you to try. Kohlrabi probably. A twelve-pack of Sierra Nevada...."

"Six-pack, actually. I'm trying to cut back." Brad patted his stomach.

"...And a gallon jug of hair gel."

"This is natural...." Brad pointed first at his jet-black, well-styled hair and then at Port. "You're just jealous."

Brad opened the door and left. Port picked up the paper. Talia bounded across the room and sat on the edge of his chair. Butter jumped up onto the spot she'd been occupying on the couch. Port tapped her knee, still looking at the paper. "Let's trust each other from now on, okay?"

She nodded, her mouth too dry to speak.

The side door opened. Port dropped the paper. It floated down to the floor. They looked up. It was Ted. Talia bent, picked up the paper and handed it to Port.

"What's that?" Ted said. "You two passing love notes? Let me read it. I bet it's not as good as the erotic haikus I write for Darla."

"Ted, I know I just asked you to take my mother to the airport, but I'm afraid I'm going to ask for your services again. I am in need of some high caliber hacking."

"Name it, Port Reduction Sauce. Hey, what's this?" Ted grabbed the paper out of Port's hand. "Hot damn. This is the tox report." He squeezed onto the couch next to Butter. She grumbled, rolled over and then put her back paws on his lap. "Whoa. That's an assload of opiates."

"Opiates? Like heroin?" Talia said.

Port nodded. "A lethal dose."

She ran a hand through her hair. "So, Buster and Nigel Zone had been doing heroin that night?" Zone didn't seem like the type to do heroin. He seemed the type to do everything else, but not heroin.

"Minnie messed up. She should have just waited a few minutes and let the horse do the dirty work for her." Ted tossed the paper at Port. "Now, you said you needed some of my finer hackery."

Port looked over at Talia and then back at Ted. "Can you get me access to the DMV?"

Talia's phone vibrated. She held a finger up and walked into the kitchen to take the call.

"Remember that creepy motherfucker you told me about?" Minnie said. "The guy in the Black Star t-shirt?"

"Yes, but I...I'm not really sure who he is...."

"His name is Walter. He's from fucking Sparks, Nevada." The way Minnie said *Sparks* made it sound like another swear.

"How do you know that?"

"Because I'm aiming my gun at him right now."

Talia bolted off the couch and ran to the garage. She wheeled the Vespa outside. Brad was still standing on the front step, his ear pressed to the door. He started to stammer out an explanation about forgetting his wallet, but she cut him off. "Minnie just called me. There's a crazed fan on her doorstep, and she has a gun on him."

"Let's go," he said.

Talia put on her helmet and waved at Brad to get on the Vespa. He shook his head and pointed at the police vehicle.

"Brad, this is a delicate situation. I don't think we should roll up in a paddy wagon."

Brad shook his head.

Talia slumped onto the Vespa seat. "Come on. Don't you think we've had enough dead bodies?"

"Jesus!" Brad stomped over to her.

She gave him the spare helmet.

He grabbed it and pointed it at her. "Fine. But I'm driving."

"No, you're not." Talia pulled the brake with her left hand and pressed the ignition with her right. The Vespa started up. She revved the engine.

"Jesus." He climbed on the back.

"Hold on tight, Detective." She swung out in a wide loop to get out of the parking lot.

He grabbed onto her waist as they hit the street. "If you see a squad car, do me a favor and dump me off the back."

*

Brad pulled out a notebook and flipped it open. "So, when did the guy leave?"

Minnie leaned against the doorjamb. She was wearing a black t-shirt, black yoga pants, and pink flip-flops. "Right after I told him exactly what I'd do to him if he didn't." She looked behind her and then back at Brad. "What the fuck are you looking at, cop?"

"Lot of mail there."

"I get mail. Is that a fucking crime?"

Brad pointed at the little hallway table behind Minnie. "That's a fancy French-looking box. Wouldn't happen to be filled with fancy French tights, would it?"

Minnie shook her head. "You've got some fucking nerve, cop, asking me about my underwear after that crazy fucker tried to rape me."

Brad held up his hands. "Fair enough."

Talia stepped in front of him. "He tried to rape you? Minnie, are you okay?"

"I'm fine."

"What happened?"

"I answered the door. This fucking guy was standing on my doorstep with his dick in his hands. He looked right at me, pointed at his dick and said, 'I'm here to take care of you.' I pointed my gun at him and said, 'The fuck you are, you fucking fuckhead.' Then I called you, but if I knew you were going to bring the cop, I wouldn't have fucking bothered."

"Sorry about that. He's hard to shake."

"It's true. I am." Brad held out his hand, palm side up. "Look, Minnie. I want you to be able to protect yourself, but I'm going to need to look at that gun."

Minnie looked at his hand and then sneered at him. "I gave it to a friend of mine."

"Can I speak to this friend?"

"He left."

"So, you're telling me that between the time you called her...." He pointed at Talia. "And we drove Barbie's dream death machine from the other side of the city, some mysterious friend showed up, took your gun and left? What? Your pleasant company wasn't enough to keep him hanging around?" Minnie glared at him. Brad looked down, ran a hand through his hair, and sighed. "All right, then. I'll come back with a warrant."

"Fuck you, fuckhead." Minnie slammed the door.

They turned and walked back toward the Vespa. Talia stopped and looked down at a row of lit candles, the flames flickering in the wind. "What time are you coming with that warrant?"

He shrugged. "I'll probably want to get breakfast before I have to deal with Little Miss Swears-A-Lot again."

"Perfect." Talia tossed him the keys, ran back to the door and rang the bell.

"Go away, cop," Minnie said over the melody of "Walk of Love."

"He's gone, Minnie." Talia turned and looked at the walkway. Brad was still standing there, holding the keys. She waved him away. He climbed on the Vespa, shaking his head. She turned back to the door. "I'm sorry I brought him, but I was afraid for you."

Minnie opened the door. "That was fucking stupid."

Minnie turned and walked into the hallway, leaving the door open behind her. Talia stepped into the house and followed her through a baby gate into a room where Ruth and Robert were crawling around, playing with toys. The women sat on two red chairs made for much smaller people. Talia pressed her knees together and tilted her legs, so her ankle was nearly flat on the floor.

Robert crawled over to Minnie and tried to pull himself up on her knee, but his legs were too wobbly, and he sat hard on his bottom. Minnie bent down and patted the fine black hair on his head. There was a long silence before Talia filled it. "Minnie, did Buster ever talk to you about an altercation with a surf gang?"

"The Surf Pinks? Yeah. He fucking hated them. He said they were ruining the sport. But then one day, he tells me that he changed his mind about the Pinks. He says they're great guys, and they're good for the Ocean Beach surfing culture." A wooden train flew across the room and fell at Minnie's feet. She clapped her hands twice. "No throwing!" She reached down and grabbed the train. "This is mine now." The babies looked up at her. Ruth picked up a wooden block and stuck it in her mouth, chewing on one corner.

"Why the turn-around?"

"I never knew why. We didn't talk about surfing much. That was his thing." While she talked, Robert grabbed Minnie's knee, pulled himself up and dropped a doll in his mother's lap.

"Minnie, is there a chance that you might be implicated in Lulu's murder?"

"Who? The stripper? Why would I be a fucking suspect?"

"There are rumors that Buster was having an affair with her. She said that he broke it off because of you."

Minnie stared straight ahead. "I didn't know about that slut. I thought Buster stuck to his fucking groupies."

"So, you didn't even...."

"I didn't fucking know about that slut." Ruth tossed a pale-yellow blanket at Minnie's feet. Minnie bent down, picked up the blanket, folded it and put it on her lap.

Talia sighed. "Who gave you that black and pink box? It seemed special."

"I don't remember a package like that."

"It was in the hall when Detective Nguyen was here, but it was gone when I came back."

"I get a lot of fucking packages."

Robert held up a board book with a cat on the front cover. He started to hand it to Minnie, but then opened it instead, pointing at the pictures and babbling.

Talia leaned closer to Minnie, so that she couldn't avoid her eye. "Please, Minnie. It's important."

Minnie leaned even closer and looked directly into Talia's eyes. "I never saw that fucking package."

"Okay." Talia leaned away. "Then what did Mark Lynn give you? It was in a black box."

Minnie laughed. "No. It wasn't *in* a black box. It *was* a black box." She stood up. "Grab a baby. I'll show you."

Minnie led her into a large master bedroom. It was decorated in all white with birchwood floors and accents of pale green. Talia was suddenly in awe of the fact that she was standing in Buster Bones' bedroom. Minnie sat on the bed. Talia stood and bounced Ruth on her hip. It didn't seem right to sit on the bed, but then Robert reached for Ruth. Talia sat next to Minnie so the babies could poke at each other.

Minnie reached into a neatly organized drawer in her nightstand and pulled out a black cardboard box. She opened it and handed it to Talia. Talia looked inside and then at Minnie. "Is this a diorama?"

"It's our family. Vincent made it." She pointed at the little painted clay figures that had been glued to the inside of the box. "There's me and Vincent. There's Joanne and Miranda. The babies. And look, Buster has a little guitar." Her eyes misted over.

"That is so sweet. He even drew your house in the background."

"He gave it to Buster to take to the studio, so he wouldn't forget his happy home. Mark Lynn found it and brought it back for me. I guess the fucking cops didn't steal it like I thought." Tears filled Minnie's eyes and spilled down her cheeks faster than she could wipe them away.

Talia couldn't hug her because she had a baby on her lap, so she put her arm around her. Minnie laid her head on her shoulder and sobbed.

*

Talia stood at the edge of the driveway. She could see patches of ocean between the houses. If she put one foot into the street and looked down the hill, she could see the scraggly trees that indicated the top of a cliff. If she lived in this little house, perched on this cliff with its scraggly trees and ocean view, she'd never want to leave. She put her hand in her pocket for the key, forgetting that she'd given it to Brad. She stood there, looking at a patch of ocean and thinking about how Buster carried around his world in a little black box while partying like Ozzy with Nigel Zone.

Her phone beeped, pulling her out of her trance. It was a text from Port that read simply, *Zone drives a silver Lexus.* She was about to respond when a call came in.

"Hi, Mark."

"Hi, Maggie. I'm calling to ask you on a real date—with waiters and food and cloth napkins and corsages. The whole thing."

"Okay, but...."

"Okay, no corsages but the rest of it is not up for negotiation."

"Good. Can you pick me up at Minnie's house?"

"You're at Minnie's? What are you doing there?"

Talia looked at the makeshift memorial on Minnie's lawn—a large wool blanket held down by a circle of black candles. "I have to go." She hung up, clicked on her photos and scrolled through them. She found the one she'd taken of Studio 9's alley. There, between the two dumpsters, was the same blanket and the same candles.

She stepped gingerly around the flowers and stuffed animals on the lawn, keeping an eye on that blanket with the oddly shaped lump beneath it. Something crunched loudly at her feet. She held her breath and looked down. It was an old cassette tape. She looked at the blanket. No movement. She took a small step.

The blanket flew, as if on its own, into the air and landed on Talia's head. It smelled like incense and old laundry. She pushed it off in time to see Star Tee running down the hill. She ran after him. He careened, feet sliding, his arms windmilling, into the intersection. A car screeched to a halt. Star Tee couldn't stop in time and landed with his body sprawled out against the hood.

The car honked. Star Tee used both hands to push himself off the hood and into a standing position. The horn honked again. He held his arms out, Jesus-on-the-cross style and closed his eyes. The car drove around him with a horn blast and an emphatic middle finger thrust out the window. Star Tee opened his eyes and looked at Talia.

She held up her hands. "I just want to talk."

"I didn't do anything to Minnie."

Talia looked him over. His cheeks looked more sunken, his eyes even more haunted than when she'd met him in the alley. "I know that, Walter. Is that your name? Walter?"

He shook his head. "That's the name Buster gave me." He started to back away.

She took a step toward him. "How did Buster give you a name?"

"He sent me a message in his lyrics." He stared at a spot behind her head. His eyes were a pale shade of green, almost colorless in the sun.

"A message?"

"Walter. Take care of her. Walter, when they take me down." He turned and sprinted away.

Chapter Twenty

"This is not exactly what I meant by a real date," Mark said.

Talia held up her egg-white and turkey-bacon breakfast wrap and pointed at Mark's apple fritter. "What? We've got food. Didn't you say a real date had to have food?"

"Yes, brought by waiters, not a barista with a septum piercing, and it should be eaten on plates, not in my car."

"What do you mean?" Talia looked around at the pile of travel mugs in the backseat and pointed at the St. Christopher's medal hanging from the rearview mirror. "I think it's got great ambiance. Besides, I tried taking the Vespa on a stakeout, and it didn't work...remember?"

"How could I forget, but I...."

"Oh! Get down. Here he comes." Nigel Zone walked out of his apartment building: a converted Victorian in a mostly residential neighborhood.

They ducked under the dashboard. Mark opened his mouth to speak. She put a finger on his lips. Mark lifted his head just enough to look in his side mirror. "He's heading for the bus stop. He must have gotten another DWI."

Following the 14-bus down Mission, Mark stayed a few cars behind and kept to the right. When the bus pulled to a stop, Talia had a clear view of the sidewalk where the riders would be getting off until a delivery truck in front of them pulled over to the curb, blocking her view. She leaned out the window.

"I hope Nigel doesn't see you hanging out the window like a Labrador retriever."

Talia fell back into her seat. "I don't think he saw me, but he's off the bus."

"Which way is he going?"

"Turn left here."

Drivers honked when they slowed to keep pace with the less than speedy Zone as he waddled down Sixteenth Street. Thankfully, he didn't turn his head to see what all the honking was about. It was only a matter of time before he did, and then he'd surely notice the Honda holding up traffic thirty feet behind him. Talia pulled out Dicko and typed "in car and following subject on foot."

"Pull over. Watch subject."

"That thing does not elaborate, does it?" Mark said, pulling into a metered spot.

Talia pointed at Zone's retreating form. "He's crossed the street. He must be going down Folsom."

They parked on Folsom several times before Zone slunk into a sex shop.

Talia turned on the radio and changed the station to KGAY. They were playing a promo for a popular segment on Toby's show called Stump the Rock God. A caller asked Toby what Janis Joplin used to mix with her Southern Comfort. Toby replied, "Sadness." There was a sad trombone sound effect, laughter and then the jingle came in: "*If it's gay and in The Bay, it's on KGAY.*"

Talia chuckled softly even though she'd heard that promo more than a dozen times. Mark guffawed, slapping the steering wheel. Talia laughed louder, more at Mark's outburst than Toby's joke. They listened to the radio for what seemed like an excessive amount of time for anyone, even Zone, to be in a sex shop. Finally, Mark said, "Maybe he's just messing with us. I'll bet he knew we were tailing him the whole time."

"Yeah. He's probably putting a banana in your tailpipe right now."

"Beverly Hills Cop. Nice." Mark smiled at her.

There was something about the way he was looking at her that made her wish that they were on a proper date and not waiting for Nigel Zone to emerge from a sex shop. "Mark, do you mind if I ask you a question about Crunch Pup?"

"I knew it! You are a fan." He leaned over and tucked a lock of hair behind her ear.

"I was wondering. Do you remember the lyric 'Walter, take care of her. Walter, when I go down'?"

He frowned. "Damn it. You're not a fan."

"What do you mean?"

"Well for one thing, that's not the lyric. It's 'Water, take and carry her. Water, worry me down.' And it's not a Crunch Pup lyric. It's Buster Bones. A hidden track. Off *Sparkle Time*, remember that one?"

"Yeah, but wait...hidden track? Is that like a secret message?"

He sighed. "Oh, very young one! Back in the day, us old-timers used to put hidden tracks on CDs that would come on maybe fifteen or twenty minutes after you thought the CD was over. Usually, it was a song that didn't fit with the rest of the album for whatever reason—maybe it was a cappella or in Esperanto or had weird lyrics. 'I'll Be Gone,' that song you misquoted, didn't fit in with the rest of the album because he had his old friend play on it." He pointed at himself and then looked down. When he looked up, he looked out the window and not at her.

"Oh shit. He's on the street." He pointed at Zone's thick form as it shuffled across Folsom.

Mark put his hand on the ignition key, but then stopped, peered through the windshield and leaned back. "He's going into another sex shop." He laughed.

She turned in her seat so she could face him. "Mark?"

"Yes."

"There was a meeting at Studio 9 the other day with Devin, Gary and a few other people. Why weren't you there?"

He laughed. "You never stop with the PI routine, do you, V.I. Warshawski?

She shrugged. "It's not a routine. It's an important case."

"I know...it's just there are some things you don't understand."

"Like what?"

"Have you ever been in a close group of four friends?"

She shook her head.

"Well, they tend to split up into two groups of best friends who hang together. For us, it was Devin and Gary and then me and Buster. After the falling out, it was Devin and Gary and then Buster and Minnie..." he sighed. "With me on the outside of it all. So, for Gary and Devin to meet without me is just par for the course."

"Gary said it was an impromptu Buster memorial."

He narrowed his eyes and looked away, shaking his head a little. "He's been in there for a really long time."

Ten minutes later, Zone finally left the second sex shop and hailed a cab.

The cab traveled up Folsom, through Leather Alley, past the bars flying rainbow flags above their windowless fronts and fetish leather stores with names like Soma Buzz and Kittens with Whips. When they turned onto Leavenworth, they crossed Market and drove into the Tenderloin, past a group of men and women slouched under a theater awning fumbling with crack pipes as the business crowd walked in wide circles around them. The neighborhood improved as it slanted up the hill. The crackheads stuck to level ground; walking up hills was for the wealthy and healthy. Talia pointed out the window. "This is my neighborhood."

"Really?" Mark made a slow lane change to avoid a double-parked laundry truck. "Do you call it the Tenderloin or the Tendernob?" he said, referring to the neighborhood name that was a mash-up of Tenderloin and Nob Hill. The Tendernob wasn't quite at the top of the hill, but wasn't at the bottom either.

"Tendernob, of course," she said with fake indignation.

Zone didn't stop in her neighborhood. When the cab turned onto Lombard, they speculated that he was going to have an early drink at the Bird's Nest, but the cab kept driving: through the Marina, over the Golden Gate Bridge and into Marin. It finally pulled over in an upscale residential neighborhood. Mark pulled into a spot across the street from where Zone had gotten out of the cab.

"Why did you pull over here? He'll see us." Talia sunk down in her seat.

"Because I know where we are."

Tap tap tap.

Mark opened his window.

"Marky. How's it hanging, mate?" Zone leaned into the car. He smelled like cheap booze and cherry-scented air freshener. "Ah! I see you're making-out with a bird. Care if I join in? Wait. I know you. Honey tits! No. What was it?" Zone looked up and scratched his neck. "Pudding knickers? No. Vanilla something?"

"My name is Axel Foley."

"Vanilla Legs!" Zone leered at her. "What are you doing slumming with this guy when you could be slamming with DaZone?"

"Ah, the lovebirds!" Doc Gray pushed in beside Zone. "Our friend Nigel got a little drunk last night, so I drove his car with the promise of paying for his cab." He nodded at Zone. "Which, by the way, I just did."

"Is that what you did, mate?" Zone looked him up and down. "I thought you tried to cut his bleeding face off."

"You caught me." Doc Gray held up a pair of shears. "I like to garden. I find it relaxing. Come on in. I'll show you my yard." He gestured with the shears toward a gray and green bungalow across the street with a silver Lexus parked in the driveway. It looked freshly washed but was covered in various dings, dents and scratches.

*

The sun shone on the crumbling stone patio bordered by an overgrown but colorful flower garden, glinting off the odd bit of mica in the concrete or shiny-backed honey bee sniffing at the lavender. Talia had been living in the fog for so long, she'd forgotten that real summer could be found just a few minutes over the bridge. She looked up. A ribbon of thin, fast-moving clouds floated past the sun, blocking its light before moving on. She scooted her chair a few inches into the shade of a lemon tree.

Zone must have thought she was scooting toward him because he leaned over and whispered, "Ditch the twat and I'll drive you home, but don't tell your Johnny Law. I'm supposed to be off the road."

"But you're not off the road?"

Zone held a stubby, long-nailed finger to his lips. "I'm a naughty boy."

"You didn't happen to drive to the Kylie Kismet concert two nights ago, did you?"

"Kylie bloody Kismet? That little trollop who was hanging on to Buster like he was the last bit of meat on the bone? Not bloody likely. Besides, two nights ago, I was in the same place I'm going to be tonight. The place where we met, Vanilla Legs."

"Did you drive?"

"Did I?" Zone stared blankly at the sky. "No. I didn't. I took a cab home. I remember because I vomited in it." He ran a hand over the salt-and-pepper stubble on his cheek. "At least, I hope that was a cab."

Mark shook his head. "You are a piece of work, Nige."

"Do people drive you around in your car a lot?" Talia said.

"Of course." Zone held his arms out wide as though he were the Greek god of getting driven around. "Especially the lightweights like Devin and your man here." He waggled a finger at Mark.

Doc Gray walked out with a tray of glasses. "Lemonade from my own tree."

"No vodka?" Zone took the glass and sniffed at it. "But then how will I get pissed?"

Doc Gray sighed as he handed out the other glasses. "I want you to promise me you'll stop partying so much, old friend. I don't want to lose another patient."

Talia's phone vibrated. It was Brad. She excused herself and stood behind a cobweb-covered hedge to answer the call.

"Hey, Talia. Have you had lunch yet?"

"I had a late breakfast. Why? Are you going to take me out for lunch?"

"No. I need you to ID a body for me, and I don't need you barfing all over my crime scene."

*

On their way over the Golden Gate Bridge, Toby called. He had been looking into the Surf Pinks when he came across a tweet about them suiting up at Ocean Beach. "They're there right now, Tea. Want to go investigate?"

"Meet me at Studio 9."

"What are you doing there?"

"Nothing good, Tobe."

When they arrived at the studio, Brad walked over and clasped a hand on Mark's shoulder. "Hey Mark! How's it going?" Without waiting for an answer, Brad turned Mark by the shoulders toward the studio entrance. "See that woman over there?" He pointed at a petite woman in an oversized SFPD windbreaker. "That's Detective Garcia. She's a big Crunch Pup fan. Go give her an autograph."

"You're trying to get rid me, aren't you?"

"Why would you think that?" Brad patted him on the back, nudging him away. "Go on now. She's a busy public servant. Don't keep her waiting."

He turned to Talia and winked at her. "You're either working your suspect, or you brought a date to a crime scene. Either way, I'm impressed."

Talia glanced over at Mark, who was trying to escape an overzealous hug from Detective Garcia. "You said something about a body."

He put his hands on her shoulders and looked in her eyes. "Listen, this is a gnarly one." He pushed down slightly, as though he were trying to keep her from running away. "Don't go in there and contemplate his humanity. Don't try to identify random bits of goo. That's a road that leads straight to Barf City. Just go in, look at the stiff and get back here. Okay?"

Talia meant to say, "Of course. I got this." But only managed to say, "Ahf...."

Brad leaned closer. She could smell the mint from the gum he was chewing. "Listen, you can do this. You're a professional. Well...not now but you will be when you get out of that alley." He gave her a little push. Talia took a few steps, then turned back and nodded once to let Brad know she could do this. He pointed at the alley.

She walked past the side door of Studio 9 and looked down. The rock was still there along with a smattering of cigarette butts, but she didn't see a dead body. Was this Brad's idea of hazing the new girl? The only spot in the alley she couldn't see was on the other side of the dumpster across from her and to the left. She took two steps and saw it.

She stumbled backwards, gasped, and then clamped a hand on her mouth as though she had disturbed the man slumped in a pool of blood. She looked him over—careful not to contemplate his humanity. He was a dark-haired man wearing a red shirt. A throng of chills ran up and down her arms just as her face broke out in a hot sweat despite the breeze swirling through the alley. Doc Gray's sunny garden seemed a hundred miles away.

She couldn't remember what Brad had said to her, only the weight of his hands on her shoulders. She took a step back and looked again. She'd been wrong. His shirt wasn't red, it was soaked in blood. His hair wasn't dark, it was gone...along with the top of his head. She was aware of an odor that made her think of seafood. Before she could think any more about the odor and rate it as good or bad, she pulled her shirt over her mouth and nose so the only part of her face that was exposed was her eyes. For some reason, that helped. She thought of herself as a being made up of no brain, soul, body or stomach...only eyes. Eyes that could look at a dead body and take in its parts—deep-set eyes, sunken cheeks, long, lanky arms, the unmistakable outline of a star beneath the large blood stain.

She turned, as a jagged red ring expanded and contracted at the edges of her vision. With each step, the exit stretched out in front of her, and just as she thought she'd never get back out onto the sidewalk, she emerged—victorious and about to throw up. She ran toward an ashcan, bent over it, retched and spat. She thought for sure she was going to vomit, but then she reminded herself that she was eyes, only eyes. She turned toward the wind-swept bay and took in a large gulp of air.

"Was that the guy?" Brad was standing next to her.

"That's him. I'm sure of it." Hoping her voice sounded calmer than she felt.

Brad nodded. "Interesting. He had an ID on him. His name isn't Walter. It's David Beeman. He wasn't from Nevada. He was from Pinole—a local boy."

Mark jogged over. "Are you okay?" He put his arms out, but Talia stepped back, trying to avoid the real possibility of puking on his shoes.

"Of course she's okay." Brad slapped her on the back. "She's a pro." He turned to Mark. "So, did you give Detective Garcia your autograph?"

"*My* autograph? No." He shook his head. "I tried to, but that woman over there seems to be under the impression that I am Richard Marx, and I didn't want to disappoint her." The woman waved and blew Mark a kiss. He caught it, put it in his front pocket, and then pulled it out and showed it to Brad. "See this? This is Richard Marx's kiss."

A car pulled up behind Mark's Honda and honked. Brad turned toward the sound. "What fresh hell is this?"

Mark shrugged. "La Marseillaise?"

Talia smiled. "It's the Blue Meanie."

"Hey, Tea! Shake a leg," Toby yelled and then, after glancing at the gathering of uniformed officers, lowered his voice slightly to a stage whisper. "I'm in a red zone."

Brad pointed at Toby. "Who is that and what is he doing here?"

"That's Toby. I told him to meet me here," Talia said.

Brad shouted at Toby. "What's going on? You two working on a lead?"

"What's going on here?" Toby shouted back. "Another dead body? Can I look at it?"

"Get out of here." Brad waved at Toby's car like a traffic cop.

Talia jogged toward the car, glad for the rush of crisp air filling her lungs and chasing the nausea away. She opened the car door. "Hey Mark! Thanks for the date." Mark smiled and blew her a kiss. She caught it and put it in her pocket.

Chapter Twenty-One

As the Meanie drove along Golden Gate Park, into The Sunset, and toward Ocean Beach, a thick white fog bank rolled toward them.

On the beach, Talia pulled her jacket around her and stomped on the icy sand, feeling the cold through the soles of her shoes. To the right, she could see the bright, rainbow-shaped sails of the kite surfers who skated along the waves near the Cliff House. Far to the left, the hang-gliders were hovering in the air like seagulls over the cliffs near Daly City. Straight ahead, the plovers chased the waves as the wind whipped along the water, sending fluffy foam skittering along the sand.

"Check it out." Toby pointed straight ahead at something out in the water. "Do you think those are the Pinks?"

Talia could only see a dark, dotted line out near the horizon. "I can't even tell if they're surfers or sea lions." Talia pulled out Dicko and typed, "Need to interview surfers, but they're too far out."

A map appeared on the screen. A red line ran from where they stood to a spot marked with a bright yellow star, a few blocks up Judah Street. They decided that it would be easier to get to the yellow star on Judah than to that dotted line way out near the horizon. After a ten-minute walk, Dicko flashed the message: *You are here.*

They looked up at the sign. "Smokey's Surf Shop"

Talia checked Dicko. The screen was dark except for the words *rent surf equipment* in white block letters. They stepped into the cluttered little shop that was filled with racks and racks of thick black wetsuits and smelled of rubber and patchouli. The clerk hooked them both up with wetsuits and boards. He threw in a little waterproof pouch at no extra charge. "For your cell phone," he said, pointing at Dicko. They brought the gear back to the Meanie and took turns changing into their wet suits. Once Toby had stopped yelling about the indignity of wearing fetishwear in public, they plunked onto the cold sand, which was considerably warmer with the wetsuits.

Dicko buzzed an alert. Talia checked it. "Oh shit."

Toby groaned. "What is that bitch telling me to do now? Do I need to vote Republican or something? I won't do it." He turned away, crossing his arms.

Talia put the screen in front of his face. He read the directions out loud. "Get in the water and paddle out to the surfers. Well, duh, Teabag. What did you think it was going to say?"

"I don't know." She looked out at the dark gray, almost black, water. "Stand on the beach looking like a surfer until one of them comes to you?" She typed the words *too scared* into Dicko.

"What does it say?"

"It says, 'even in the middle of sheer terror, it is important to behave as manly as possible.'"

"That's a tall order for this duo." Toby put an arm around her. "You don't have to do this. We can just walk to the nearest bar and ask them if they serve kinky sea lions." Talia leaned her head on his shoulder. He patted her head and said, "Minnie probably did it anyway. Let's get real."

Talia thought about Minnie's face when she looked at that little black box with her family in it. She stood, hitched her surfboard under her arm and said, "Let's do this fucking thing."

Talia ran down the sand, took three steps into the water and then ran back to dry land. This happened three more times before Toby put his hands on her shoulders and looked in her eyes. "Look, bitch. An hour ago, you were alone in a dark alley with a gross body. If you can do that, you sure as shit can go for a little swim."

A few minutes later, she was paddling her board out past the crashing waves to a relatively calm spot where the water rolled gently beneath her. It helped to clear her mind of everything but a single mantra (a trick she'd learned in yoga class): *let's do this fucking thing* over and over, but that was a bit too wordy, so she edited it down to *paddle paddle paddle.*

"When the fuck are we going to stop fucking paddling?" Toby yelled over the sound of the wind and waves.

"Paddle paddle!" Talia yelled back.

A dark, hulking figure glided toward them. Talia peered at it, thinking, "paddle paddle paddle."

The hulking figure grew closer revealing itself to be three surfers in a V formation. They crouched on their surfboards in what was either the "about to catch a wave" position or the "kill the newbies" position. The surfers advanced and hit her surfboard with a thunk. She fell into the water. For about a second, she allowed herself to think that she was going to die there in the ocean, sliced up by the motor of a passing boat. Then she started another mantra: *swim, swim, swim.*

Strong fingers grabbed her arm. She struggled against them but was violently pulled out the water. She screamed.

"Bitch, stop screaming."

"Toby?"

"Who'd you expect? Aquaman?" Toby pulled her up onto his surfboard. She looked around for her board, but it was lost. She straddled the board, coughing up water, and trying to catch her breath. "Talia?" Toby said.

"Yeah?"

"Why the hell were you screaming 'fire' just now, in the water?"

"Was I?" Talia coughed. "I must have...oh, they teach you that in self-defense class because no one will come if you yell 'rape.'"

"How about yelling 'I'm drowning?' or...oh good lord!" Toby was looking at something over her shoulder. She turned. Two more surfers (crouched in what she now knew was the "drown the newbies" position) were speeding toward them.

"Shit!" Talia grabbed Toby. Toby wrapped his arms around her.

They held their ground—floating above the waves, shaking in fear and holding on to each other until Toby screamed, "Fire! Fire! Will someone please call the fire department? I'm about to get killed by a gay surf gang. I mean...fire!"

Talia buried her head in the crook of Toby's shoulder. The wave swelled beneath them and then a male voice yelled "Hey!" right before the collision.

They tumbled into the icy water. Right as she hit the water, she did something stupid. She thought about sharks. She thought about how surfers got attacked by sharks because their slick, black wetsuits made them look like seals. Talia tried to kick her legs in the most unseal-like way possible, which was barely at all, so she began to sink at an alarming speed. She pushed all her thoughts, especially ones about sharks, out of her head with her *swim swim swim* mantra, but it was more of a *swim swim seal legs swim shark bite swim* mantra until something clamped down on her forearm. She flailed.

Whatever was clamped onto her arm pulled her out of the water. Talia collapsed onto the surfboard and kissed it. A small wave lapped over the board and into her mouth. She sputtered and coughed and was knocked off balance, nearly falling back into the water. She didn't have the strength to *swim swim swim* one more time. Her mantra would now be *shark shark shark here sharkee sharkee.*

"Careful, honey. You don't want to go back in the drink," a male voice that was not Toby's said.

Not Toby's voice? Had one of the Pinks saved her from drowning only to murder her on his surfboard? She looked behind her, holding one arm up defensively against the tire iron that would be poised above her head, ready to strike.

Instead, she saw a slight, fair-haired man with a toothy grin and wide-set blue eyes. "Sorry about the fender bender, sweetie. We'll get you two back on dry land in no time."

Talia turned to the right and saw Toby draped across another surfboard, flirting with the male model who was currently paddling him back to shore. Toby waved. "Hey, Teabag! This is Brent."

"Hi, Brent." Talia did not wave but held onto the surfboard with both hands until they got to shore.

They'd barely emerged from the water when two men rushed over to them with blankets. It was two of the surfers who'd buzzed them. They each had a pink diamond sewn a few inches above the right breast on their wetsuits. "Surf Pinks," she murmured.

"Sh. Save your energy," Brent said. "You'll need it to keep warm." He looked up the beach. "Finally."

A man ran toward them, holding a large paper bag. "Don't worry, my little victims of disaster, I'm coming."

"That's Mario," Talia's blonde rescuer/attacker said. "He's got a flair for the dramatic."

"Hush, you." Mario sat cross-legged in the sand next to Toby. Talia saw he also had a pink diamond on his wetsuit. "Okay, I've got two skinny lattes, but tragically...." Mario paused, inhaling sharply. "They were all out of cinnamon. Ugh! I know." He handed each of them a cup. "What kind of coffee shop runs out of cinnamon?"

"Oh, my god," Toby said. "This latte is awesome."

"Are you sure? It doesn't simply reek of lack of cinnamon?"

"It's very good," Talia said, but was just glad to be alive and had no opinion on the latte other than the cup was keeping her hands warm.

Mario stared at Toby. "Can I ask you something?"

"Of course." Toby held his coffee cup close to his face, inhaling the steam.

"Are you Toby the Flaming Rock God?"

"The one and only, baby." Toby grinned.

A squeal louder than anything heard on the dance floor of a Castro club during Pride Week went up the beach, frightening a group of plovers. "I told you guys," Mario said, and then turned to Toby. "We're all huge fans!"

"Oh, good," Talia said. "Then you're not going to kill us?"

*

Toby pushed open the door of The Undertoe, the fog-muted sunlight cutting a dim swath through the darkened bar. "Look, Tea!" He pointed at the line of surfers, wetsuits pulled down to their waists, sitting at the bar. "They serve sea lions here." They piled into a dark corner booth, and over a round of beers, the Surf Pinks told their side of Irina's story.

"Your rivals actually call themselves the Homophobes? In San Francisco?" Talia said.

"I know. Can you believe it? None of the OB surfers have been particularly welcoming, but The Homophobes have been actively and violently trying to kick the Pinks off the beach for years." Steve, Talia's rescuer, pointed to a long, jagged scar that ran the length of his forearm. "One of those beasts gave me this."

Mario shrugged. "We didn't know who Buster Bones was, but he was a dead ringer for one of the leaders of the Homophobes. I'd blame myself, but it really wasn't my fault. How am I supposed to know what Buster Bones looks like?"

Steve pointed at Mario. "Now, if Cher decided to go surfing...."

"Oh, that would be fabulous!" Mario grabbed Steve's index finger and shook it back and forth. "Do you think Bob Mackie would design her wetsuit?"

"See, this is why you need to educate yourself about classic rock." Toby shook his head. "Cher is not going to go surfing. She isn't even going to button her own fringed jacket."

Brent tapped Toby on the arm. "I know about classic rock. Remind me to show you my Van Halen tattoo sometime."

Talia took a sip of her beer and put the glass on the table with a *clunk*. "I heard that Buster changed his mind about the Pinks, though. When was that?"

"When we saved his life." Brent leaned back and casually put a hand on Toby's shoulder. "Like with you two today...only then it wasn't our fault."

Steve leaned toward Talia. "Sorry again about that. We feel just awful."

"You two were all hunkered down like a couple of sea lions," Mario leaned toward her, both hands gripping the edge of the table. "We didn't see you until we were on top of you...and then when we came back to see if you were okay, we expected you to be paddling, but you weren't, so we miscalculated and.... Oh! It was all so horrible." He threw his hands to his face.

"It's okay, Mario. We shouldn't have even been out there. We're noobs." Talia patted his arm and turned to Brent. "You were saying you saved Buster's life?"

Brent nodded and took a sip of his beer, slipping his arm around Toby's back. "He was a good surfer. He had to be to surf here. Ocean Beach is brutal. You two saw that, first hand. But on this particular day, Buster was out in conditions that even scared us, and we aren't easily scared."

"It was crazy that anyone was out there," Steve said. "The sets were coming in double overhead."

"He wiped out. His board landed right on top of him." Brent slapped the table. "And then a wave pulled him under and just beat the crap out of him. He was dead meat if we didn't help him. Homophobe or not, we weren't going to let him die. We got to him and got him to shore. His shoulder was banged up pretty good, so we put him in the back of Mario's PT Cruiser and drove to the hospital. On the way, he calls his private doctor and the guy meets us at the door and whisks Buster inside, past reception. That was when we realized that he was no Homophobe."

Mario raised his eyebrows. "He was a rock star with some very expensive medical care."

"Fat load of good it did him." Steve leaned back and put his hands behind his head. "He sucked as a surfer after that."

"What do you mean?" Talia said.

Steve shrugged. "I don't know. He just wasn't as good as he...."

"Talia?" A male voice called from the front of the bar.

Talia squinted into the gloom, trying to make out the dark form walking toward her.

"There you are! Thank fucking Vishnu." Ted leaned on the table in an overly dramatic show of relief.

"Well hello, tall, dark and super-duper sexy." Mario scooted closer to him. "I just love a man in glasses."

Ted grinned. "These old things?" he said, adjusting his black-rimmed glasses. "I just wear them so no one knows I'm Superman."

"Ted, how did you know where I was?"

"Dicko sent us a distress signal." He pointed at the waterproof pouch still hanging from her neck. "I installed it with a sensor that knows when it's been knocked around or been underwater for too long."

"But it was in a surf pouch," Talia said.

"Doesn't matter. It measures pressure as well as moisture."

"Ooh! He's as smart as he looks. Please tell me you're not straight, Clark." Mario rested his chin in his palm and gazed up at Ted.

"To the bone, sweetie." Ted held his arms up, showing off his wiry, Doctor-Who-t-shirt-clad body.

Mario clutched his chest. "Tease!"

Talia picked up her beer but clunked it back down without taking a sip. "Ted, you said 'us.' Did Port ask you to come here?"

Ted picked up her beer and sipped. "When Dicko sent out the distress signal, it also turned on the mic. Port heard you screaming about sharks and fire and stuff. He panicked."

"He panicked?" Talia stood up and ran out of the bar. Once on the sidewalk, she blinked in the fog-filtered sunlight. She shielded her eyes with her hand and scanned the street for the handicapped van with the prayer flags in the back window. She spotted the Interceptor on the other side of Taraval. She looked behind her at Ted, who was walking out of the bar. "Oh. You got it fixed."

"Huh? Oh. Not exactly. It's got sort of a Fred Flintstone system of braking."

"You used your feet?" Talia pointed at his dusty, black boots that were so scuffed in the front, the leather curled back in long, scraggly strips.

"And ruin my Docs? Hardly. Coasting, shifting into neutral and then park." He rubbed the back of his head. "I avoided the bigger hills."

"What's so important that you drove all the way here without brakes?"

Ted put his hands on her shoulders and looked in her eyes. "Look, I know how the guy feels. If I heard Darla being drowned or set on fire or whatever the hell happened to you, I'd go nuts. Get this, Gidget, he thought you were toast. Crazy or not, dudes are dudes. We need to protect our women, even if they aren't technically our women and even if we have to do something they don't like...."

"What are you talking about, Ted?"

"I guess I'm saying you're fired." Ted sighed. "Sorry, kid. I need to take Dicko."

Her hand shook as she pulled the little black device from the waterproof pouch. She began to hand it to him but stopped. Maybe it was the "dudes are dudes" crap or the fact that he called her Gidget. She bent her elbow and held Dicko at her shoulder. "Bullshit! Less than a month ago, I was so afraid of even being in ankle deep water that a guy who never leaves his house had to leave his house to save me. And today, I paddled the fuck out into cold, deep and probably extremely sharky water, and yes, I screamed. Because I'm afraid of water, obviously, but I still did my job, didn't I?"

"Yeah, but it's just..."

"I bet if it had just been Toby out there screaming, you would think it was funny, right?"

Ted started to laugh. "Well, sure, that would be hil..." He looked at Talia and stopped laughing. "But I see now how wrong that is."

She tossed Dicko at him and walked toward the Muni stop.

"Right on, Billie Jean!" Ted yelled. "Fair is fair!"

She stopped. Spun around on her heel, walked back to Ted, snatched Dicko out of his hand and said, "Screw that. He's going to have to fire me to my face."

"Hey Talia! Do you want a ride?" Ted called to her as she walked toward the L winding slowly up the block, the single headlight cutting the fog.

She put one hand behind her and held up a middle finger.

*

By the time Talia arrived at the door to the warehouse, some of her fire had dissipated. She raised her hand to knock on the door, but stopped. She looked behind her. Darla's car wasn't in the parking lot. She glanced at the hide-a-key. She was technically fired. It wouldn't be right to just walk in. It wasn't right, though, that she'd been fired. She grabbed the key, unlocked the door and threw it open. Once it was open half-way, she felt a thick resistance, as though there were a sandbag blocking the door. She heard a low grunt. Butter barked.

She looked inside. The resistance wasn't a sandbag. It was Port. He was sitting on the floor underneath the pot-holder window, hunched over, his legs splayed, Butter at his feet. The dog yelped at her excitedly and then licked Port's head. He didn't respond.

"Port! Holy shit!" She knelt next to him.

"Hello. I um..." Port sucked in a mouthful of air that whistled sharply as it hit his throat. "I mean...oh. I was worried about you...." He clutched his chest.

"I'm calling an ambulance." She reached for her phone.

He grabbed her arm. He was remarkably strong for someone who looked like he was having a heart attack. "Please don't. I couldn't bear the humiliation of six paramedics struggling to get me onto an extra-large gurney."

"I'll request seven paramedics."

He took a deep breath—less wheezy this time. He smiled weakly. "I just over-exerted myself trying to get to the door. I thought I could do it. I've done it before. The last time I heard you screaming in the water, remember?"

She nodded. "Of course."

"Talia?"

Something about the way he said her first name made her heart jump and do a high-dive into the pit of her stomach. She took a breath. She meant for it to be a deep breath, but it was a shallow, halting breath. "Yes, Port?"

"Would you mind terribly pouring me an *enormous* Dewar's on the rocks?"

Talia walked into the kitchen, and made two drinks—one with diet club soda, one without. She sat on the floor next to him and handed him a glass. She leaned her head on his shoulder. There was something about being close to Port that gave her an immediate warm and comfortable feeling, even as she could feel his shoulder bones jutting into her cheek.

Port was quiet except for the ice clinking in his glass as he drank. Finally, he said, "Do you remember the second time Minnie came here? When she brought her brood with her?"

"Of course."

"There was a moment when she so eloquently pointed out that I was bat shit crazy."

"I remember."

"She was right." He tapped his empty glass gently onto the floor.

"That's the last of it," Talia said.

"Not to worry. I've prepared for this situation." Port lifted his arm about an inch and pointed toward the office. "There's a bottle of Dewar's in the bottom drawer of my desk."

Talia didn't want to leave her cozy spot on the floor. She turned, and in a move that felt both brazen and completely natural, kissed his shoulder. She stood and walked over to the desk and opened the drawer. Empty. She looked back at Port. He looked smaller than ever. She was reminded of the first time she saw him and thought he was a child. "It's cashed."

He laughed softly. "Feel along the right side of the drawer, toward the bottom."

"Nothing...oh wait." Talia felt a small square button, about the size of the tip of her finger. She pressed it and the bottom opened up, revealing a secret compartment that contained a bottle of Dewar's. She picked up the bottle and tucked it under her arm. There was something underneath it—a dried flower. There was something underneath the flower. A photo. She pinched the corner between her thumb and index finger and carefully lifted it. She brushed a few pieces of the disintegrating flower from the photo as she walked back to Port.

"Who's the girl in this picture?" She handed him the photo.

"My old partner. Julia Lake."

Talia sat down and leaned against him. She looked at the photo. The girl was straight out of central casting for a tough but pretty female cop—dark haired and dark eyed with a wry, crooked smile.

"We didn't have the kind of relationship where we took pictures of each other, so this is all I have." Port looked down at the photo for a long time. "She has a funny smile, see. And she's got one dimple. Right here." He placed his index finger on his right cheek. "The camera didn't pick it up, but I know it's there." His voice cracked. "We were at one of Ted's parties. For reasons only known to Ted, the theme of this party required guests to bring a zucchini and wear a silly hat. Julia had been wearing her four-year-old nephew's cowboy hat. That was why I took this picture, but she took it off right before the flash. She's holding it behind her back. That's the reason for her smile, and the reason I've kept this. It's like the two of us still have a secret." He let the photo drop from his fingers and onto his lap.

Talia held up the bottle. He held his glass toward her. She poured him a shot. He held the glass without taking a sip. "I haven't always been like this," he said. "Do you remember, a few years ago, a young college professor was found shot in her office over at SF State?"

"I remember that."

"It was all over the news—a high-profile case, just like the one we're on now. It was frustrating. We had no motive. No leads. Bupkes. We'd decided to go to the school and talk to her students again. There were a lot of them, over seventy, and they'd already been interviewed, but like I said, we had bupkes." He put his hand down on the floor and pushed himself up from his slumped position. "To save time, we split up. I took one side of the dorms and Julia took the other. It seemed fair because, well, we figured we were wasting our time anyways, so we might as well be quick about it. You know what I mean?" He looked at her, his eyes pleading with her for something. Approval?

She nodded. "Of course."

"My last interview." Port raised his glass to his lips but then put it back down. "My very last interview. I walk into the kid's dorm room. He's a small, mousy kid—curly, red hair and big square glasses...the kind you might wear ironically if you were hip, but this kid was not hip. I sit on his bed. It's unmade—dirty clothes all over it. Typical dorm room. He's squirrely, nervous, but I figure he's got a bong or something under his bed. I pull out my notebook, and I ask him about the professor. He pulls out a gun and shoots me."

"Holy shit."

Port raised his glass again. This time he drank until the glass was empty. He picked up the bottle and poured a shot into his glass. He offered the bottle to her, but she shook her head. "Convalescing was hard. Everything hurt. It hurt to stand. It hurt to walk. Some days it hurt to lie in bed. The only thing that didn't hurt was eating, so that is exactly what I did. And Julia...well, she wasn't going to stick around to watch me become...what I've become."

"I'm sorry, Port. I didn't know." Talia had been slowly moving toward Port as he told the story until her face was barely an inch from his. She could feel the warmth of his breath.

Port pulled away, but only slightly. "So, this kid, this messy, frizzy-haired kid, killed the professor and then shot me, and do you know why?"

"Why?"

He shrugged. "I have no idea. The only word I ever heard him say was 'guilty.' Now, he's on the short end of a very long sentence, and he still...." The ice cubes clinked as he drained his glass. "Let's just say that no motive was ever revealed." He reached for the bottle with a grunt.

Talia grabbed the bottle from him and poured them both another shot. She took a sip and then looked into her glass, watching the ice melt into the booze. Finally, she said, "Did I ever tell you why I panicked, that day on the raft?"

"No, but we don't have to talk about it if you don't want. It wasn't exactly my finest moment either."

"Are you kidding?" She put her arm through his arm, and grabbed his hand. "You were my hero."

"Your hero who nearly had to be airlifted from the rescue site." He looked in her eyes.

She smiled. "I was researching a part. Kitty Genovese. Do you know who she is?"

"The secretary who was killed outside of her apartment building back in the fifties?"

"Sixties."

"Right. I read about her at the academy. Sad story."

Talia nodded. "Well, when I was researching her, I stumbled on a similar case. It happened in...Florida? I think. Somewhere in the South. Anyway, this woman gets into a fender bender on a bridge. The guy she hit was a big guy, and he was pissed. He got out of his truck. He pulled her out of her car, threatened her with a tire iron, and somehow ended up stripping her naked on the bridge in front of bumper-to-bumper traffic."

"Jesus." Port breathed out in a low whistle. "They didn't teach us about that one at the academy."

"And the crazy thing was that no one helped her. I'm sure they were scared because he was so big, but supposedly some people cheered. She jumped, or was pushed and then...I guess a boat was passing by, and she was ripped apart by the blades of the motor." She paused. She looked down at their hands, clasped together, and took a deep breath. "After reading that, I started having nightmares. All the time. I dream that I'm that girl. That her death is my death, and sometimes I think those dreams are going to come true."

Port gripped her hand tighter. "I get that. I'm afraid of my death, too. So afraid that some mornings I can't get out of bed. But look at you—you faced your fears, and you're still here."

She looked into his eyes—deep brown and ringed with gold bands that caught the sun from the tiny window. She knew something with razor-sharp clarity. She could kiss him. She could give him one brief kiss on his lips and nothing would change. It would just act as an exclamation to all this: the floor, the Dewars', the picture, her dreams.

He must have been feeling the same thing because he leaned in just as she did, and they kissed. It was just one kiss. Natural. Casual. As though they'd done it every day, a kiss hello or a kiss goodbye. There was more tenderness in his lips than passion. He pulled away, but she leaned her forehead on his. There was a heat between them in the small triangle of space they'd created with their bodies. A triangle of space that could easily be closed.

Talia imagined herself doing just that. She pictured her hand, reaching out and grabbing the collar of his sweater and pulling him roughly toward her, just to close that space between them, then putting her lips on his, so she could...what? What would she do? Put her tongue in his mouth? Push him down on the floor? Straddle him? Reach her hand down the front of his sweatpants as he struggled to lift his arms so he could put his hands on her? The whole thing sounded horribly painful and awkward.

She looked into his eyes, and he sighed, his breath so close it felt as though it had been her sigh. "Port, I have to tell you something. Mark and I...."

"Miss Green, if you're going to tell me about your dating situation, please don't." He pulled away. "It's none of my concern."

"But I just wanted to...." Talia stopped talking so she could concentrate on not bursting into tears. She wanted to put her head on Port's shoulder but leaned against the wall instead.

There was a loud bang that rattled the warehouse. Port put one arm protectively around her.

"Ah shit!" It was Ted.

"What was that?" Port said.

"The Interceptor and its Fred Flintstone brakes," she said.

Ted banged in the side door and ran into the room. "What are you doing on the floor?

"Drinking." Talia held up the bottle.

Chapter Twenty-Two

It was late, and the Bird's Nest was so crowded, Talia had to turn sideways just to get inside. She tried to walk toward the bar, but she was stuck in a sea of drunks.

"Not a chance. I think Minnie's going to get off," a male voice said. "The evidence against her is circumstantial. I'm not saying it's right. It's just a fact."

Talia turned toward the speaker. It was someone close by and to her left, but all she could see were shoulders and backs of heads.

"Are you kidding me?" a young female voice answered. "There's video. That's hardly circumstantial evidence, and even if it were circumstantial, evidence is still evidence, and it's still admissible. They're going to lock her up and throw away the key."

"She's going to get a slap on the wrist," the male voice said. "You two are making it sound like they're going to bring back the death chamber."

"Absolutely I think she might get the death penalty," another female voice said. "Just because there's been a hold on it in California doesn't mean it's abolished. Minnie is a serial killer at this point. You'd better believe that the DA is going to ask for the death penalty. I would."

Talia tried to push her way through the crowd so she could see who was speaking. She could only manage to move a few inches, but she caught a glimpse of the male speaker as he said, "What are you ladies? Pre-law?" He was young, twenty or so, and dressed all in dark blue, gray and black. He was sneering at someone, but she couldn't see who.

The person in front of Talia dropped something and bent to retrieve it. Talia could see the female speakers. They looked familiar.

They were laughing at the man sneering at them. "Try post law," one girl said, and Talia recognized them. They were the girls in short skirts who couldn't get past the bouncer when she had come here with Toby. Talia wanted to go talk to them and ask them about Minnie's chances of getting the death penalty, but she had a feeling she wouldn't like the answer.

She needed a drink. She turned toward the bar. Zone was standing right in front of her, clutching a neon blue cocktail in one hand and a glowing cell phone in the other. He looked like a fuzzy disco light. "Vanilla Legs! Back for another slice of Zone pie, then, are we? I'm off to the bar, what are you drinking?"

She glanced at the glowing drink. "Anything but what you're having."

He turned and yelled into the center of the throng, "Out of my way, wankers!" as he pushed his way through.

Something hit Talia's shoulder. She bent and picked it up. A silver high-heeled shoe.

"Hoo hoo! Psst!"

Talia turned, but the crowd had backed her up to a wall. There was nothing behind her but a dark coat check room and a sign that read *closed*.

"Hoo hoo!"

Talia leaned into the coat check window and peered at the shadowy form until she noticed a faint yet familiar frizzy quality to the outline. "Linda?"

"Sh! Be cool. No one knows I'm here. I want to keep it that way."

Talia turned around and leaned her elbows against the counter. "Did you follow me here?"

"Not you, no." Linda Varela poked Talia's elbow and said, "I can't trust anyone. Neither can you."

Talia looked toward the bar and watched Zone snap his fingers at the increasingly irate bartender. "You can trust me. I didn't show anyone else that manuscript. Did I?"

"That's what I'm trying to tell you," Linda said. "You can't trust anyone. Not even me. I didn't give you that manuscript because of what was in it; I gave it to you because of what wasn't in it."

"What wasn't in it?"

"It...I was trying to help someone, but I don't want to help him anymore."

The music faded out and they could hear Zone's ranting. "Bloody hell! Who do I have to blow to get service in this festering bowl of...."

Someone else yelled, "Nigel!" and the music picked up again.

"Who was that?" There was fear in Linda's voice.

"Nigel Zone." Talia stood on her tiptoes to peer over the crowd to see Zone screaming at the blue-haired bartender. He threw a pile of napkins on the floor, and the bartender crossed his arms, shaking his head. "I'm sure he'll get tossed soon. Who were you trying to help, Linda?"

No answer. Talia turned and peered into the coat check room. Linda was gone. When Talia turned back, Zone was standing in front of her holding two glasses of champagne. "The bartender was being a right cunt, so I had to get pretty boy to order for us. Mark, you already know Vanilla Legs," Zone said, pointing at Talia. "In the biblical sense, of course.

Just so we're clear, if you get the urge to swing, I could be persuaded."

Mark locked eyes with Talia. "Not going to happen, Nige."

Zone downed his drink and then grabbed Talia's glass and drank it as well, losing about half of it down his chin and into his graying chest hair. "Gah! Is that whiskey?"

"No, it's champagne. At least it was."

"It's bloody strong." He swayed and pointed at a spot next to Talia, then closed one eye and managed to point closer to where she was actually standing but still a few inches off. The lights flicked from dim to bright. Zone squeezed his eyes shut.

"Last call for alcohol!" the bartender yelled.

The lights dimmed. Zone opened his eyes, first one, then the other. "Right. I'm off." He spun around on his heel, stumbled and then barreled through the crowd toward the bar.

"Hey, why are you here with Nigel?" Mark smiled and leaned toward her. One wavy lock of hair fell over his eye, and he pushed it away. Talia wanted to put it back so she could watch him do it again. "Are you still following him?"

"No. I wanted to ask him a few questions."

"Yeah, me too." A group of drunks hooted, cackled and swayed a few inches from the back of his head. "You're wasting your time. Nigel is a prick, but he isn't your killer."

"Look, I know Zone doesn't seem like a criminal mastermind, but his car is at the center of everything, so...." She looked toward the bar. Someone familiar was pushing through the crowd toward them. She looked at Mark. "Were you here with Doc Gray?"

"No...I...Oh, hey, man." Mark turned and clasped Doc Gray's hand with one hand and patted his shoulder with the other. "What are you doing in this hellhole?"

"I came here to commiserate our latest loss with Gary, and now I think I need to pour him into a cab." He pointed to the bar. Talia looked where he was pointing but could only see shoulders.

Mark nodded. "Poor guy. He and Lulu were close."

Talia looked at Mark. "Were they an item?"

Mark scratched his head. "I don't think so. Lulu had an on-again, off-again thing with one of the Male Revue dancers. A big guy. Gary isn't exactly a saint, but he usually stays away from large boyfriends."

"Who, Carlo? That guy is bad...." Doc Gray leaned toward her just as the drunks behind them hooted and swayed, pushing him, and he put a hand on Talia's shoulder to keep from falling into her. She could smell his cologne; it smelled metallic and expensive, like gold. "Sorry." He righted himself. "No. Gary and Lulu weren't dating, but they had a semi-platonic relationship that went beyond sex. He won't be getting over that poor girl anytime soon."

Talia stood on her tip-toes and tilted her head to the side. She spotted Gary through the crowd. From her vantage point, she could only see a sliver of Gary: one of his arms, his shoulder and the side of his face, but even that sliver looked extremely drunk. Just then, he lurched forward and out of her sight. Did he fall? Talia craned her neck and spotted him zigzagging toward the bar.

"Whoa! I'd better stop him before he tries to order last call." Doc Gray turned and side-stepped his way through the crowd.

"I wonder if I should...." Mark ran his hand through his hair but elbowed someone behind him. "Oops. Sorry."

"Yeah, you are." The broad-shouldered blonde sounded irked, but when she spun around and saw Mark, she smiled. "Hey! You're whatshisname!"

"No. I just look like him."

"Oh." She snapped her fingers with a loud pop. "No! You are him...but what is your name?"

"Orville."

She turned to her friends. "Hey guys! What's his name?" Before her friends could answer her, someone pushed past them and bolted toward the door.

It was Gary. Talia and Mark bolted after him. When they got to the sidewalk, Gary was gone. "There's an all-night donut shop he likes to go to. Up here." Mark led her quickly down Lombard as sirens blared in the near distance. After a couple blocks, they silenced. Something rustled behind Talia. She turned. There was nothing there. She kept walking. The rustling was there again. Close. Like someone was right behind her. She spun around. Nothing. That's when she realized that the rustling was coming from the hood of her zip-up sweater. She stopped, took the sweater off and examined the hood.

Mark stopped. "What's wrong?"

Talia pulled a something out of the point of her hood—a coat check ticket with *p24* scrawled in red ink across it. Linda Varela must have shoved in in there. Talia turned it over. Other than *p24* there was nothing else. Talia looked around. The sidewalk was empty except for a couple getting into a parked car and a man selling *Curbsides* a half a block up. "Nothing, let's go...." More sirens. An ambulance sped toward them and then away.

Two large men burst out of a doorway to their right. "This way, bro!" The men yelled the word "bro" a few more times as they hulked past them and lumbered toward the Bird's Nest.

"Let's find Gary, pour him into a cab and then go to my place. It's just a few blocks away." Mark picked up her hand and let his fingers intertwine with hers. "I can put on a pot of coffee, and we'll pull an all-night case-solving session. What do you say?"

Talia smiled at him and pulled her hand away. "All-nighter? What happens when the caffeine wears off? Do you drive me home, or do I sleep on the couch with your cat?"

"You haven't tried my coffee. It never wears off." He pointed at her. "Wait...how did you know I had a cat?"

"Let me guess...." She reached over and picked a few stray black hairs off his jacket. "He's a black long-hair with some indie rock name like Wilco or Costello." Mark held out his palm. She dropped the hair in it. "Am I right?"

Mark looked at his palm and smiled. "You could not be more wrong. I thought you were a detective." He hooked her arm with his and started walking, pulling her along. He leaned down and whispered in her ear. "His name is Captain Beefheart."

"Watch it," a calm, gravelly voice said.

They looked up just in time to avoid walking into a man in a blue, stained ski jacket. "*Curbside.*" He held up a paper.

Mark reached into his pocket, pulled out a dollar and handed it to him. The man held up the paper again, but Mark waved him off. "Sorry about the near-collision, man. Have a good night."

"Appreciate it." The man held up the dollar. "God bless you."

They walked past the man but then Talia stopped. "You didn't take a paper."

"Of course I didn't. I never take them because...."

"Because they only give out a limited number of *Curbsides.*" She ran a hand through her hair, pulling it out of her face, and thought about the homeless man she'd mistaken for Toby. The man who'd abandoned his stack of papers on the sidewalk in front of their apartment building.

Mark nodded. "I never take the paper. That would be rude."

"Exactly." Talia continued walking. "One *Curbside* is actually worth a lot more than one dollar...."

"So?" He sped up his pace to keep up with her and passed her.

"So...I think maybe I should stay at your place tonight because the Kah!" (Talia was going to say, "The killer knows where I live," but said "Kah!" when she walked, throat-first, into Mark's out-stretched arm.)

"Oh! Sorry, but look!" He pointed across the street at about a dozen officers who were swarming a black SUV parked next to the wrought iron fence that separated the Marina from the Presidio.

A uniformed officer stretched a length of yellow and black police tape from the car parked in front of the SUV to the one parked behind it. As he did, he sealed in the small space between the two vehicles, capturing a plainclothes detective in his flimsy trap. Brad grabbed the tape and yanked, reeling the officer toward him. "You and I are going to have to get a safe word if this keeps up, Lew." He tossed the now-crumpled tape to the officer and walked away. As he did, Talia could see into the open trunk of the SUV for only a second before a woman with a camera stepped into her line of sight, but one second was more than enough.

Talia lurched behind a parked car. She sat on the curb and spat on the ground. She pressed her hand on her forehead and stared at the sidewalk until the wave of nausea began to subside. She took a deep breath, but the sidewalk swam out of focus and started to spin—first one way and then the next. She covered her mouth with her other hand and told herself that she was just eyes...only eyes...until the world became clear again. She put her head between her knees, retched and spat.

"Are you okay?"

She looked up. Mark crouched in front of her. She took a deep breath and then another until the urge to vomit passed. "That was Linda Varela in that trunk," she whispered.

"Jesus. Are you sure?" Mark stood up to look through the windows of the parked car, but Talia pulled him back down.

"I don't want Brad to see us. I keep showing up at his crime scenes."

He nodded. "Here. Let's try it from a different angle." He lay flat on the sidewalk and looked under the car. "Holy shit." He looked up at her, his face as pale as hers felt. "That's Gary's car."

"What?" She pushed aside some gravel, a few eucalyptus leaves and broken windshield glass. She pressed her cheek against the asphalt.

Mark pointed under the car. "Look. Gary's car has one of those happy-family stickers on the back. You probably can't make it out from here, but Gary's stick figure has a little bass guitar and Kristen's is wearing high heels."

She couldn't make out the sticker, but she could see Brad talking to Detective Garcia. She heard him say, "Get eyes on Johnson" before a boxy white coroner van drove up, blocking her view.

Mark sat up and brushed the gravel off the front of his jacket. "I don't know why it's here, though. He never drives that thing when he plans on drinking...even a little." He was looking at something to the left of the coroner van. She followed his sightline and watched a line of uniformed men and women fan out past the wrought iron fence and into the darkness of the Presidio. Mark pointed toward them. "We'll have to walk past them to get to the donut shop."

"Let's just go back to your place," she said.

"Yeah? You sure?" He pushed a lock of hair behind her ear and then traced a finger along her jawline, sending a shiver of sparks along her skin.

"Nothing is going to happen."

"I know," he said.

*

As Mark led her up the stairs to his apartment, she thought about what the miniskirt lawyer had said, "Minnie's a serial killer." She thought about the way Minnie cried on her shoulder. She knew Minnie wasn't the killer, but the killer was close, as close as Talia had been to Linda while she was whispering at her, fear in her voice, from the dark cover of the coat check closet. As close as the killer had been when they found Lulu's body.

When Mark opened the door, she grabbed him and pulled him to the floor. She straddled him and grabbed him by the collar. She pulled his face to hers and kissed him. He leaned up toward her. She wrapped her arms around his head and back as they kissed. He ran his hands along her back and through her hair. She felt a warmth that filled her insides and little shivers of sparks all over her body.

When it was over, lying on the floor, still trying to catch her breath, she realized something. She threw her arm out and hit him in the chest. Hard. "Oof!"

"Ooh! Sorry. It's just that...." She turned and looked into his eyes, at that small yellow speck that shone out from the blue, and said, "I know who the killer is."

Mark got up to get them a blanket. While he was gone, a large black cat walked over to her, sat down on the floor as close to her face as possible and stared at her with glassy green eyes. She scratched his chin. "Beefheart, I presume?"

"Don't let him bother you. He doesn't know he's a cat." Mark put a blanket over Talia and sat down next to her, pulling part of the blanket around his shoulders, like a couple of kids on a camp-out.

"What does he think he is?"

"I don't know. Lizard, maybe?" He grabbed the cat's face and shook it slightly. The cat closed his eyes and purred. "So, who is the killer? And please don't say Nigel."

She shook her head. "I've known it wasn't Zone for a long time. He's too drunk and dumb. But it had to be someone who had access to his car. Which meant it had to be either Devin, Gary, Doc Gray or you. But only you and Doc Gray had both access to Nigel's car and opportunity to kill Lulu."

"You think I killed Lulu?" He laughed nervously, but his eyes were filled with genuine hurt.

"No. Because of two things. First, only an idiot has sex with a killer on his kitchen floor, and I am not an idiot."

He laughed, a genuine laugh, not a nervous one, and wrapped her up in his arms. He kissed the top of her head. "So, what's the second thing?"

"Linda Varela."

"Ha! I couldn't have killed her because I was with you, right?" The blanket started to slip off their shoulders. He pulled it back up. "You're my alibi, Maggie."

"You didn't have opportunity, of course, but there's also motive. Doc Gray and Linda were dating."

"Dating? Really?"

"Maybe dating isn't the right word, but they were involved in some sense. When I saw his garden, I noticed that he was growing the same kind of flower she had in her office. And then right before she was killed, she told me that she had taken something out of Buster's book to protect someone. Someone she wouldn't name, but when I saw that note she left me..."

"Note?" he said.

"Page twenty-four. I knew she was talking about Doc Gray. She'd taken him out of the book, all except for one sentence, which I'm willing to bet is on page twenty-four." She reached down to pet the cat, who had fallen asleep on her knee.

"Yeah, but what could she have possibly taken out of Buster's book? Doc Gray wasn't anymore debauched than the rest of us."

"Really?" She raised an eyebrow at him.

He laughed. "I mean them. I've been a choir boy."

"It was actually something that Toby said to me. Doctors get the best drugs."

"Yeah, but so did Buster." He shrugged.

She studied his face. He didn't believe her. Doc Gray was still his friend. "I'm sure, but not the kind of pain killers Doc Gray prescribed Buster for his surfing injury. At first, he probably took them only for the pain, but then he got addicted. When he died, Buster's body was filled with enough opiates to kill five men."

Mark pulled away from her a little so he could look at her. "But why kill him if the pills were going to do the job?"

"Because then Minnie wouldn't be implicated. Doc Gray would."

Mark took a deep breath and held his head in his hands. Finally, he looked up and said, "I think I should call Gary. Make sure he got home safe. I'm sure he did, but you know...just in case."

Chapter Twenty-Three

The door of the Bird's Nest was closed and sealed with a padlock. Footsteps echoed from about a block away, but no one was around except for a homeless man urinating loudly in the alley across the street. Mark pounded on the door. "Shit!"

"We open at ten a.m."

They spun around. It was the blue-haired bartender. He'd traded in his tuxedo for a peacoat and a messenger bag. "Sorry, man...I wasn't trying...I need your help." Mark put his hands together like he was praying and then pointed them at the bartender. "There was a very drunk guy here tonight—dressed in black, black hair, five o'clock shadow."

The bartender gave him an odd look. "Are you talking about your bass player, Gary Meyers?"

"Yes. Did you see him?"

"He left with that guy who is always drinking with one or more of you. You know who I mean?"

"Tall and blonde or short and ugly?" Mark said.

The bartender sighed. "Not Nigel Zone. The other guy." He turned and walked away.

Talia called out to him. "Excuse me!"

He turned around, but left one foot pointed in the direction he was walking.

"Have you seen a silver Lexus?"

He shrugged and started walking away. Without turning, he pointed at the alley across the street. "There's one right there."

The silver Lexus was parked a few feet into the alley. Talia narrowed her eyes at the tinted windshield but couldn't see if anyone was behind the wheel. The headlights lit up. The engine started.

"Run!" Mark yelled pointing at the Honda that was parked half a block away.

Talia ran as fast as she could, but lagged. Mark reached out. She grabbed his hand. The sound of their feet hitting the concrete was pierced by the screech of tires spinning on asphalt. The smell of burnt rubber pushed her to run faster. Mark dropped Talia's hand. He pulled out his keys and fumbled with them. He managed to hit the door unlock, just as she reached the passenger side.

Talia was pulling the door shut when headlights flooded the car. She inhaled, bracing for impact. There was a dull crunch as the Lexus clipped the Honda's side mirror, sending it skittering along the street as it sped past. She exhaled. Mark started the car. They clicked their seatbelts. He stomped on the gas and chased after the Lexus that was already out of sight. At the top of the hill, the Honda caught some air. The landing was not smooth, but they could see the Lexus about four blocks ahead of them. Mark stepped on the gas.

They closed the gap but were still a few blocks behind the Lexus when it stopped suddenly in an intersection, spun out awkwardly, and then turned left. Mark guided the Honda onto Mason Street with a quick tap of the brakes and a half-turn of the wheel. The two cars sped down the hill toward Fisherman's Wharf. The rows of upscale apartment buildings and converted Victorians soon turned into blocks of nautical themed t-shirt shops, hotels and restaurants. During the day, the Wharf was packed with cars, bikes, pedicabs and pedestrians but at this time of night was deserted.

Mason Street ended at Jefferson, but the Lexus kept speeding and clipped a large, steel mooring cleat, spraying an arc of bright orange sparks. Mark drove through a pedestrian walkway into a large parking lot that dead-ended at the San Francisco Bay. As the Lexus drove closer to the pier, it sped up and crashed into the lobby of the crime museum. Mark stepped on the brakes. There was a loud crack and then something rained onto the windshield with a soft clatter. It looked like a flock of small, dead birds.

Talia looked out the windshield. The birds were the splintered remains of the wooden cut-out of the condemned gangster that had been on the roof of the crime museum and was now scattered on the parking lot along with broken glass and rubble from the lobby. Mark turned on the wipers and the splinters of wood flicked off. He clasped the door handle. "Do you have a gun?"

"No, do you?"

"Excuse me." Mark reached between Talia's feet and rummaged around under the seat, coming up with an aluminum squeegee (the kind people use to clear the condensation off their windows on foggy days). He held it up. "Ready?"

"Almost." She leaned over and kissed him. "Let's do this thing." She opened her door.

They crept toward the driver's door of the Lexus, Mark in front, holding the squeegee above his head. Mark stopped, turned and pointed down. Talia nodded, ducked down and crawled under the window. Mark mouthed the words *one* and then *two*. Talia pulled the door open on *three*. He swung the squeegee back like a baseball bat. A scream came from inside the Lexus.

"Killer! Help! Killer!"

Mark lowered the squeegee.

"Marky Mark?! You're the killer? I'm shocked. And you're planning to kill me with a bleeding squeegee? I'm insulted."

"What are you doing here, Nigel?"

"Parking."

"Zone, do you know...." Talia began.

"Vanilla Legs!"

"Hi. Do you know where Gary is?"

"No. But I thought I heard someone singing Beatles songs in the backseat."

Mark looked. "There's no one in the backseat."

"Are you sure?" Zone turned around. "He sounded very small. I think he was an elf. Or Prince. Maybe he's his bleeding gho...."

"Sh." Talia held up a hand. "Do you hear that?"

They were silent until Zone broke the quiet with a large belch. "Sorry."

Mark shook his head at Zone.

"Pop the trunk," Talia said.

Zone mashed his hand randomly on the dashboard. "I don't know how to do that, do I?"

"I'll do it." Talia reached into the car. As she did, she saw a rectangle of black cardboard on the passenger seat, just large enough to fit over a license plate.

"Don't be fresh now, Vanilla Legs." Zone held up his hands but otherwise made no attempt to help.

Talia and Mark ran around to the back of the car and lifted the door to the trunk. Gary was curled up in a ball, his head resting on the spare tire. "*Meeeechelle, My Belle.* Hey! Who turned on the lights?"

"How did you get in the trunk?" Talia held her hand out for him to grab, but he just stared at it.

"Get in here? I've always been here. I was born here."

"Man, am I glad to see you." Mark put his hand out for Gary to grab.

Gary beamed. "Hey, Markle! What are you doing here and when did you get the second head? It looks good on you."

Mark grasped Gary's arm and pulled, but Gary tugged Mark until his upper body was in the trunk. Talia squeezed next to Mark, leaned into the trunk and slipped her arms under Gary's knees. Mark grabbed Gary by the shoulders. He struggled like a toddler having a tantrum as they dragged him out of the trunk and plopped him onto his feet.

Gary stood squinting at them and wobbling back and forth like an air dancer outside of a used car dealership. "I'm sorry, Markle."

"That's okay," Mark put his arm around him.

"No! You don't get it. We were going to write a book. For Linda. We didn't ask you because we knew you'd say no. But she and the Doc were...cahooting. I'm sorry, man." He draped himself in a sloppy hug around Mark's torso.

"That's okay, Gare. I just need to get you home before Kristen kills us both."

"Ah shit! You called her? Why would you do that?"

"Because Talia figured out who the killer is." Mark dragged Gary one step forward.

Gary stumbled back two steps. "Was it me?" He lurched to the side and leaned on Mark.

Talia ran over to Zone, who was slipping in and out of consciousness. She clapped her hands in front of his face. "Hey! Did you put Gary in the trunk?"

"Who is Gary?"

"You know who Gary is. Somehow, he ended up in your trunk. Think." She clapped again. "You drove to the Bird's Nest. You got out of the car. Did you lock it?"

Zone didn't answer. She clapped again. "I'm awake. I'm awake, you loony bird. It's just that's the weird thing, isn't it? I didn't drive to the Bird's Nest. I took a cab. And then when I got kicked out by those bastards, I tried to hail another cab, but I was too tired to hold my bleeding hand up in the air. So, I go in the alley to take a wazz on the bouncer's car, and as my stream is hitting the bleeding thing, I realize it's my car." Zone laughed, and the stench that emanated from his mouth smelled like a sewer filled with bourbon. "I open the door, and oh happy day, the keys are in the ignition."

She ran back to where Mark had Gary by one arm, struggling to keep him upright. She hooked her elbow around Gary's other arm.

Talia looked at Mark and said, "Doc Gray must have put Gary in Nigel's trunk."

"Why didn't he kill him?"

"Because he saw Linda. I think...." There was a noise. Talia looked out towards the Bay Bridge. She listened but could only hear a persistent foghorn and waves lapping at the pier.

"Talia?"

"Sh!" She heard it again: glass rattling. She looked toward Pier 39 and saw the source of the rattle. A homeless person was pushing a shopping carriage full of bottles on the extra-wide, tourist-friendly sidewalk. She exhaled. "I think he put Gary in the trunk when he saw Linda leaving the club. She was running away from him, but she wasn't running fast enough."

"Jesus." Mark hooked his arm around Gary's waist and hitched him up a few inches.

"Doc Gray must have taken Gary's keys, and then followed Linda, shot her and put her in Gary's trunk. But the police arrived sooner than he hoped, and he had to wait for them to clear out. By the time he came back to kill Gary, Zone was there."

Mark exhaled. "That meant we were there too."

Talia nodded and looked around again. She peered at the homeless person, but he was too far away to see clearly. "Let's get out of here."

Gary squinted at her. "Who's going to kill me, Maggie?"

Mark started to pull him forward. "Kristen, buddy. Kristen is going to kill you."

They could hear approaching sirens as they dragged Gary to the Honda.

*

After she told Port her theory about Doc Gray, Port checked page twenty-four of the manuscript, and it was there—the line about Doc Gray and Buster playing liar's dice and snorting coke. Doc Gray was the killer, they were sure of it, but they still needed to figure out how he killed Buster if the police were going to believe them. Talia poured them some coffee to make up for the fact that neither one of them had gotten any sleep. As she was walking back into the office with the cups, Port's phone rang. It was Brad. Port put it on speaker.

"This is just a courtesy," Brad said. "I'm just calling to tell you I'm about to arrest your client for Lulu's murder."

Talia looked at Port. He held up one finger. "Evidence?"

"Evidence?! She's got truckloads of motive, no alibis and all the murder weapons. And remember those tights?"

"The ones you wore in Barstow?"

"Very funny. We did a search of her place and found an empty box of tights from a place in Paris called Chez Frou-Frou or something like that. You know what else we found? That gun she claimed to have lent to a friend. It somehow magically appeared in her nightstand."

Port leaned his head back and groaned.

"Was that a groan?" Brad's voice filled with emotion. "How do you think I feel? Before breakfast, I'm standing on the broad's doorstep, listening to her tell me that she threatened some poor bastard with her gun, I leave, only to find the very same poor bastard with his brains splattered all over a dumpster before I even get a chance to finish my organic acai oatmeal bowl."

Port sighed. "Shitty."

"Very shitty!" Brad yelled. "You know how I feel about breakfast. Oh, and before I can get past Minnie's team of lawyers to arrest her, I find yet another stiff in the Marina."

"Before you arrest her, can you come over and hear me out?"

"I have to get this maniac off the street, Porty." Brad sighed; his tone was quieter. "And you and your little amateur sleuth are just getting in the way."

"Sorry, Bradley." Port hung up. "Well, we'd better...What's wrong? Miss Green? You look pale."

Talia took a deep breath. She felt pale. "It's all my fault. I've messed it up."

"What are you talking about? You did nothing of the sort."

She tried to take a deep breath, but it wouldn't work. She had to take air in halting gulps. "The dead bodies, Port. Brad's right. I don't know what I'm doing, and people are dying because of it." The warehouse stretched out in front of her. Her hands loosened their grip on the coffee cups and a few drops hit the floor. She turned toward the door. The little potholder window seemed to be getting smaller and smaller.

She heard something. It was Port. He was saying "Shhhhh...." The sound hit her ears like a life preserver. "Now, now. Take a sip of your coffee. Don't sip mine. You won't like it."

She took a sip and swallowed. The coffee was cold but sweet and felt good in her throat.

"There, now sit down." His voice was soothing and commanding at the same time. Talia sat at her chair and pushed Port's coffee cup to him across the desk. "I've known Brad for a long time, and he's a great cop, but cops have a set of rules they need to follow. Those rules are mostly bullshit. It's just like the armored car heist. The cops had to look at Victor Diaz because he had a rap sheet. We followed our hunch, and who was right?"

She took another sip of the sweet coffee. "We were, but...."

"And who is right in this case? Brad, who thinks Minnie did it just because there is indisputable video evidence of her doing it? Or you, the so-called amateur sleuth, who figured out that Doc Gray has to be the killer despite absolutely no solid evidence whatsoever?"

She took a deep breath and let it out. "Me."

"So, when you think about it, Brad is actually in your way, right?"

She put her head on the desk. Ted had said that only crazy could talk down crazy, so maybe that made her crazy because she felt better. She sat up and said, "Right, so let's do this thing."

Port nodded. He pulled his laptop over and opened it up. "Now, Doc Gray's motives for killing most of his victims is at least somewhat clear. Buster was going to expose him as a pill pusher and cause him to lose his license. Linda had been helping him and then turned against him, so she had to go. Lulu was close to Buster and probably saw something or heard something. David Beeman, the obsessed fan, was in the alley on the night of the murder and most likely saw him enter the building."

"The motive for this one, however, is murkier, but I actually think this is the glue that holds our theory together." He clicked a picture of a dark-haired young man in a graduation cap up on screen. "Benjamin Cohen. Look at him there, graduating top of his class, soon to become what many of his peers call a quote very good doctor with strict adherence to a code of ethics unquote. It's a reputation that has garnered him one of the most coveted personal doctor gigs in the country. Kylie Kismet. But you said that he and Miss Kismet are dating, right?"

"Right. Why? Do you think Doc Gray wanted Kylie Kismet?"

"Yes, but only in a professional sense." Port pointed at the image of Benjamin Cohen up on the screen. "If he were dating his client, wouldn't his code of ethics make him quit his job?"

Talia looked up at the screen. "Yes, but I think only a few people knew that they were dating...."

"Could one of those people have been Buster?"

"She gave me the impression that she'd started dating him after Buster was killed."

"Do you believe her?"

Talia tapped her fingers on the desk and thought about the way Kylie told her that she had *finally* met someone. "No. I don't."

A door slammed, and Darla walked into the room with a fussy Belisa.

"We just figured out The Who," Port announced.

"That's great," Darla said absently, putting Belisa into a bouncer that she referred to as The Nuclear Option. Once strapped in, Belisa would be simultaneously rocked and bounced while teddy bears holding red balloons rotated in a soporific circle in front of her. Darla twirled one of the bears. "Look at the bear, *mija*. Silly bear. Look at her. Please...."

"Yes. So, now we just have to figure out The How."

"Uh huh." Darla looked blankly at them. "I'm going to go check the changing table." She sprinted down the hall.

"So, let's break this down." Port clicked Benji's photo off the screen. "Doc Gray gives Buster a monster dose of pain killers and then tells Minnie that her husband has been doing drugs with Zone. Minnie goes to the studio and does...something...for the strange duration of exactly one minute."

Talia nodded. She didn't see a reason to tell him about the Jeopardy song and reveal Minnie's secret.

Port clicked one of the pictures Talia took of the alley next to Studio 9 up on the screen. "Doc Gray knows the security cameras can't see him once he's in the alley. He goes there dressed as a homeless man. His disguise is still in the alley in this shot." He put his cursor over the discarded jacket and then moved it over to the dumpster, near where Star Tee's body had been found. "The fan, David Beeman, sees Doc Gray change into his security guard disguise."

"The Imposter." Talia nodded.

Port looked up and rubbed his chin. "But why doesn't he kill him then? Why leave a witness?"

Talia shook her head. "Doc Gray didn't know he was there. He was sleeping under a blanket held down with candles."

"Ah. Yes." Port nodded slowly. "A unique camping set-up, so Doc Gray sees it again later...at Minnie's house?"

Talia tapped the desk and thought about her run in with Star Tee at Minnie's house. She thought about Minnie, reaching into her nightstand for Vincent's diorama. Talia was sure the gun wasn't there. "Minnie was telling the truth when she said she gave away the gun. She gave it to Doc Gray. He was the friend she was talking about. Probably also the friend who gave her the tights in that black and pink box."

Port rubbed his hands together. "Here we go. So, Gray uses his keycard to get in and hides in the utility closet until Minnie leaves. On his way out of the closet, his security guard disguise is caught on the nail. He kills Buster, breaks into the security room and rewinds the studio footage."

Talia looked up at the bulletin board where the square of fabric used to be. "That can't be right."

"Why not?"

"Because the security guards at Studio 9 wear tan uniforms. Not blue."

"I wonder if they wore different...."

He was interrupted by the sound of Belisa crying. Darla stomped down the hall and toward the bouncer. Port continued talking, but quieter. Talia leaned closer to hear him over the sound of Belisa's crying and Darla's shushing. "Maybe they wore different uniforms at night? The tricky part is figuring out how he managed to doctor the video without...."

"Where the hell is it?" Darla stood in the living room, bouncing Belisa on her hip, their faces mirroring separate but equal panic. "I'm going to look on the changing table again." She ran down the hall, still bouncing Belisa.

"Maybe we're wrong," Port rested his chin on his thumb and rubbed his cheek with his index finger. "Maybe Doc Gray didn't dress up as a security guard at all. There wasn't supposed to be one on duty, so it seems it would attract more attention than he'd want."

"Then why did Star...I mean David Beeman...call him The Imposter?"

"I'm not sure, but I...."

"Wait!" Darla burst into the room with a screaming Belisa. "This baby is teething, and the only thing that makes her feel better is her fucking Ninja Mouse, but I can't find her fucking Ninja Mouse, so unless you want this baby to cry all day, you'll stop your stupid murder investigation and help me find the fucking mouse!"

Port held up his hands. "Okay..."

Belisa wailed, her hands clenched in little fists, her eyes darting wildly around the room.

"It's not okay!" Darla balled her free hand up in a fist and shook it.

"Where did you last see it?" Port managed to make his voice sound soothing while still being heard above the screaming as he clicked a few keys on his laptop.

"Yesterday. In her high chair." Darla relaxed her hand just enough so she could point at the chair. "She had it there after lunch, right before we went to Minnie's. When I came back it wasn't there, but she didn't ask for it at bedtime, so I didn't worry...." Darla's voice cracked.

"Wait." Port looked up from his laptop. "You saw Minnie at lunchtime yesterday? Talia saw her at breakfast. That doesn't leave a lot of time..."

"Port, I love you like a brother, but if you don't shut up about this goddamn case I swear...."

Talia walked over to her and took the crying baby out of her arms. Maybe it was the novelty of a new person, but Belisa's crying slowly abated as Talia alternated between bouncing and swaying.

Port put a black and white video up on the screen. It showed the corner of the kitchen where the high chair stood in front of the refrigerator, taken from the perspective of the camera Talia had found behind the coffee maker. The Sombient cam. He fast-forwarded until they saw Darla walk into the kitchen with Belisa, feed her, and then leave—all in fast motion. Port pressed pause. "There. Look!"

Darla squinted at the screen. "There's the mouse, just like I said, but what happened to it?"

"Let's find out." Port fast-forwarded again.

Talia leaned in to look. Even Belisa seemed interested. They all giggled a bit when Port shuffled into the kitchen in rapid motion. Port blushed. "I haven't moved that fast in years." Darla put her hand on his shoulder.

Suddenly, there was a dark blur moving across the kitchen.

"What happened?" Darla said.

Port rewound and played it back at normal speed. They watched Ted walk on-screen, grab the mouse and walk off-screen.

The side door opened. "What did I miss?"

"Ted, your timing has never been worse," Port said.

"Okay...." Ted backed away slowly.

"Don't let me kill him." Darla picked up Port's coffee cup, raising it above her head. "I just need to maim him."

Ted hid behind Talia and Belisa. "Hey!" Talia said.

"Whatever it is, I can explain!" he yelled from the safety of his hiding spot.

Darla pointed the cup at him. "Don't use our baby as a human shield, you ass. Give Ninja Mouse back to me, and I'll let you walk out of here."

"What the hell are you talking about you crazy, yet very sexy, woman?"

"You're caught on tape. Red handed!" Darla pointed at the video. It was still running.

Ted looked at the screen and then at Port. Port nodded. "This is serious stuff, Ted. We put the murder investigation on hold, and we were getting close."

"Fast forward this a bit for me, will you, Portermouse?"

Port did as he was told.

"Okay, keep going. Any second now we are going to see.... Ho! Lookie there." Ted pointed. The video showed Ted walking back in and putting the mouse on the high chair.

"But what happened to it?" All the anger seeped out of Darla's voice and was replaced with defeat.

Port fast-forwarded until they saw another blur. He stopped and brought it back to reveal the real culprit. "Mangy mutt!" Darla ran toward where Butter was snoozing on her bed in the living room. "Where is it?"

Butter slunk away and hid under the desk. "Smart dog," Ted told her with some authority.

Darla picked up Butter's bed and shook it. Various household objects fell out, including Ninja Mouse. "My dog is a kleptomaniac," Port said, pointing at Butter's pile of ill-gotten gains. "Is that my corkscrew?"

Darla, victorious, held up the mouse. She paused, looked at it and then at Ted. "Oh, Mason."

"I didn't want her to think that she was the only one." Ted walked over to her and put a hand on her shoulder.

Darla looked into his eyes. "Here." She handed him the mouse. "Go wash the dog slobber off of this before you give it to our child."

Ted ran into the kitchen.

Port and Talia looked at each other and then at Darla. Even Belisa stared saucer-eyed from her perch on Talia's hip.

"What is happening?" Port said. "Darla, are you not killing Ted?"

Darla looked toward the kitchen and smiled. "No, Port. I'm not killing him. Not at all."

Ted ran out of the kitchen and over to the desk. "Here's the little guy who'd been causing all this trouble." He held it up for them to admire.

"Oh! Good work, Ted." Port nodded and smiled.

At first Talia didn't notice anything but then she saw two little stitches on Ninja Mouse's top lip in the same spot as Belisa's little vertical scar.

Ted handed the mouse to Belisa and took the baby out of Talia's arms. "Poor little thing is tuckered out from nearly driving her mother to homicide. Someone needs to go back to bed." Ted started to walk toward the nursery.

Darla followed him. "Yeah. Me."

"Let me tuck the baby in, and then it's your turn, woman." Ted patted Darla on the butt with his free hand.

"I'm glad we looked at that tape," Talia whispered to Port.

"I'm glad I fast-forwarded…." Port stopped. He looked at Talia and grinned. "I just figured out The How."

Chapter Twenty-Four

When she came back in with more coffee, Port had taken down the Ninja Mouse video and put up the Studio 9 video.

"What are you doing?" Talia said.

"I am cueing this up to the point where Minnie is supposedly killing Buster." Port leaned back. "Here, what do you see?"

"I see Minnie hunched over Buster."

"Do you see Minnie killing Buster?"

"Maybe?" Talia shrugged. "It's hard to tell."

"Hold on." Port fast-forwarded through the video. "I'm looking for the point in the video where everyone would have stopped watching."

"Like a hidden track?"

"Hmm? Oh. Yes." He smiled at her. "Exactly like a hidden track. That's a good way to put it." He turned back to the video. It showed nothing but Buster's lifeless body for a long time until, finally, there was a blur. Port rewound. The video showed a paramedic running into the studio and rushing to Buster's side. "What do you see?"

"A paramedic."

"What's he doing?" Port said, watching Talia and not the video.

"Trying to resuscitate Buster? I guess."

"Okay, I'll just let this play. You tell me everything you see." Port pointed at the screen. "Quick. It's running."

"Fine. Okay, the paramedic is still working on Buster. He looks like he's giving up. He's leaving." Talia looked at Port. "That's it. He's gone."

Port pointed at the screen again. "Keep watching."

"Oh, he's back, and he's brought a partner and a gurney and some equipment. I think that's a defib machine. They're both working on Buster. Now, they're looking at each other like, 'Whoa! We just found a dead rock star. The chicks are going to be all over us.'"

"That might be bit of a reach but to be honest, not much of one. Now, look at the split screen." Port put the dark, grainy video of Minnie hunched over Buster's lifeless body on one screen and the dark, grainy video of the paramedic hunched Buster's lifeless body on the other. "Why do we assume that Minnie is killing him and the paramedic is saving him?"

"I guess because Minnie is the pissed-off wife of a slutty rock star and the paramedic is a...well, he's a paramedic."

"Is he?" Port pulled up a shot of the paramedic when he first entered and zoomed in. He juxtaposed that with a shot of him entering the second time. "Why do we think these two men are the same person?"

Ted walked into the room and looked up at the screen. "What are you guys looking at?"

"Two completely different men," Talia said. "It's so clear, now. I mean this second guy is about twenty pounds heavier, and he has a goatee, not a beard."

"Yes." Port nodded. "And here, if we add in the partner."

"That's three different men," Ted said.

Talia stared at the image of the first paramedic, trying to detect hints of Doc Gray's features. "Can we get a better look at his face? The first guy."

Port zoomed in. "He must have known the camera was going to get a shot of his face, hence the hat and beard."

Talia studied the image. Only a sliver of cheekbone was visible between the dark, fake beard and the sunglasses. It was enough. Talia nodded. "It's him."

"Who him?" Ted said.

"Him, Doc Gray."

"Really? He looks like Doctor John in a paramedic uniform." Ted squinted at the screen. "I take that back. That isn't a uniform. That's a costume. I probably have a similar one at home in my costume closet. See? The guy on the left is wearing a jumpsuit. The two other guys have on a pant and shirt combo."

Talia slapped the desk. "Costume closet!"

"What? I like to dress up. Is that a crime?"

"No, I mean, Lulu had a costume closet. It was filled with stripper costumes. Male stripper costumes that probably belonged to her boyfriend, Carlo."

Ted nodded. "Ah yeah. I remember that closet! I was wondering why Lulu had all those big, unsexy costumes."

"A stripper costume?" Port said. "That seems a bit...."

"Of course it's a stripper costume. Look how crappy it is." Ted leaned over Port, so he could access the keyboard. On each shot, he zoomed in on something on their chests. "See, these guys have these intricate little patches, with this weird medical symbol on it."

"A caduceus," Port said.

"Whatever. But this guy is sporting something that looks like a snake having sex with the letter *T*. Which is fine because all it needs to do is sort of look like a paramedic uniform for a three-minute strip routine."

Port nodded. "Or for a grainy security video."

Ted walked closer to the screen and stood up on his toes to get a better look. "See that radio on his belt, though? That's real." Ted turned around and faced them. "It's a police scanner."

"So he'd know when the real paramedics were arriving," Talia said.

"Yes, and so he could time his entrance as well as his exit." Port lifted his index finger an inch from the desk in a subpar attempt at pointing. "Look at the little pocket on his hip. Notice anything odd?"

"Yeah. It's useless. It's only big enough to hold a condom." Ted scratched the side of his head until his glasses tipped sideways. He left them like that for a few seconds before straightening them. "So, I guess I'll take that back. It's not completely useless."

Talia rolled her eyes. "It looks as though there should be another one on the other side, but it must have torn off when he left the utility closet," Talia peered at the screen. "What's that in his right hand? Can you zoom in?"

Ted zoomed in. "That looks like one of those little hammers that doctors *claim* they use to check your reflexes. Is there anyone really stupid enough to fall for that scam?" Ted threw his arms up in frustrated disbelief. "Obviously, they're hammering tiny muscle-control implants into your knee."

"You are mistaken, Ted," Port said.

"Whatever. Don't come crying to me when you become part of our Grand Supreme Ruler's personal horde of zombie soldiers...or worse! Zombie janitors." Ted pantomimed an exhausted zombie mopping a floor.

Port shook his head. "No. I meant you are mistaken because that hammer is not for checking reflexes or zombie implants, for that matter. It's the murder weapon—the lever that was used to tighten Buster's necklace around his neck."

"Oh yeah." Ted stood on his toes again. He stuck out his tongue. "Ick. That costume looks worse the more I look at it. I can't believe he fooled everyone for so long with it."

"No one was looking for the deception because they were convinced of Minnie's guilt," Port said.

Talia rested her chin on her hand and looked up at the image of Doc Gray in a fake beard and stripper costume. "He fooled me the other day when he disguised himself as a guy selling *Curbsides* outside my building. I didn't figure it out until last night."

Port looked at her. "Wait. You didn't tell me about that. He knows where you live?"

"Don't worry. We...uh...didn't stay at our place last night."

"Where did you stay, Cagney? At Lacey's house?" A look of recognition crossed Ted's face. "Oh! I get it. You were banging Mark Lynn last night. You finally hit that, huh?" Ted did a cowboy-riding-a-horse dance around the room, yelling "hitting it, hitting it!" Which was sufficiently mortifying, but as he did, the metal chain that connected his back pocket to his front pocket slapped against his hip rhythmically as he danced, which somehow made it worse.

"Stop!" Port yelled. Ted stopped. The chain swayed a bit as he stood and stared at Port.

Port wasn't looking at Ted. He was looking at Talia. "Toby called me looking for you late last night. I was under the impression that he was at your apartment."

Talia shook her head. "That's impossible. I told him...." She tried to remember herself saying the words, or texting the words: "Toby, the killer knows where we live," but she couldn't. The only words that rang in her head were the ones Brad said to her when he told her not to contemplate Star Tee's humanity while she was identifying his body. Toby's humanity was not something she would be able to ignore if she had to identify his body. The last time she saw Toby, he was with Brent. Maybe he'd gone home with him. Toby barely slept at their apartment. He was always either working or getting lucky or both.

"Talia," Port said gently. "While we were talking, Toby told me he was feeding the cat. You have a cat, right?"

A cat? That sounded familiar. Someone having a cat. Her brain was filled with images of Toby's lifeless body: lying on the floor, propped up against a dumpster, stuffed in a trunk. She pushed the images out and replaced them with an orange short-hair cat meowing at his dish. She put her hand on her forehead and fought the urge to vomit. Even if Toby had gone home with Brent, he still would have gone home to make sure his precious little Kirky got his breakfast on time. She pulled out her phone. Her fingers were shaking, but she made the call. It went straight to voicemail.

She barely heard Port say "Talia, wait..." as she grabbed her purse and ran out the door. She looked around. Where had she left the Vespa? She panicked. She didn't want to have to explain to Toby that she couldn't save his life because she'd had to wait for the bus. Then she saw it parked on the other side of a van that looked vaguely familiar.

She was reaching for the handlebars when she felt a hot, prickly feeling across the top of her back. Before she could turn around, a strong hand yanked on her neck. Her purse hit the ground. She heard a tiny click, and hoped that Dicko was sending an alert. She looked up and saw the tire iron. Fear sunk through her bones like oil. She tried to twist from Doc Gray's grip, but he had her in a headlock.

"Ah ah. You don't want to do that. I know just the right spot on your pretty skull to hit, so you'll know you've had your brains bashed in just before you die." The tone of his voice was professional and practiced. "Now, let's go." He pulled her backward.

Then Talia remembered something the instructor told her in self-defense class (the same one where she'd learned the fire trick): *Never let an attacker take you to a secondary location. He might kill you if you resist, but he's definitely going to kill you at the secondary location.* Talia dug in her heels. "Where's Toby?"

"Toby? I've never heard of her." He tightened his arm around her neck. The cold, metallic edge to his cologne seemed sharper now, as though he was trying to cut her with his scent.

Talia fought the nausea rising in her chest. "My roommate! You better not have hurt him, you prick."

"Why would I hurt him? He told me right where to find you."

He was lying. He must have been. He thought Toby was a girl. What if he was telling the truth? Toby had been her best friend since freshman year at college. The idea of him being in the position she was in now, or worse, made her panic. She lurched, trying to break his grasp. He yanked her backwards and dragged her, her feet digging long trenches in the gravel. She screamed.

A door slammed. "Hey man," Ted said, doing a passable impersonation of a calm person. "It's okay. Don't hurt her, man. We can work this out." As Ted was speaking, Doc Gray readied the tire iron above the crown of her head. Ted's calmness wavered a bit, saying the word *work* for just a bit too long, so that the *er* sound was all stretched out, as if he'd affected a southern drawl for the sole purpose of talking down a killer.

Doc Gray laughed and continued dragging her toward the secondary location, where he was most certainly going to kill her. Talia commanded her limbs to fight, kick, punch, jab...anything, but the tire iron hung above her head, looking just as it had in her nightmares. Any small movement she dared to make felt as though she were trying to move through wet cement.

The door opened again, but this time with an odd creak instead of a slam. Talia looked up. Port was standing sideways in the doorway. There was a pained expression on his face as he gripped the doorjamb. Sweat trickled down his forehead as he wobbled forward a couple steps. "It's okay, Doc. I understand." His voice was calm.

"Right, and I understand that you and Tex over there are going to stay where you are, or I'll smash her face in." As he spoke, Doc Gray's elbow trembled around her throat, just a little, but was it trepidation or adrenaline?

"I understand that you were the doctor for one of the biggest rock stars in the country and that made you a rock star in your own right." Port took another slow, wavering step. He looked like an old man who'd lost his walker.

"Hey Frankenstein, I said, back off."

"I'm more of a Hulk than Frankenstein." Port smiled and held up his hands. "You gave Buster whatever he wanted because he was the boss, and after the surfing accident, he wanted pills. Lots of them. You liked your job. What could you do but write the scrips?" Port took another slow, careful step. "Buster uses you as his walking pharmacy and then he sells you out." Another step.

Doc Gray must have noticed Port's snail like progress. "Hey, watch it."

Port stood still and held his hands out again. "He came to you, right? And showed you what he wrote?"

"He wasn't asking me if he could publish it!" Doc Gray snapped. "He was telling me. Telling me...after everything I did for that shit."

"The timing was unfortunate." Another step. "The biggest doctoring gig in the biz was about to open up. Buster told you that Kylie Kismet had started dating her personal doctor, Benjamin Cohen. You knew about Cohen, and you knew he had integrity. You figured he would step down as her doctor." Another step. "But he didn't."

"Even a sap like Cohen couldn't resist a gig like that." Talia could feel his pulse, steady and determined around her throat. "Rock stars don't hire doctors anymore. We're a dying breed. Everyone wants God-damned gurus and yoga teachers these days. But Kylie doesn't need a guru. She needs someone who knows his way around an insulin shot."

"So, you took out Cohen, knowing that Nigel Zone would take the fall for it."

"Wrong." Doc Gray dragged her a few steps back. "The cops are going to find Minnie's DNA all over that car."

"Of course. Minnie is the perfect scapegoat. You framed her for Buster." He took a half-step forward. It was like a twisted game of red light, green light. "And the fan." Another half-step. "And Linda." A tiny step. "And Lulu. You didn't mean to kill her, did you? But she argued with you when you told her to keep her mouth shut about the costume she gave you." One step. Port was nearly close enough to jump Gray and rescue her, if he were capable of jumping. "Didn't she?"

Doc Gray laughed, and that slick, oily feeling gushed back into Talia's bones. "I knew I was going to kill that whore before I banged her." Talia moved her foot, trying to position it behind Gray's leg. He gripped her tighter, lifting her heels off the ground.

"You..." Port's voice cracked. "You won't get away with it."

"Come on, Doctor Maxwell. We may not be rock stars, but someone will probably notice if you murder us. In broad daylight." Ted's voice sounded calmer, as though coming up with a silly nickname for the killer had taken away some of his power.

"Will they?" Doc Gray's arm pressed against her windpipe. "Or will they notice that Minnie used her own tire iron to bludgeon the three detectives who bungled her case and then put their bodies in her van and rolled it into the bay?"

At the word "bay" Talia looked out over the gray water, dimly illuminated by the sun creeping up behind the clouds. She looked away. Port was looking in horror at something above her head. She looked up just in time to see the tire iron coming at her. She closed her eyes.

"Big mistake!" Port yelled.

She waited for the blow, for her head to be bashed open, and hoped there wouldn't be much pain. She heard Port suck in a raspy breath and say, "Your plan worked too well. The cops are picking up Minnie right now."

There was a pause, and then Doc Gray said, "Damn it. I thought I'd have more time." He laughed, and it sounded like a knife scraping against metal. "But that's not your problem, is it? I'll figure something out after I kill you."

Butter sprang out of the warehouse.

Browf browf browf!

Talia had to assume that Doc Gray was distracted, at least for the moment, by an obese dog browfing at him. She put one leg behind his leg and grabbed the crook of his arm and pulled with both hands, moving his arm just half an inch, but it was far enough that she could turn her face toward his armpit. With her face pressed against his body, she felt that she was going to suffocate, but with one good tug, she slipped his arm off her head like a sweater that had shrunk in the wash (just like they'd taught her in self-defense class).

She was marveling at her escape when she felt a searing pain on her scalp. Doc Gray had her by the hair. He tugged, hard, pulling her back. Something whizzed past her head. It hit Doc Gray in the shoulder, then hit the ground and shattered. Port's coffee cup. Talia didn't need to look to know that Darla was up from her nap just in time.

Taking full advantage of this second distraction, she pushed Doc Gray's fist into her head until his fingers released their grip on her hair (another self-defense trick). She lunged toward Port. Doc Gray brought the tire iron down, swiftly. Port reached toward her, but he stumbled. Talia grabbed his arm just as the tire iron connected with a horrible thud and a blast of pain. She lost her grip, and Port hit the ground. She fell on top of him.

Talia couldn't see anything. Her face was mashed into the gravel next to Port's shoulder. She heard a siren, then squealing brakes and a door opening. "Police. Don't move." Brad.

She pried her face off the ground and brushed the pebbles off her cheek and nose. "Are you okay?"

Port lifted his head and shoulders off the ground with a grunt. He looked up at her and smiled, just like he'd done on the day he'd carried her off that raft. "Don't worry about me. Did he hurt you?"

There was a pain in her shoulder so intense she wasn't sure that it was still attached to her upper arm. She smiled back at him. "Nah. Just my shoulder. I'll live."

Port collapsed back on to the ground and closed his eyes. "Good. Let me know when the forklift arrives."

*

Talia pulled into Deadman's Gulch. She took a deep breath and let it out. Today was the day she would play Mark's new album for Port. That meant that today was the day she was going to tell Port that she and Mark were dating. She'd planned on doing it a few days ago and chickened out, but today was the day.

She turned and grabbed the white bag from the Vespa's basket. It was from the diner near her apartment and filled with the usual—two egg-white omelets, one with fat-free cheese and one with full-fat cheese and butter. After Darla and Belisa moved in with Ted, Talia had taken over the fattening-up-Port duty. Reaching into the basket had tweaked her shoulder. She rubbed it as she stepped off the Vespa and onto the gravelly driveway.

She looked at the warehouse. The newest addition caught the morning light. It was an ornate brass doorbell that played "Walk of Love." Minnie had given it to them as a thank-you present, along with invitations to Buster's funeral. Ted had begged Port to give him his invite. Port told him that it didn't work like that; it was a funeral, not a Kylie Kismet concert.

It was close, though. Buster's funeral was the biggest event San Francisco had seen in a century—bigger than any Giants World Series or Forty-Niner Super Bowl. The city shut down for an entire day. People came from all over the country and crowded into the streets around Grace Cathedral, where only family, friends, and the highest echelon of rock-and-roll royalty were granted entrance. Toby had garnered a press pass, and he and his producer Karen had set up with the throng of reporters in the park next door, doing a play by play of what he called "the mourning circus."

Talia and Darla were lucky to be allowed in but had to stand in the back. Crunch Pup had served as pallbearers, so Mark sat near the front. Talia stood on her tip-toes and tilted her head so she could see him. On his way to his seat, Vincent turned and looked at Mark. Mark waved, but Vincent put his head down and shuffled down the aisle with his sister, clutching a black box to his chest.

A few days after the funeral, Red Robin Publishing announced that Minnie was releasing Buster's story and donating the proceeds to Benji's rehabilitation and to the families of all Doc Gray's victims—even Lulu. Minnie hired Darla to write an epilogue about Buster's murder and Doc Gray's trial and conviction. Darla called the chapter *Final Jeopardy*.

The door opened and a woman walked out of the warehouse. She was tall and thin, wearing expensive yet casually professional clothes. "Hello." Talia smiled and waved.

"Morning." The woman nodded and walked purposefully toward her car. Talia stared at her. She had a strange urge to run over and stick her head through the woman's open window and ask her...what? When she was going to finally cure Port?

"I know what you're thinking, Talia."

She spun around. It was Brad. "Whoa. I didn't mean to startle you." He held up his hands. "I just came by to get Port's take on a case I'm working on. I've been waiting for the shrink to leave, so I could go in." Brad waved at the dark gray sedan that was driving past them and out of Deadman's Gulch.

"So, that's the...."

"Port's head doctor, yeah. The first time I met her, I asked her a ton of questions. She answered most of them with a very nice, very professional 'none of your business.' But she told me one thing about this crazy body-dysmorphic thing that Port has. She said that he might get better tomorrow, he might get better in ten years, or he might never get better, and that everyone in his life needs to be prepared for that."

She nodded. "So, you...uh...you said you had a new case?"

"It's not really a new case." He sighed, his dark brown eyes filled with emotion. "I just found out something new in an old case. The SF State case. It's about the scumbag who killed Detective Julia Lake."

"Julia Lake is dead?"

Brad tilted his head and looked at her. "Julia Lake was shot and killed in a dorm room at SF State by a student named Zachary Flood. Didn't Port tell you?"

“I guess he left that part out.” She looked down and kicked the gravel at her feet. She felt Brad’s hand pat her shoulder and then heard the *crunch crunch* of his footsteps as he walked away. When she looked up, Brad was holding the door for her.

When they walked into the warehouse, Talia looked at Port sitting in his giant chair, looking smaller than ever and decided that today was not the day to play Mark’s album.

Port smiled at them. “Ah. You need our help again, Bradley?”

“Don’t start yet,” Talia stepped into the kitchen. “I need to put on a fresh pot of coffee.”

“Good,” Port said. “It’s been too quiet here lately.”

Acknowledgments

Thanks go to my husband, Jon, for laughing at all my jokes and treating my characters like old friends of the family, my script doctor Jody Handley for her skillful doctoring and for shortening Dickopedia to Dicko, my proofreader Karen Spiegelman for each and every sticky note, and to Leslie Dotson Van Every and Jennifer Otter Bickerdike for being my first-draft cheerleaders and for having names that look great on an acknowledgment page. I'd also like to express my gratitude to Matt Potter and Truth Serum Press for seeing the potential in my book and helping me to get it there.

Also from TRUTH SERUM PRESS
and PURE SLUSH BOOKS

https://truthserumpress.net/catalogue/

- *Kiss Kiss* by Paul Beckman
  978-1-925536-21-8 (paperback) 978-1-925536-22-5 (eBook)
- *Dollhouse Masquerade* by Samuel E. Cole
  978-1-925536-43-0 (paperback) 978-1-925536-44-7 (eBook)
- *On the Bitch* by Matt Potter
  978-1-925536-45-4 (paperback) 978-1-925536-46-1 (eBook)

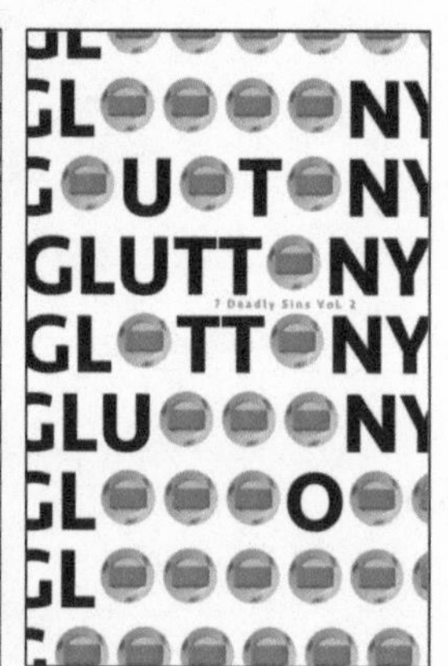

- *Inklings* by Irene Buckler
  978-1-925536-41-6 (paperback) 978-1-925536-42-3 (eBook)
- *Gluttony 7 Deadly Sins Vol. 2*
  978-1-925536-54-6 (paperback) 978-1-925536-55-3 (eBook)
- *Lust 7 Deadly Sins Vol. 1*
  978-1-925536-47-8 (paperback) 978-1-925536-48-5 (eBook)

Also from TRUTH SERUM PRESS

https://truthserumpress.net/catalogue/

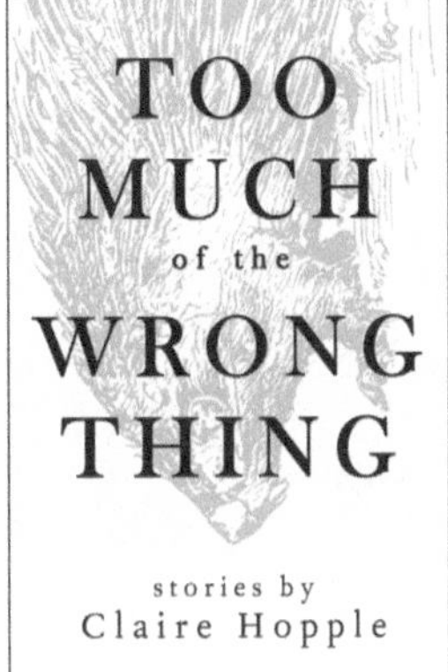

- *Track Tales* by Mercedes Webb-Pullman
  978-1-925536-35-5 (paperback) 978-1-925536-36-2 (eBook)
- *Too Much of the Wrong Thing* by Claire Hopple
  978-1-925536-33-1 (paperback) 978-1-925536-34-8 (eBook)
- *True Truth Serum Vol. 1*
  978-1-925536-29-4 (paperback) 978-1-925536-30-0 (eBook)

- *Hello Berlin!* by Jason S. Andrews
  978-1-925536-11-9 (paperback) 978-1-925536-12-6 (eBook)
- *Deer Michigan* by Jack C. Buck
  978-1-925536-25-6 (paperback) 978-1-925536-26-3 (eBook)
- *Rain Check* by Levi Andrew Noe
  978-1-925536-09-6 (paperback) 978-1-925536-10-2 (eBook)

Also from TRUTH SERUM PRESS

https://truthserumpress.net/catalogue/

- *Luck and Other Truths* by Richard Mark Glover
  978-1-925101-77-5 (paperback) 978-1-925536-04-1 (eBook)
- *Wiser Truth Serum Vol. 2*
  978-1-925536-31-7 (paperback) 978-1-925536-32-4 (eBook)
- *What Came Before* by Gay Degani
  978-1-925536-05-8 (paperback) 978-1-925536-06-5 (eBook)

- *Based on True Stories* by Matt Potter
  978-1-925101-75-1 (paperback) / 978-1-925101-76-8 (eBook)
- *The Miracle of Small Things* by Guilie Castillo Oriard
  978-1-925101-73-7 (paperback) 978-1-925101-74-4 (eBook)
- *La Ronde* by Townsend Walker
  978-1-925101-64-5 (paperback) 978-1-925101-65-2 (eBook)